TWICE SHY

By
Patrick Freivald

JournalStone
San Francisco

JournalStone books may be ordered through booksellers or by contacting:

JournalStone
199 State Street
San Mateo, CA 94401
www.journalstone.com

The views expressed in this work are solely those of the authors and do not necessarily reflect the views of the publisher, and the publisher hereby disclaims any responsibility for them.

ISBN: 978-1-936564-50-7   (sc)
ISBN: 978-1-936564-57-6   (hc)
ISBN: 978-1-936564-58-3   (ebook)

Library of Congress Control Number: 2012941730

Printed in the United States of America
JournalStone rev. date: October 26, 2012

Cover Design: Denise Daniel
Cover Art: Philip Renne

Edited By: Dr. Michael R. Collings

ENDORSEMENTS

DEDICATION

To The Redhead(tm). You're why I write.

ACKNOWLEDGEMENTS

To Phil, Mark, Jake, Brooke, Amy, Mom, and all of my beta readers, for the support and for telling me what sucks. To the Mansers and the Wastoids, who might not have many answers, but sure know how to party.
To the reader who gave this book a chance.

You rule.

Check out these titles from JournalStone:

That Which Should Not Be
Brett J. Talley

The Void
Brett J. Talley

Cemetery Club
JG Faherty

Jokers Club
Gregory Bastianelli

Women Scorned
Angela Alsaleem

The Donors
Jeffrey Wilson

The Devil of Echo Lake
Douglas Wynne

Pazuzu's Girl
Rachel Coles

**Available through your local and online bookseller or at
www.journalstone.com**

CHAPTER
1

Tiffany "Fey" Daniels smoothed the black lace down over her
fishnets. "Picture day sucks," she said, tugging the dress down to
expose the silver ankh hanging at her waifish neck.

It's worse when you're dead, Ani thought.

She rolled on blood-red lipstick to avoid answering, blotted
it and threw the tissue into the trash. She glanced at Fey. Tiny
frame, ghost-pale, black dress, black lipstick, black nail polish,
black-dyed hair and too much mascara. In another life they could
have been twins. "You look good, Fey." Her tongue stud clicked off
her teeth.

Fey sized her up and snorted. "You should eat more." She
walked out of the bathroom. Ani turned up her iPod and let *Kill
Hannah* drone at her as she finished her makeup. With a sigh for
what couldn't be, she stuffed the headphones into her purse. She
tromped out after the queen of the Ohneka Falls Upper School
emos to join the line of juniors waiting their turns in front of the
camera.

* * *

A blinding flash and it was done. The photographer turned
the monitor so that she could see it. The screen showed a gaunt,
pale girl in a long black wig, a nose ring, three rings in her left
eyebrow, and innumerable earrings. The black mascara was

halloweentacular: a dead-eyed raccoon in a long-sleeved black dress. The woman gave her a doubtful frown. "We can take another..."

"It's fine. Whatever." Ani walked out of the gym as the bell rang.

Trig time, she thought. *FML.*

* * *

She sat in the front of the class so she wouldn't have to look at anyone. 'SOHCAHTOA TEST TOMORROW!' splayed across the assignment board in red dry-erase marker. She copied it into her agenda and practiced breathing, using the beat of her pacemaker to time each inhalation. She felt Mike Brown's gaze burning into her back.

She closed her eyes and saw his, green and dazzling as they played under a sunny sky. She strangled the memory. He was a jock, forever off-limits now that she was condemned to live by her mother's rules. She might as well have moved to another planet.

High heels shredded her reverie. "Nice boots, Cutter. Salvation Army?" Devon Holcomb's murmur was acid. Devon was a senior—athletic, blonde, and popular—everything Ani could have been. Devon gave her a viper's smile as she stalked past and pecked Mike on the cheek, bending low to flash too much leg. Mike flushed and glanced away, and Ani turned to the front of the room as Mr. Gursslin began the lesson. It was review for the kids who didn't pay attention the first time.

She closed her eyes and mentally worked on her most recent secret composition, a poppy dance number to make Ke$ha proud, and blocked out the sounds of flirting from behind her.

* * *

She didn't have to work, so her mom gave her a ride home in the Audi. Her mom's athletic frame had suffered a little since her job change, and her curly auburn hair was gray under the dye. *She might be the only school nurse in the world who drives an Audi.* They rode in silence, honoring their unspoken deal. Ani didn't complain about the rules, and Mom didn't complain about the medical practice she had given up to protect her daughter.

Dinner conversation was functional. Her mother ate off of her own plate, and another sat in front of Ani just in case someone dropped by. It all smelled like nothing.

"Did you finish your homework?" her mother asked between bites of chicken salad.

"Yeah. I have a trig test tomorrow, but it'll be easy. I finished English in study hall." She sat with her hands folded in her lap, black fingernails against white skin.

"Work?"

"Not tonight. I'm working five to ten tomorrow." The incense in The Dragon's Lair clung to her clothing, which helped obscure the formaldehyde smell that permeated her skin, and the game store was one of the few places where no one would look twice at an emo girl.

"Good. You should get in the bath." Her mom shoveled another bite into her mouth.

"Mom!" Ani didn't quite stifle the whine.

Her mom set down her fork, patted the corner of her mouth with her napkin, and stood. Ani tried not to roll her eyes as her mother grabbed her head and looked in her mouth. "Your gums are still receding. Formaldehyde doesn't do any good if you're not in it, so if you have down time, you need to be in the bath. We can put on some music. Something you like. I'm working on a new mixture, something that works as well but won't toughen up your flesh so much."

In the end they compromised. Ani watched *Dancing with the Stars* while she wrote out what she had composed in her head earlier in the day, practiced piano on the Baby Grand for forty minutes, and dragged her feet up the stairs to the bathroom. She set the iPod to B.o.B, turned on "Genius," and cranked the speakers. She took off her clothes and slid into the bath, a slippery mixture of noxious chemicals and crushed ice that would keep her body from decaying any further. She pressed the 'close' button and the hydraulic lid slid into place, pressurizing with a soft hiss.

If they found out she was a zombie, they'd burn her.

CHAPTER
2

Cold rain sloughed off Ani's umbrella as she waited in the pre-dawn gloom. Trig identities floated through her brain, entwining and interfering with the melodies she was constructing to the falling drumbeat. A low rumble triggered the end of her peace for the day. She opened her eyes and stepped aboard the bright yellow bus.

She shook out the umbrella, closed it, and stepped over the white line. She froze. Mike sat in his old seat. He hadn't sat there since they'd transitioned to the Upper School at the end of 10th grade, a year after she'd died. She tried not to look at him, his perfect eyes, and sat across from him—as she had for eleven years.

"No ride today?" she asked.

She caught the headshake in her peripheral vision. "Senior Picnic. Devon left for Darien Lake an hour ago." He smiled. It was dazzling. "Nice weather for it."

She looked out the window at the drizzle. Anywhere but at him. "They let seniors drive to Six Flags?" In her imagination the yellow VW careened off a bridge and erupted into a fireball on impact. "I wouldn't have guessed that." She looked at him, anxious.

His smile turned timid, almost nervous. Under high cheekbones, his square jaw sported a hint of stubble that he probably didn't need to shave, and his lettered jacket emphasized his muscular frame. The scrawny boy she had played with a lifetime ago was gone, replaced by this man, this stranger that she could never have, never get close to.

"What?" he asked. She realized she'd been staring.

She looked out the window. "Nothing. Just remembering."

He shifted, turning away from her a little bit as the bus stopped. "I wonder..." He cleared his throat. She didn't dare interrupt. "I—"

A shape interposed itself, blocking her view. Fey sat next to her and handed her an ear bud. "Black Rainbow. Totally wretched." Despair and relief warred on Mike's face. Fey glanced across the aisle as Mike looked out the window, then reached up and closed Ani's mouth with a finger. "You're catching flies."

They rode the rest of the way smothered in music as bleak as the weather.

God, I hate this crap, Ani thought.

*   *   *

By noon the sky had cleared. It looked like the senior picnic wouldn't be a complete disaster. Ani stood outside the cafeteria, trying not to smile as she basked in sunlight through the window. UV rays would damage her skin, and she couldn't just moisturize with aloe. Her mother's injections stimulated some healing, but not enough. Never enough.

A male voice rang out from down the hallway. "No way! She doesn't sparkle!" Immature chuckles accompanied the jibe. She ignored them and closed her eyes. Every day it was harder to feel the warmth. As they got closer, it was clear they weren't going to leave her alone.

"Hey, did you screw Edward?"

"Yeah, you like them popsicles?"

"Quiet, guys, she might go cut herself."

"Are you gonna cut yourself, freak?"

She kept her eyes closed, hoping they'd keep walking. She gasped as someone slammed into her. She stumbled forward and her foot exploded in pain, even as her head bounced off the glass. As the contents of her purse spilled, she heard a teacher yell a warning. Footsteps scattered.

She knelt to the ground and picked up her makeup, her ID, and the unmentionables she didn't need but couldn't avoid carrying. As she grabbed her mascara, a hand closed over hers. She looked up, startled, right into those green eyes.

Mike looked worried. "Are you ok?" he asked. She nodded. "You hit the window pretty hard."

She reached up and touched her head. She felt the cut and swore under her breath. She kept her face calm. "I'm not bleeding or anything. Jerks."

He brushed his thumb over the cut. "You've done worse on the swings."

She pulled her head away and stuffed the rest of her belongings into her purse.

"Those guys are a bunch of assholes. Don't let them get to you."

She jerked away from him. "Jocks are jerks. I know the type."

"Not all jocks," he said, reaching for her arm. She turned and staggered away from him.

"Yeah, all jocks." She walked down the hall consumed by tears that couldn't fall.

* * *

Her mother looked up as Ani limped into the nurse's office.

"What happened to you?" Her mother circled around the desk to lead Ani to a bed. As Ani sat down, her mom pulled the curtain, then removed a small phial from her purse. The liquid was sticky and pungent, a regenerative ointment reserved for the military and the rich. Her mom clucked and scowled as she applied it first to a cotton swab and then to Ani's forehead. "You have to be more careful. This stuff is only so good."

Modern medicine had come a long way since the Zombie Virus outbreak seventeen years before. After ZV was contained in the United States, her mother had spent her life making sure it would never happen again, and with that experience, she had gained access to all of the state-of-the-art medicines: ZV suppressors, regeneratives, synthetic antibodies. Neither of them had expected to need them quite so desperately.

Ani unlaced her boot as her mother finished dabbing and applied a Band-Aid. "Some jerks pushed me into a window." She pulled off the boot. She didn't want to look.

"Oh, honey!" her mother exclaimed. She looked down.

Her pinky toe was at a right angle. She looked away.

Her mom spoke in a bare whisper. "I'll tape it for now, sweetie, but we'll have to do some surgery tonight. I don't have anything for a broken bone." A sickening crack accompanied a jolt of pain. It faded to a slow burn as her mom wrapped her pinky and the toe next to it in tape. Her mom stood, kissed her forehead, and patted her on the shoulder. "That's good for now. Go back to class."

Ani's eyes widened. "Oh, shit, my trig test!" She shot to her feet and stumbled out of the room, boot in hand.

"Watch your language!" her mother called after her.

"You know you can write her up, Sarah," the secretary in the next room offered as Ani shuffled down the hall.

* * *

Ani hustled into Mr. Gursslin's room ten minutes late. "Miss Romero," he said. He looked at the clock, shook his head, and nodded at her desk. The test was already on it. She put the pass on his desk and hurried to her seat.

Mike flushed but didn't look up.

The test wasn't too hard. She finished as the bell rang and hurried out of the room, grabbing Mike's arm as he went past. "Hey..."

He spun and towered over her. "Hey what, Ani? I thought you didn't talk to jocks."

She frowned. "I just wanted to say I'm sorry. That sucked, and I was in pain, but there was no excuse for what I said." His delicious masculine smell overwhelmed her; sweat and musk and—she stopped breathing.

He looked down the hall, where Fey scowled at them. "Well, just remember that just because you wear black and hate life doesn't mean you can't also be an asshole, too." His timid smile reappeared. "Right?"

She smiled back. "Sure, Mike. Sorry again."

He walked away as Fey stepped into his place.

"You'd better have life insurance," she said, looking down the hall after him.

"Excuse me?" Ani had almost forgotten to start breathing again.

Fey rolled her eyes in the direction of Mike. "Poaching Holcomb's boyfriend. She'll claw your eyeballs out and leave your corpse on the side of the road." She rolled her eyes again. "Not that you stand a chance with either of them."

Ani scoffed. "Rude, much?"

Fey's eyes widened. "Speaking of 'doesn't stand a chance,' head off Dylan for me, would you?" She whirled around and stalked down the hall, her high heels clopping over the din of the student masses. Ani turned around as Dylan moped up behind her.

He was tall, blue-eyed, and skinny, with an Edward haircut and a permanent scowl. He lifted his chin and brushed his hair out of his face, flashing a silver bracelet. "Hey," he said, his stare following Fey's retreat.

"Hey," she said back.

"Where's Fey going?" His eyes didn't leave Fey's ass until it was around the corner.

"Class, I guess."

Creepy-quiet to begin with, Dylan had started wearing black and cutting himself to impress Fey and had since slid off the deep end. Stealing, smoking, taking X, vandalism, and very bad poetry had yet to change Fey's opinion that he wasn't worth her time. His only use as far as Fey was concerned was stealing cigarettes from the gas station. His dad had been a HomeGuard technician before he died in the war, and Dylan was surprisingly good at breaking and entering—but he charged five bucks a pack.

He glanced up and down the hall. "You hear the new Paramore track?"

She shook her head. "My mom froze my iTunes account. Now I got to work the skating parties with her until I pay it off."

"Skating parties, huh?" His blank gaze floated to her face. It always felt like he was looking through her instead of at her. "At the middle school? Don't you work at the Lair?"

She rolled her eyes. "Mom works the skating parties and wants the help. She doesn't care if I have the money. Look," she said, touching his arm, "I got to get to class. See ya."

"Yeah," he said. He didn't move, so she pulled her hand away and walked off.

When she looked back, his unblinking stare stretched down the hall after the memory of Fey.

* * *

Ani sat on the bus, looking up every time someone climbed aboard. Eventually, she saw Mike—getting into Devon's yellow VW. *Damn it. They're not supposed to be back yet.* She looked away as they kissed.

Fey patted her leg. "Life sucks. Get used to it."

CHAPTER
3

Ani slouched at the table, affecting her best "The world sucks and I hate you all" pose. Three hours of pop music and wailing little kids was the definition of emo hell. She loved it. Her body screamed to move to the beat, and she wanted to skate with the kids, feel their energy as they circled the gym. She'd always liked kids, and she liked middle-schoolers more and more as she got older. *Maybe I'll become a teacher once I escape this hellhole,* she thought.

She tried not to smile at her mom. Her mother hated pop music and didn't much care for little kids. As a birthday present, she had agreed to find a reason to force Ani to come to the middle school skating parties for the rest of the school year. If Ani ever had a question about her mother's love, this answered it.

A sixth-grade girl in a yellow dress and pigtails skated up to the table. Beaming, she ordered a peanut butter cup and bottled water over the noise.

So cute, Ani thought. She could feel the energy flowing out of the girl, hear the pulse of her heart drumming in her ears. She seemed so *alive.* Ani handed over the goods and sent her on her way with a smile that couldn't be helped. She turned to her mom to thank her.

Her mom smiled, then looked over her shoulder and closed her hand into a fist. It was a code signal. *Animal.* Ani turned around. Mr. Bell, the middle-school principal, had brought his terrier into the gym and was headed to the refreshment table. Ani's chair flew backward. She hurried to the bathroom and locked herself in the stall to await the "all clear."

She didn't know why animals hated her. *You're the walking dead, freak.* Okay, she knew why, but she hated it. Dogs were great ZV detectors. So were cats. And birds. Anything, really. Experiments had shown that all life was repelled by ZV carriers, and would go to almost any lengths to get away from a zombie. On the bright side, the lack of bacteria slowed down tissue decay, and Ani never got mosquito bites.

She didn't know how she'd contracted the virus—it was believed wiped out in North America over a decade before—and she didn't know why it hadn't turned her into a mindless, brain-eating machine. If her mom knew, she wasn't talking. But the other symptoms—necrotized flesh, animal psychosis, dulled sense of taste, touch, and smell—those were in full force. She missed Roscoe. He'd been a good dog.

Her mom whispered through the door, "We're good."

Melancholy, Ani stepped out into the pounding bass beat and tried to enjoy the rest of the evening.

CHAPTER
4

Homecoming week: a glorification of all things jock. *Might as well strap steaks to the nerds and set them loose in a tiger pen*, Ani thought. It was "Opposite Day," which as far as Ani could tell was blanket permission for homophobic jocks to cross-dress like cheerleaders and prom queens. One of the AV tech kids had shown up dressed in a varsity jacket and football helmet—he'd gone home to change after the team had pummeled him. He'd probably carry the nickname "Helmet" for the rest of his high school career.

Emo kids didn't have school spirit. It was far too positive. Ani wore black, of course, and as usual she was invisible when not a target. Being a girl helped. Dylan and Jake took way more crap than any of the girls did. Most of the time the girls were left alone, except by the emo guys, who gave them a very different type of attention.

"Hey," Dylan said, "do you know if Fey's going to the dance?"

That's so cute, Ani thought. She stifled the happy thought and rolled her eyes. "You'd have to ask her, Dylan. I'm working three to eight Saturday. There's a Magic booster tournament at the Lair." And afterward, if she could figure out a way to escape both the emos and Devon, she'd try to talk to Mike at the dance. She handed Dylan a five-dollar bill.

He shuffled his feet, his intense stare unsettling. "People still play that, huh? If I had some old cards, could you sell them for me?"

Mike walked out of history and headed for his locker in a cheerleading skirt. He had blue and white pom-poms tucked under his arm.

"No," Ani said. "I..." She tried to step around Dylan, but he stepped with her. "I just work there. Bring them in, and Travis will buy what's worth anything."

"Hey, thanks." He stepped closer—too close. He smelled like old patchouli and Old Spice. He barely moved his lips. "There's Fey. Find out for me, would you?" He dropped a pack of cigarettes into her hand and walked away before Fey caught up.

Ani glanced around for teachers and then handed Fey the smokes.

"You're a life saver, Ani. Payday's Friday. I'll catch you back then."

"Mom's dragging me to Open House on Friday," Ani said. "I have a C in English and she wants to talk to Mrs. Weller. Why don't you bring it to the bonfire?"

"You're going?" Fey asked. Her bloodshot eyes rolled upward. "There's nothing better to do in this town anyway. Billy J's smuggling in some vodka for the soccer team. It could get interesting."

Ani nibbled her lower lip. "Could be fun to watch."

"And laugh at," Fey said.

* * *

Mrs. Weller's room was cleaner than it had been all year. Every pen had its place, and every paper was filed. It looked like the walls had been scrubbed.

"Sarah, Ani, come in," Mrs. Weller said, offering her hand. "I'm so sorry we couldn't catch up during the week, but Ani's grade isn't where it should be, and I'm a bit concerned."

Great. Right down to business. Ani did her best to not get defensive as they discussed her work ethic.

"We read *The Crucible* in eighth grade, Mom. It's too boring to read a second time."

Mrs. Weller raised an eyebrow. "And you don't think you might get more out of it with several more years of school under your belt, young lady?"

"I didn't get anything out of it the first time—"

Her mother's scowl stopped her in her tracks. "If you're going to be flippant, do it elsewhere. I'll meet you in the Band Room in five minutes."

"Fine," Ani said, snatching her purse off the floor. She stomped out of the room. Her mom probably thought she was acting. *That book sucks.*

She slunk into the Band Room. Voices murmured in the back—Mr. Bariteau entertaining parents. Ani sat at the piano, closed her eyes, and put her fingers on the keys. Chopin's *Ballade in G Minor* fit her mood—alternating melancholy and whimsical, violent and breathless, cheerful and mischievous. She screwed up a few times but nothing big, and the little piano couldn't do it justice. All in all, a passable job.

She finished, and applause startled her. Her eyes snapped open to find Mike, his mom, her mom, Mr. Bariteau, Dylan, and several people she didn't know, all watching her. A tear hovered on her mom's cheek. Ditto Mr. Bariteau. Dylan stood in the doorway, mouth open. She looked around for an escape route.

Her mom brushed away the tear. "That was excellent, sweetie."

"Oh, is that your daughter?" a woman in a blue jogging suit asked.

"I... need to go to the bathroom." She ducked between the chattering adults and out into the hall. Mike didn't follow her. Dylan did.

"That was amazing," he said. "I had no idea you could play like that."

She shrugged. "I've had lots of practice." *It's amazing what you can do when you don't get tired.*

"No kidding." He brushed his bangs out of his eyes. "It hurts to hear such beauty. Or see it."

Oh, great, Ani thought. The last thing she needed was Stalkerboy's attentions focused on her. "Hey, I don't know about the dance, but Fey's coming to the bonfire."

His face stayed a dispassionate mask, but the barest twinkle crept into his eyes. "Oh, yeah? I might show up, if I don't have something else going on."

Ani snorted. "What else could possibly be going on in a town the size of a postage stamp?"

They arrived at the bathroom. Instead of taking the hint, Dylan leaned against the wall. "Sometimes I get pretty wrapped up in my poetry. It's pretty consuming, you know? All that darkness needs an outlet. If not words, what?"

Are you staring at my ankles? "Sure, Dylan," she said. "Maybe you can let me see some of it some time." *Why did I just say that?*

His eyes molested her body on their way to her face. "Really?"

"Yeah, maybe sometime. Look, I really got to go."

He backed up from the doorway. "Oh, right, me too. See you tomorrow. At the fire."

"Sure, Dylan." She stepped through the door into blessed silence.

* * *

Friday was School Pride Day, and if she wore a blue-and-white T-shirt under her black turtleneck, and only her mother knew, then that was what it had to be. Sometimes the little things mattered.

* * *

The official, school-sponsored bonfire ended at ten when the chaperones went home and the firemen put out the fire. The unofficial one started at ten-fifteen, in the woods behind Finster's barn, far enough from the road to not draw undue attention. How people could drink themselves silly, stay up to all hours, and then play sports in the morning was beyond her. Ani didn't sleep anymore, but she didn't play sports, either.

Her mom bought liquor and smokes for her, which she "stole" for the other losers. In the back of the crowd, she sat Indian-style next to Jake and handed him a half-full bottle of Captain Morgan. "Have you seen Fey? She owes me ten bucks."

He pulled off the cap and took a swig, careful not to smear his black lipstick. "Yeah. She's scoring some X from Roberts."

Chuck Roberts was the poster child of the modern American dream. Twenty-four years old, he had somehow graduated without passing any classes his senior year. Banned from school grounds after serving two years for statutory, he still used drugs to pick up teenage girls. Ani didn't want to think about how Fey was paying him. It made her queasy.

Jake took another swig. "Wow. You hear about that guy in Rushville?"

She watched a cascade of sparks escape into the heavens as a pallet collapsed in the fire. "No. What guy?"

"It was all over the news. Some redneck meth-head gnawed a cop's thumb off when they tried to arrest him. They quarantined the street, had to test everyone for ZV...." He took another swallow. "Can you imagine waiting for your test results, knowing there's a flame crew right outside?"

Ani's stomach knotted. *Yes.*

"No," she said. "That's awful."

He drummed his legs with his hands. "It's pretty funny if you think about it. It was just meth—"

Fey plopped down next to her, a ten-dollar bill between her index and middle fingers. "Told you I'm good for it."

Ani grabbed the bill and stuffed it into her pocket. Fey smelled like jasmine, and underneath, something primal, enticing. The unpleasant feeling in Ani's stomach intensified. *What the hell is wrong with me?*

Movement in the darkness caught her eye. Dylan crept up behind Fey with a tiny shake of the head toward Ani. His movements were feral, like he was stalking prey. She gave him a weak smile.

Fey rolled her eyes without turning around. "Dylan, if you touch me, I swear to God you're going in the fire." She stuck a cigarette in her mouth, which Jake lit for her.

Dylan frowned, his hands balling into fists, then slumped to the ground behind Jake. Ani's stomach cramped. Dylan smelled like blood. Like meat.

Oh God, I'm hungry.

She stumbled to her feet and staggered into the brush, her pacemaker pounding in her ears. She caught snippets of their conversation over the growing need in her gut.

"...the hell did I do?"

"...too much, Captain...."

"...the hell alone, douche...."

She fell to her hands and knees. She needed to get away, or she'd burn. She started to crawl. *I can't. I'll kill them all.* The brush, black and orange in the firelight, faded to throbbing red. *I'll bite them, and then they'll eat each other.* She curled into a fetal position, crippled with sobbing, desperate gasps. *The police will come, and they'll kill... They'll burn.... They'll... taste... so... good....*

She sighed in relief as her fingernail dug into her wrist. She focused on the tearing skin, the angelic release of pain. She shuddered, and her eyes rolled into the back of her head. The nail gouged a perfect line across her wrist, and then another, and another. With each cut she transcended further above the hunger where it could not touch her.

When she opened her eyes, Dylan was there, staring in rapturous horror.

"Get away from me," she spat, and ran into the darkness.

CHAPTER
5

October second was a chilly Saturday, a chance to try on her new leather trench coat. The cowhide was a little stiff, and it smelled like her mom's Audi, but it blocked the wind that seemed to bother everyone else so much. She hadn't yet figured out how to fake a shiver, but the cold air felt good. She hadn't felt this good in ages.

Ani couldn't have gone to the Homecoming Parade without blowing her credibility as a life-hating loser, but her mom volunteered as First Aid at the games, so she was able to catch the JV and Varsity girls before she had to go to work. A lot of those girls used to be her friends, but they had abandoned her the moment she became a social liability. Mom's rules weren't negotiable—no sports, limited sunlight exposure, and bulky, body-covering clothes were necessary if she was going to survive long enough to be cured.

The lab hidden in their basement wasn't for show. *If there's a cure, Mom will find it. She knows more about ZV than anyone.* Ani pushed away thoughts of the bonfire—the hunger—and ran her thumb along the razor blade in her pocket. *Just in case.* There were some things Mom didn't need to know.

She stood off to the side and watched the girls play. Every ounce of her being wanted to be on the field, kicking the ball, running, being part of a team. She hated to admit it, but Devon was a great offensive midfielder. *Let's hope she slips and breaks a bone. Or five.*

Keegan Taylor stepped up next to her. "Explains a lot."

She looked at him sidelong. Interactions with jocks were never good, especially jocks that had had a crush on her in eighth grade.

"What does?"

"You. Standing here, looking at a bunch of girls."

"I'm not the one who wore a skirt to school on Monday." The girls executed a near-perfect defensive play and stole the ball. Devon took it at midfield and passed it forward.

"The whole team wore skirts. You're the one staring at the girls."

"So now I'm a dyke?" Her brain scrambled for a witty retort and came up blank. "Sure. Whatever you say, Keegs."

He scowled. "What the hell happened to you, Ani? You used to be cool."

The game was a rout. She didn't clap as the home team scored an easy goal, then turned to look him in the eye. "Life sucks. Then you die." *And then it really sucks.*

She left him scowling on the sidelines and walked to work.

* * *

Travis was an okay boss, but he loved to hear himself talk. He rambled on about responsibility and customer service, and Ani fought the urge to yawn or roll her eyes or hang herself. The third time 'unsupervised game store kid' knocked over a display item, Ani had thrown him out of the store. His mom had freaked out at her for dumping her child on the street—oblivious to the fact that she was the one who had abandoned him in the Dragon's Lair while shopping down the road—and then Travis came in and freaked out at her for upsetting the customers. It was almost a relief when Dylan showed up with his Magic cards.

As he walked in the door, Ani interrupted Travis mid-freak. "Customer!" She danced out of earshot and leaned against the counter in front of Dylan. He put the cards on the counter and Ani scooped them up.

She had to use the price guide to sort them into 'crap' and 'not-crap' before handing them over to Travis. A full third of them were from the current set. She tapped one with a black plastic fingernail while Dylan stared at her covered wrists. "I thought you said these were old."

Dylan blushed and looked at the gaming tables, then away.

"Mine are. I stole some from my brother."

She chewed her bottom lip to keep from talking and sorted a few more. He pointed at one. "That's one I stole. It's worth twenty bucks." He licked his lips as his eyes drifted back to her wrists.

Time to go, Dylan. "You're a bad liar. Fey might bite if you were a bit more real."

"You know what?" he said. "FUCK you!" Face twisted in rage he scattered the cards and stormed out. Travis hollered at his heels as he fled down the sidewalk. Ani had the cards re-sorted before her boss got back, red-faced.

"What the heck was that?" Travis asked.

Ani shrugged. "Just trying to give him some advice."

Travis pointed at the kids in the back. "I can't have your friends yelling obscenities in my store. Parents catch wind, and then who pays my bills, huh?"

"He's not my friend," Ani snapped. *Not even my pretend friend.*

"Sure he's not," Travis said. "Don't let it happen again."

"It won't." She dropped the worthless cards in the trash and handed him the rest of the stack. "You owe him ninety bucks."

* * *

6:50 p.m. The dance started in ten minutes. A night watching hormone-crazed teenagers molesting each other under the eyes of teachers, who were trying to pretend they didn't see anything, wasn't Ani's idea of a good time. She wanted to be one of those hormone-crazed teenagers, hot and sweating on the dance floor. Failing that, she'd paint.

She was half-done with a watercolor of tiger lilies when a throaty rumble shook the house. A car horn sounded. She pushed back the curtain with a pinky finger and saw a maroon '87 Caprice Classic idling in the driveway. *Dylan.* She wiped her hands on a towel and went outside.

He turned down the music as she approached the car, tiptoeing bare-footed through the gravel. The titanium pin in her pinky ached, dull and distant, and the rocks pricked the bottom of her feet.

"Hey," he said. "I'm sorry about earlier."

"Mmm," she said. She didn't much feel like giving him the

satisfaction. "You almost got me fired."

"I said I'm sorry."

"I heard you."

He sat there, staring at the steering wheel. She waited. He didn't say anything. She leaned her elbows on the door and put her head in the car.

"What do you want, Dylan? I'm busy."

"Will you go to the dance with me?"

Ani cleared her throat. "Excuse me?" *You didn't just ask me to go to the dance with you. No. Nuh-uh. That did not just happen.* She tried to think of excuses, and her mind went blank.

"Fey's going to be there, helping her step-dad DJ."

"Oh," Ani said. *Thank God.* "And why do you need me there?"

He threw up his hands. "I can't go by myself. Fey won't give me the time of day, and Keeg and his friends will leave me alone if I'm with a girl."

"Or they might go *Carrie* on both of us."

"Yeah, I won't let that happen. Will you come?"

She sighed out the breath she'd been holding. "Shit. Yeah. Um… On two conditions. One, we never, ever talk about last night."

He nodded. "What's two?"

"Tomorrow you apologize to Travis for swearing in his store."

"Oh, please," he said. "He's a total douchebag."

Ani *tsk*-ed. "Suit yourself." She pushed away from the car and picked a few careful steps back toward the house.

"Hey!" Dylan called. "Wait! Okay."

She turned around. "Okay, what?"

"Yeah, okay. I'll do it."

"In person. While I'm there."

He hesitated. "Deal."

Dammit. "Okay. Give me five minutes." She walked inside and shut the door. It took longer to convince her mom than to pick an outfit.

* * *

Dylan's car smelled like old french-fries. She was glad to have big chunky boots between her feet and the garbage on the floor. She noticed a smudge of yellow paint on her knuckle and sucked it off.

Dylan manhandled the gearshift into reverse. "You smell delicious," he said.

Ick.

She looked out the window. "It's incense from the Lair. It clings to your clothes." *And masks the nerd-funk.*

He backed out of the driveway. "Well, you still smell nice."

She sighed for effect. "If you hit on me, the deal is off. Stay focused."

He put the car in drive and hit the gas, too hard. The trombone-blast of his decrepit exhaust system echoed through the neighborhood. "I was trying to be nice," he said through gritted teeth.

"Well, don't. This isn't a favor, this is *quid pro quo*."

"Quid what?"

"Never mind. What's the game plan?"

"Uh… Game plan?"

She put her hand to her head and closed her eyes. "Yes. Game plan." She turned to look at him. "You want Fey to like you. She thinks you're a creepy obsessive fairy-chaser who went emo to get in her pants."

Dylan blushed. "Ouch."

"Yeah, so what's the game plan?" She glanced at the speedometer. He was going sixty in a thirty-five. *Never a cop when you need one.*

"Um..." He took a hard left at twenty miles an hour. "Will you dance with me to make her jealous?"

"Not a chance."

"Why not?"

Because you're a creepy obsessive fairy-chaser who went emo to get into Fey's pants. "Because then we really will be fresh meat. Besides, it wouldn't make her jealous. Emo kids don't dance at dances. They just hang in the back and look miserable."

He laughed, short and mirthless. "You're pretty jaded."

"Yup," she said.

* * *

They walked into the gym together, but not so close as to look romantic. Nobody seemed to notice either way. The room was dark and the bass cranked so high that the floor shook. Ani didn't see Mike or Devon anywhere, though Devon's cronies sweated it up under the strobe lights while trying to ignore the underclassmen at their heels.

Dylan made a beeline for the speakers. *Subtle.* Ani followed a few steps behind. Fey's step-dad wore giant earphones and bobbed his head to the beat, his eyes closed. Fey sat against a subwoofer, knees to her chin, and rubbed her back in slow circles across the vibrating fabric. She had a sucker in her mouth, and red drool had puddled on her leg.

Dylan elbowed Ani and jerked his head at Fey.

Ani stepped between Fey and the lights and yelled. "Hey!"

Fey opened her eyes and smiled, her teeth red. She slurped the sticky juice off her lips, then pulled the sucker out of her mouth. "Hey, Ani." She reached out and touched Ani's leg, staring wide-eyed as her hand rubbed the black fabric. "That feels amazing."

"It's called denim," Dylan said. Fey smiled at him and he smiled back. *It's called ecstasy.* Fey closed her eyes and dropped her hand, brushing her fingertips across the floor. "When are you done here?" Fey didn't respond. He scowled at Ani, then looked back at Fey. "Fey?"

Without opening her eyes, she swatted in his direction. He stepped back, then tried again a few minutes later. And again the song after that, to the same result.

He stormed over to the corner and crossed his arms, glaring at the floor. Ani followed and put her hand on his shoulder. "I'll kill that stupid bitch," Dylan said through clenched teeth. "Nobody ignores me. Not me. Nobody."

Ani widened her eyes and took a step back. "Whoa, Dylan. You need to chill. She's just rolling."

He sat, arms folded, and ground his teeth through song after song, eyes locked on Fey. He seemed oblivious to the stares and ignored Mr. Betrus when he tried to engage him in conversation. With nothing else to do, Ani sat on an amp while Fey pet her leg. *Awesome.*

As the dance wore on, Fey became less and less squirmy, and by eight forty-five, she was asleep. At nine-fifteen, her eyes snapped open and she sprang to her feet.

"Ani, hey. I'm starving, you want something?" Without another word she walked out of the gym.

Ani looked at Dylan, but the corner was empty. She followed Fey out to the concession stand.

The dance ended with no sign of Dylan, so Ani hitched a ride home with Fey.

The next day, Travis got his apology, so the night wasn't a complete loss.

* * *

Thursday was a half-day, and they had Friday off for parent-teacher conferences. English was up to a B+, but math had slipped to a B-. AP US History held strong at an A-. Music and Art were, of course, A's, and Gym was a D. There was no pleasing Mom with less than academic perfection, so she sat through a tag-team lecture from Mr. Gursslin and her mother.

Saturday and Sunday were the Fall Foliage Festival, where tens of thousands of people who lived with trees all around them for some reason converged on Ohneka Falls to gape at the foliage, eat greasy food, and play overpriced games with lame prizes. Everyone who lived in the village proper either cashed in on the festivities or got the heck out of town for two days. Her mom, unfortunately, was the former type.

If anyone else saw the irony of an independently wealthy cardiologist-turned-ZV-researcher-turned-school-nurse running a funnel cake stand, they never mentioned it. For as long as she could remember, Ani spent the weekend in her front yard as a Fall Foliage Traditional Kettle-Fried Funnel Cake slave, selling sugar-coated deep-fried batter at a six-thousand-percent markup. Only now it was Mom who ran the register and passed out the food, and Ani who did the frying.

The heat didn't bother her. She didn't sweat, and if the awning sheltered her from the sunlight, at least it was nearby. The tent kept the sea of humanity at bay, and if now and then she dragged a razor across her arm to release the tension, it was a small price to pay for spending two normal days with her mom.

The SATs were that Saturday, too, and that meant Devon was out of town. Mike spent the morning helping out, just like old times. They joked and laughed and she forgot herself, ignoring her mother's occasional frowns. Mike hip-bumped her as he sidled past, and she giggled. It felt so good to laugh. Drowning in his presence, she turned to hand her mother a stack of funnel cakes and froze.

Devon stood outside the tent, fists on her hips, her eyes ablaze. Mike was a deer in headlights.

Devon's voice was clipped. "Michael? Can I speak to you?"

Mike forced a pained smile. "Yeah, babe. How was the test?"

She stood her ground, glared at Ani, and then back at Mike. "In private?"

Mike untied his apron, set it on the counter, and walked out of the tent without saying 'goodbye.' Devon was bitching in muted tones before they'd taken two steps.

"Sweetie?" her mom asked.

Mike slumped his shoulders as they walked away.

"ANI! I need four more cakes."

Ani started, then handed her mother the cakes in her hand. Mike didn't even look back as she returned to her station. Her feet tangled and the world tilted. Arms flailing, she tried to catch herself as her chin slammed into the counter. Her hand hit the pot handle, and it flipped off the stove. Her mother screamed.

Four-hundred-degree oil gushed onto her side as she rolled out of the way. It sizzled as it soaked through to her skin, and she clawed her clothes away from her body. She heard panicked shouts and a fire extinguisher discharge but was too distracted to find their source.

She staggered to her feet to find a crowd gaping at her. She held her clothes out, away from her body, and gave a sheepish smile. "I'm okay! It's okay! It didn't make it through my clothes." Her mom's furious eyes followed her as she rushed inside to change.

She stripped to her bra in the bathroom, and winced as she touched the grey, shiny patch on her left ribs and abdomen. She winced as she poked at it, and again as the door flew open.

Her mom glared at her in the mirror. "Ani Romero, you need to watch what the hell you're doing." She dropped to her knees for a closer look and examined the injury. She pressed at the flesh around the burned spot with latex-covered hands. Ani didn't flinch. "Can you feel that?"

Ani nodded. "Yeah."

She moved onto the damaged skin. "And that?"

Ani shook her head. Her mom prodded further, and the entire area sagged, then sloughed off. Her mom sprang back as the meaty chunk slapped onto the floor. Ani shook in horror.

She could see ribs, stark white against her gray, lifeless innards. *Is that my liver?* She touched the lowest exposed bone, and her mother slapped her hand away.

"Don't touch," her mom said. "I'll get a bandage." She walked to the door, then looked back, her eyes watering. "Don't touch." She walked out.

Don't cry, Mom. You never cry.

Ten minutes later, she stepped outside to a chorus of cheers from people who thought she'd been crippled. Her mom waved them off, and Ani tried to ignore the odd sensation of her internal organs rubbing against the bandage. They closed shop for the day.

* * *

That evening, Jake came to the door, his eyeliner smudged across his temple. He peered into the house and spoke in a whisper. "Hey, Ani. Can you score any more booze?"

"No," she whispered back. "Mom's already wondering about the rum. You can't just come around here."

He leaned in close, a mischievous smile touching the corner of his mouth. "What's for dinner? BLTs?"

"What?" She'd made her mom some mac and cheese about an hour before. *Oh, no.* "Go away, Jake." She closed the door in his face.

Her mom called out from the basement. "Who was that, honey?"

She slipped behind the bookcase and tromped down the stairs. The lab smelled clean, antiseptic. The cinderblock walls were stark white, and racks of chemicals, labeled in block letters and shelved alphabetically, sat by type. Three giant, glass-door refrigerators stood against the far wall, lined with vials and Petri dishes of biological substances, and a yellow-orange cabinet labeled "DANGER: FLAMMABLE" sat in an insulation-lined corner, across from the fire extinguisher.

Her mom looked up from the confocal microscope, saw the look on Ani's face and frowned. "What is it, honey?"

Ani tried to keep the disgust out of her voice. "Mom, Jake thinks I smell like bacon."

Her mom's eyes widened. "Ani, we have to do something ."

Ani shook her head. "No, he didn't realize it was me." She slumped onto a stool. "He thought we were having BLTs." She hated pouting, but she couldn't help it.

Her mom took off her lab coat and stripped off her latex gloves. "Oh, sweetie," she said, walking around the table. She tossed the gloves into the biohazard bin. "We'll get that taken care of as soon as I finish this rejuvenation test." She gave her a hug, and held it. After a moment, Ani pulled away.

"Mom, the bath isn't working."

Her mother raised an eyebrow. "Yes, it is." She took out a syringe and a bottle of appetite suppressant, filled the needle half full, and squirted out the air. "Do you have any idea what shape you'd be in without the new regeneratives?"

"Yeah, Mom, it's better than the straight formalin, it really is..." She paused as her mother pushed back the wig and injected the serum into her brain. A small prick, and the familiar rush of warmth flooded her. "But I'm freaking falling apart here."

Her mother set down the syringe and threw up her hands. "What do you want from me, Ani? I can't both work on another new bath and work on a cure. The bath's good enough as long as you're careful. If you keep out of harm's way, maybe we can avoid home school."

Ani gasped. "Mom, you *promised*. Social interaction stimulates my cerebral neurons. It's *essential*."

"I know, and it is, but things can change if you don't stop getting hurt. Your safety is top priority." She pulled on a new pair of gloves. "No more mooning after Mike. No boys. No friends over." She put on her lab coat. "And cut Jake off for a while. I'm not having him die in a DWI just so you can fit in." She walked over to the microscope, then smiled to take the edge off of the lecture. "Go practice your piano. I'll call you when I'm ready to deal with that... bacon smell."

CHAPTER
6

Monday was Columbus Day. A day off from school, wasted in study for the PSATs on Wednesday, after which Ani ran Warhammer night at the Lair. The customers kept asking her questions as if she played the game. *Boys and their little metal dolls.* Even emos looked down on the war-gamers. The thirty-year-olds with neck beards and beer guts were the worst. *Creepy.* She was almost glad to get in the bath.

She spent all day Tuesday worrying about the essay test in AP History, then nailed it. Three hours at the Lair, then home to study. *So much pressure for a test nobody cares about once you take the SAT.* She laughed. *Mom cares. Mom always cares.*

* * *

Ani walked out of the cafeteria feeling pretty good.

"That was brutal," Mike said as he stepped up next to her. His emerald eyes looked flat and lifeless under the fluorescent lights.

"I think I did okay," Ani said. "Did you study?"

He shook his head. "How do you study for a test like that?"

Fey grabbed her arm as she opened her mouth to reply, and dragged her toward the bathroom. She didn't dare look back.

Inside, Fey pulled a bottle of pills from her purse, popped one in her mouth, and offered it to Ani. *More drugs, Fey?* Ani shook her head, so she capped it and put it back. "What the hell was that?" Fey asked.

"Uh..." Ani said. "He was... Uh... we were just talking about the test."

Fey rolled her eyes. "You. Are. Pathetic." She punctuated each word with a poke in the shoulder. "*I* was talking about the test. What the hell did that have to do with anything?"

"I don't know," Ani said. She checked her makeup. *Haggard and hideous. Perfect.* "College, I guess."

"Huh," Fey said. "You going?"

"To college?"

Fey rolled her eyes. "No, to the freaking moon."

Ani bit her lower lip, thinking. "I think so. You?"

Fey shook her head. "What for? So I can learn to sit in a cubicle the rest of my life? There is no future. You live, you die—that's it. Done. Just try not to get hurt too much on the way."

I'm sure those pills are helping, Fey. "Yeah," Ani said. "My mom wants me to go. Maybe music or something."

Fey smiled, her eyes glassier by the second. "Music's cool. You could do that." She looked around the bathroom at the cracked ceramic tile and old grout. "Escape this crapfest anyway. I'll die before I become a townie."

* * *

Ani rounded the corner and swore under her breath. Devon stood there, leaning against Ani's locker with one hand, talking to Leah and Rose. To the untrained eye, they looked nonchalant—just three girls pausing for a chat. To Ani they looked like lions circling a wounded antelope.

Rose's eyes flickered to her and away, and a tiny nod alerted the other two to her presence. Leah tossed her blond hair back as an excuse to look over her shoulder. Devon didn't mark her at all. There wasn't a teacher in sight. Not even a janitor.

Almost without volition, Ani's feet shuffled forward, the walk of the condemned toward the gallows. Three feet from her locker, the three girls still hadn't moved. Ani slid her way past Leah and, without looking up, said to Devon, "Please move, I need to get my books."

Devon didn't move and kept talking. "So anyway, Mike and I were making out last night, and *finally* he gets my bra off without help."

Rose's laugh was forced. "It took him four months to get to second base?"

"No," Devon said. "He got to second base on our first date. This is the first time he did it without help. He's so cute."

From behind her Leah said, "No kidding. I wish I had a boyfriend like that."

"Yeah," Devon said. "He's been my boyfriend for *four months*." She crowded Ani, forcing her to step back into Leah. "It's *amazing*. He feels *so good*."

Ani looked up into Devon's hate-filled blue eyes.

"Did you hear that, Cutter?" She was so close that strands of her light-brown hair hung in Ani's face.

Ani looked at her locker. "Can I get in my locker? Please?"

"Oh," Devon said. "This is your locker, Cutter? I wouldn't want to get between you and what's yours."

"Don't tease her," Leah said. "She might slit her wrists."

"Aw, shucks," Devon said. "That'd be such a shame."

"Mrs. Weller's coming," Rose warned.

They turned their backs on her and walked away, gossiping, all signs of malice having vanished. Ani opened her locker and knelt down to trade out her books, hiding her face. A shadow fell across her, and she looked up.

The pity in Mrs. Weller's eyes didn't help.

"Are you okay?" she asked.

"No," Ani said. "Just go away, please."

Mrs. Weller stood there, watching her. Ani shoved her music theory notes into her locker and pulled out her Trigonometry and US History books.

"Please?" she whispered.

Mrs. Weller knelt down next to her. "You're a very strong person, Ani. I've never seen you cry. Everything will be better after high school. I promise. Meantime, if you need to talk, my door's open." She stood and walked away.

Ani's eyes itched. It was as close as she would come, ever again.

* * *

When Ani got home from Dungeons and Dragons night at the Lair, her head throbbed. If she ever had to listen to one more stinky middle-aged dork tell her breasts about his '20th level cleric with a mace of holy smiting' or whatever crap ever again, she was going postal.

Her mom was in the kitchen, the contents of her purse scattered across the table. Keys, lip balm, pepper spray, mints, tampons, loose change, tissues, and a small revolver lay in a heap. Her mom was eating a banana, running the paring knife through the fruit and taking each slice with her teeth.

Ani raised her eyebrows. "Purse explosion?"

Her mom looked at the piles of stuff. "Just reorganizing." She plucked a crumpled envelope from the heap and held it out. "School picture make-up day is November first."

Ani took the letter and rolled her eyes theatrically. "Not likely, Mom."

Her mom nodded at the letter. Ani read it and looked up, furious. "That's asinine."

Her mom shrugged. "They lost the disk. The whole junior class has to be re-done."

Perfect. Just freaking perfect.

CHAPTER 7

The following Friday was "Family Fun Night" at the elementary school, and Ani painted faces, "forced" to do it by her mean old mom. It was sort of a pre-Red Ribbon Week kickoff, and all of the volunteers wore their ribbons: bright crimson for drugs and AIDS, lavender for cancer, purple for domestic violence, periwinkle for eating disorders, green for the environment, yellow for the troops, rainbow for GLBT pride, and safety-vest orange for zombie preparedness. You had to look hard to see the red ribbons for which the week was named.

Ani had cut new lines into the grey flesh of her wrists, now raw and red because of the regenerative cream. Her mother thought it was just to fit in with Fey and her crowd, and because of that, she disapproved but accepted it as necessary. She didn't know that Ani had taken to doing it when she knew she'd be around a lot of people in close quarters, to ease the tension in her mind. The appetite suppression injections made control possible; cutting made it easy.

She was dimly aware of Fey, Dylan, and the rest of the emo crew lurking toward the back of the haunted house, determined not to have fun whether dragged there or not. She was much more aware of Devon and her friends at the dunking booth, proffering their tan, swim-suited bodies to raise money for the Sports Boosters. *Something else I'll never do.* It had been almost two weeks since the deep fryer, and while the skin-grafts and regenerative cream had helped, the left side of her abdomen was pulled tight against her ribs and scarred an unhealthy pink.

She sighed and let her thoughts go. She painted whatever was asked. Grape vines crawling up a young girl's cheek, a spider perched on a little boy's eyebrow.... The squirming canvas and the crappy brushes made it more of a challenge than she expected, and it was super-fun. She clacked her tongue stud against her teeth as she worked.

She was startled to see Mike when she looked up. She glanced over at Devon, who didn't seem to be paying attention, and flashed her eyebrows at him. He held the hand of a young boy with adorable John Lennon glasses, no more than three or four years old. His vibrant blue eyes burned holes through her reflection; black mascara and maggot-pale skin. They quivered, uncertain. His fear made her want to cry.

He bravely stepped up and asked for a heart on one cheek and a rocket-ship on the other. She got to work, her stomach knotting with Mike so close. He was somewhat standoffish with his posture, but the conversation was pleasant.

"This is Bill. Debbie's son." Debbie was his dad's most recent live-in girlfriend, one of a million he'd cycled through since he'd left Mike's mom when Mike had been in fifth grade. Mike lived with his mom, but spent one weekend a month with his dad in the city—it was supposed to be more, but never was.

"Your dad brought you?" *That's a nice change.*

He shook his head. "No. He asked me to watch Bill for the weekend. Apparently he's very busy 'remodeling' with Debbie, and didn't want kids underfoot."

"Gross," Ani said. "Is he at least paying you?"

Mike snorted. She finished the heart, showed it to Bill in the mirror and, with his approval, started on the rocket ship. She painted the grey base as the knotted feeling rose in her stomach. Something about Mike made it difficult to control herself. She pushed the feeling away; she had a few minutes.

"So how's soccer?" Not a good topic, but it would distract her.

"Uh... Over, Ani. We just lost in sectionals."

I know, she thought. *3-2 in overtime vs. Red Jacket. I just can't let you know I know.*

"What do you care, anyway? You've barely been to a game in two years. Not since..." Palms up, he motioned to her clothes and body. "Not since this."

"I don't care, Mike. I was just making conversation." The knot in her stomach tightened again. It wasn't all nerves. She patted Bill on the shoulder, showed him his face in the mirror, and hustled to the bathroom, ignoring the rest of the line.

Inside the stall she drew lines across the top of her left wrist, each cut grey, dead, unnatural. The pain was dreadful, terrible, perfect. She closed her eyes. Her body shuddered in release as the blade crisscrossed over old wounds, slicing half-healed scar tissue with bursts of delicious agony.

After three cuts, she felt better. These were deeper than the last, and the flesh separated more than she'd intended. Annoyed with herself, she pulled the needle and thread from her purse and started making sutures.

"Ani?" *Oh, crap.*

Her eyes widened. "I'll be out in a minute, Mom!" She stitched faster.

"Are you okay?" There was real worry in her voice.

Just what my social life needs, Mom. You yelling at me in the bathroom in front of what few friends I actually have.

She didn't try to keep the annoyance from her voice. "I'm *fine.* Just give me a minute."

The door slammed, then silence.

* * *

Wind clutched at her clothes as she got in the Audi. Ani hadn't even shut the door when the interrogation began. "What was that about, young lady?"

"Nothing, Mom."

Her mom adjusted the rear-view mirror and pulled out onto the neon-washed street, headlights flashing off fallen leaves scattering in the wind. "It's never *nothing.* I know you didn't have to use the ladies' room, so spit it out. What were you doing in that stall?"

"Jeez, Mom, chill out—"

Her mom slammed on the brakes and the car lurched to a stop. Her eyes were cold fury as she held up a finger. "I will never chill out.

Never. And you will be honest with me. *Always*." Ani waited in sullen silence for her mom to drop her hand, but she didn't. "You're young, so you might sometimes forget that our deal is a deal, and so it works both ways. All of your privileges are subject to your compliance with the rules. Understand?" She dropped her hand. Ani looked at her lap.

"I understand."

"You will follow the rules, or they will find out and they will burn you. It's not your fault you were born a carrier, it's mine, but it is your responsibility." She put the car in gear.

"I know, Mom."

"Good." The car started moving. "Now answer the question."

"Mike was being a jerk. I just wanted to get away from him for a minute." *Sorry, Mom, there's some things you just wouldn't understand.* "I just want to be normal again." *At least that was true.*

Her mom started to cry, silent rivers of water down her cheeks. She reached over and patted Ani's hand, then put her hand back on the wheel.

Ani tried not to gape in astonishment. *Twice in two weeks. Menopause? Or something else?*

"I'm doing my best, baby. You lived as a carrier for fourteen years. Nobody has ever done that. Nobody knew it was possible. I'll make it better. I'll change you back. I will."

"I know, Mom."

"I love you, sweetie."

"I love you, too." *I just wish I knew what was wrong.*

CHAPTER
8

Wednesday was the health fair, mandatory for juniors and seniors. The emos traveled in a herd for mutual protection against the barely-supervised throng. Only Dylan wore a ribbon—red, upside-down, cradling a fake joint. Ani assumed it was fake. Jake had a bag of oranges that had been soaked in vodka for a week, and Dylan had already eaten two as they wandered the aisles of booths crowding the gym.

They crossed paths with the jocks twice, and she might as well have been invisible. Mike didn't even look at her when Keegan bought an orange from Jake for five bucks. Devon didn't stop looking at her, her lips curled up in an ugly sneer. Leah and Rose muttered and glared; Ani ignored them.

A few minutes later, Devon's voice rang out over the PA. "Ani Romero and Tiffany Daniels, please report to the Eating Disorders Booth. Ani Romero and Tiffany Daniels, to the Eating Disorders Booth." Girls tittered in the background. A boy yelled, "Awww, SNAP!" from across the gym.

Fey blushed, her face twisted into a mask of rage. "You know what would be great? If that bitch died in a car fire." Ani bit her lip, stifling agreement.

"I got this," Dylan said. He stalked off in the direction of the PA system.

Fey stared after him, her mouth agape. "What the hell is he doing?"

Jake shook his head. "Can't be good."

Jake headed after Dylan while Fey and Ani made their way toward the exit, weaving through the crowd with as little disruption as possible, ignoring the stares and laughs as best they could. They were almost to the door when feedback tore through the gym, a squeal that ran right up Ani's spine. Someone tapped the microphone, and then Dylan's voice reverberated through the gym at insane volume.

"Devon Holcomb, please put on a longer skirt. Your balls are showing." The microphone cut off and the sound of a scuffle erupted from the other side of the gym, accompanied by hoots and laughter. Fey grinned as they escaped, only to be accosted by Mr. Gursslin.

"Where you going, ladies?" He looked bored out of his mind. Ani would be, too, stuck on door duty.

"Bathroom." Fey touched her finger to her bottom lip. "It's a little testosterone-y in there." Ani gave her best enthusiastic nod.

He looked them over, considering. "Tell you what. My room's open. You can hang out there until the assembly, as long as you behave yourselves."

Ani beamed. "Thanks, Mr. G!" They went upstairs and talked about nothing while Thrice blasted from Mr. Gursslin's computer. *Emo meets hardcore. Please, someone, shoot these people before they make another CD.* Ani let Fey gripe about her life while she composed another pop song in her head.

At the assembly, Jake gave them the details. Dylan got a chipped tooth and two days of in-school suspension, extended to a week of out-of-school when they found a pocketknife in his boot. Jake didn't know what happened to the joint. Keegan and Mike were given two days out-of-school for fighting, and a week's detention. Devon was let off with a warning.

* * *

That night, Ani's mom gave her permission to stay out until midnight. She sat on the playground with Fey, Dylan, and Jake, drinking Genesee Light that Dylan had boosted from Tops. They drank, she didn't. *A nice thing about the emo crowd: the peer pressure is pretty understated. Suicidal apathy; the anti-drug.*

"I'm telling you," Fey said, "you should press charges. And sue for damages."

Dylan fingered his chipped tooth with his tongue. "I'm not that damaged." He took a swig of beer. "Besides, they'll pay. Not with money, and not today. But I'll make them suffer."

Fey smirked. "You going to read them your poetry?"

Dylan's hands balled into fists. "You little—"

"You guys doing anything for Halloween?" Jake interrupted. Fey shook her head. Dylan shrugged.

"I'll be at the Lair," Ani said. "Travis has some big vampire party there every year, and he's paying double time. You?"

Dylan's smile was almost a snarl. "I'm going to cover myself in fake blood and shamble down the sidewalk scaring little kids."

Jake snorted. "You'll get busted."

Dylan shook his head. "Not with a mask. The cops can't catch me, even if they see me."

Zombie costumes had been outlawed in most states nine years ago, after a survivor ambushed some trick-or-treaters with a gas can and a propane torch. The ACLU took it to the Supreme Court, said it was an infringement on free speech. The Supreme Court upheld the ban on public zombie costumes, but struck it down for private events. *And here I spend most of my time trying not to look like a corpse.*

"What if someone shoots you in the head?" Fey asked.

Dylan's eyes sparkled. "Can you imagine? That'd be awesome."

Fey rolled her eyes.

* * *

Red wine in bottles labeled "blood." *Hors d'oeuvres* shaped like eyeballs, fingers, ankhs, and werewolf claws. Ani had never seen so many Twilight haircuts and undead slut costumes in her life, and the Lair was packed with sweating, heaving bodies. Travis had been holding vampire parties for twenty years, but in the past few, they'd just exploded. That the youngest person there was at least thirty just made it all that much more pathetic.

Blood-red candles and strobe lights were the only illumination. The pulsing, flickering beat clashed with the haunting violin melodies of Leila Josefowicz on the cheap stereo. Even with the doors propped open, it was steaming hot. The whole place reeked of incense, perfume, and body odor—much like the black velvet cape Travis had talked her into wearing. She looked at the clock.

Ten thirty. An hour and a half left. She put her hands in her sleeves and ran her fingertips along the crisscrossed scars. She'd pulled the stitches out a week earlier, and they'd left no marks. She took a woman's coat to the stock room—at least at this party, nobody commented if you didn't smile.

As she hung the coat, a hand touched hers. Travis jerked his hand back. "God, you're like *ice*."

"Poor circulation," she said.

Travis' face was blotchy, his eyes glassy with wine, and he stood so close she could feel his breath on her face. He looked at his fingers, rubbed them together. "I guess." He closed his eyes tight and leaned even closer, then popped them open. Ani wondered if double time was worth an uncomfortable moment with her intoxicated boss. He licked his lips. "I need you to get another two boxes of *hors d'oeuvres* and get them in the oven. We're getting low."

Thank God. "Sure thing," she said, ducking past him.

She slipped out the back door and savored the cold night air. A siren wailed in the distance, and she idly wondered if someone had shot Dylan. She cut around the store into the alley, where Travis had stacked the food. A cat hissed at her, then bolted for the street.

"It's chilly." She jumped at the voice, then turned around. A figure smiled in the shadows, and the street light picked up straight teeth with a chipped incisor. *Dylan.*

"I thought you were scaring little kids," Ani said. "You sure scared me."

"I can see my breath," he replied. She saw it too, a curling mist against the darkness of the cinderblock wall.

She turned around and picked up a case, shielding her face from his. "Help me with these, would you?" She turned around and shoved a case in his arms. He took it, but didn't stop looking at her. She picked up the other box and walked toward the door, keeping her back to him.

"What about you?" he asked.

She neared the corner. "I'm stuck here until midnight."

A hand on her arm spun her around. The box tumbled to the ground next to his. He grabbed her by the shoulders and stared into her eyes. His were blue flecked with gold—she'd never noticed before—and his pupils were huge. She breathed out very, very slowly, so that he wouldn't see it. She didn't flinch as he leaned in, close enough to kiss. She breathed in. His warm breath reeked of cheap gin.

"When you walked out here, I couldn't see your breath," Dylan said. He squeezed, hard, digging his fingernails into her shoulders right through the cape. His eyes blazed. "Breathe for me, bitch."

She brought her knee up into his groin as hard as she could. He grunted and stumbled back, falling to the side in a fetal position.

She stacked one box on the other and picked them both up. "Don't ever presume to touch me again, Dylan." He squirmed; his eyes rolled back so she could only see the whites.

She ducked inside in desperate panic, her heart beating in perfect, mechanical rhythm in her chest.

* * *

By midnight, she'd made five more trips to the alley and hadn't seen any sign of Dylan. The party had, for the most part, moved upstairs to Travis's apartment, and after she turned down an awkward invitation to "join in," he told her to go home. She ditched the stupid cape behind the counter, set the alarm, and left through the front door.

The night was quiet, except for the wind rustling the leaves of the few trees that still had them, and the bitter cold froze her hands through her gloves. She pulled her coat tight, not because she needed it but because someone might see her, and set off toward home. She heard a car coming up behind her, so she crossed to the left side of the road well in front of the headlights.

The car slowed as it approached. She turned to look and something splattered across her face. She smelled rotting apple, sickly-sweet and foul. Whooping laughs and shouts of "FREAK!" and "CUTTER!" accompanied spitting gravel as Keegan's rusty Camaro lurched forward. Rocks peppered her, and she slipped, trying to avoid them. Her head hit the curb at the same time as her hands.

Head ringing, she reached up and felt her face. There was a

jagged tear in her right cheek. Her finger went right through and touched her tongue. *Gross.* She fingered the wound for a moment, then got up and hurried home, her hand pressed to her cheek.

If Mom sees this, I'm never leaving the house again.

* * *

Her mom was asleep when she got home. She half-slammed the door and tromped up the stairs to the bathroom—sneaking would inevitably backfire—and her mom called out from her bedroom. "How was the party?"

"Fine. I'm getting in the bath in a minute."

"Okay, sweetie," her mom said, voice groggy. "See you in the morning."

"Good night, Mom." She walked into the bathroom, turned on the light, and shut the door. She thought about locking it, but that would just make her mom curious.

She looked in the mirror. *Oh, crap.* It was worse than she thought. The wound was a quarter-sized gash from her jaw to her cheekbone, and she could see her tongue through the hole. She poked her tongue through, then pulled it back. *That's disgusting.* No amount of regenerative cream would fix that wound overnight. She got an idea, and headed to the sewing room. *If you have to be a freak, you might as well own it.*

CHAPTER
9

The lights came up in the bath, and Ani pressed the button to raise the lid. The familiar hiss as the seal released was a relief—it always was. The coolant pump kicked on as she lifted the lid, and the gooey mixture of formalin and other noxious chemicals ran off her body into the floor drain her mother had installed between her bedroom and the bathroom.

She toweled off, got dressed, put on some vanilla perfume, and ran down the stairs. She walked into the kitchen while her mom had a spoon full of cereal halfway to her mouth. "Hi, Mom!" she said. The spoon froze, and her mom's mouth with it. Ani smiled.

Her mom reached up and touched her own cheek. "What. Did you do. To your face?"

Ani ran her hand down the fourteen safety pins in her cheek, bunched so tight that the stitches in the skin beneath didn't show. "You said I could get whatever piercings I wanted to."

Her mom set the spoon down. "That's disgusting."

Ani grinned. "It's school picture day."

"Ah," she said. "I forgot." She pushed the bowl away and stood from the table, her face tinged green. "Rebel as you must, my darling child. Just keep your grades up."

"I will."

As her mom walked into the bedroom, Ani followed her.

"Hey, Mom, I noticed something yesterday."

"Oh, yeah, what's that?" Her mom had already showered and thrown on scrubs for the day. She always wore scrubs to work, called it a perk of being a nurse.

"In this cold weather, when I breathe out, there's no mist. What if someone notices that?"

Her mom sat on the bed to put on her shoes. "Huh. Good thought." She tied her shoes, thinking. "Keep a bottle of water with you, and just before you go outside, inhale a capful or two. That should do the trick."

"Okay, Mom, I'll try it on my way out to the bus. Love you!"

* * *

Her breath fogged nicely as she waited for the bus. Kids gaped in astonishment as she got on, and murmurs accompanied her to her seat. This time they amused her—she might be falling apart, but she'd beaten the rules, and beaten the odds, again. She was still free. She could deal with Dylan. *If he even remembers anything.* She sat down and turned her head to the window, feigning sleep as the bus stopped in front of the Daniels's House.

Fey dropped into the seat beside her, and a glance revealed perfect hair, perfect makeup, a polished nose stud, and polished eyebrow rings.

"Hey, Fey. You look nice today."

"Thanks," she said. Ani turned toward her as Fey handed her the iPod's right headphone. "So do—holy shit! What did you do?" Her eyes wide, she reached up and ran her fingers down the safety pins. "That is some crazy shit, Ani." Without further comment she sat back, put the other headphone in her ear, and closed her eyes.

* * *

Dylan wasn't in school. Jake texted him, and he claimed to be hung over after waking up freezing in a dumpster. *I hope that's true,* Ani thought. In the bath last night, she'd had plenty of time to think about how far she'd go to keep him quiet. *Could I do it?* Ignorance is bliss. She wasn't even sure what "it" was at this point.

She got more disgusted looks by the end of the day than she'd had all year, and the only one that hurt was Mike's. She'd walked into

Trig and he looked up, grimaced, and looked away. He didn't say a word to her through the whole class. *Yeah, well, if I didn't do it I'd never see you again.* She'd rather gross him out than be a memory.

Fey was acting funny by the time they got on the bus. It wasn't quite the silent treatment, and it wasn't the I-don't-care-about-anything malaise. It was monosyllabic, standoffish, and grumpy. She scowled down the aisle, arms folded.

"What's up?" she asked. *Don't ever ask emo kids "What's wrong?"*

"Nothing," Fey said. She turned her body toward the aisle and didn't offer the headphone.

Ani nibbled her bottom lip. *Do I pursue this one, or let it go?* "Are you pissed at me?"

Fey rolled her eyes. "No. I'm not pissed at you. Why would I be pissed at you?"

"Then what?"

Fey sighed. She rolled her head to the side to look Ani in the eyes, then shifted her body to face her. "Look at you."

Ani looked down at herself, then back at Fey. Fey's eyes were bloodshot, her skin flushed pink under the heavy pale makeup. "I don't know what to say, Fey. What do you see?"

Fey reached over and ran a finger down her unblemished left cheek, an oddly intimate gesture. "Everyone was talking about you today. Everyone."

"Yeah," Ani said. "About what a freak I am." *And at least today I deserved it.*

"No, you don't understand, that was just the kids. They don't matter. They ain't nothing. Who cares what a bunch of morons say?"

Ani shook her head, confused. "What are you saying?"

Fey crossed her arms. "The teachers. Bariteau. Weller. Those guys. Every time someone starts talking shit, they say something nice. Ani's a good artist. Ani's a great pianist. A great composer. She works hard. She's going somewhere. She gets out of here, she cleans herself up, she gets a life."

Ani didn't know what to say, so she said nothing. Fey tapped Ani's forehead with her finger, the nail digging at her skin.

"Hey, Ani? You in there? You understand what I'm saying here? I'm not pissed at you. I'm pissed because of you."

Now she was really confused. "Fey, I... Why would that make you mad?"

"Because if I had the balls to show up to school with a bazillion safety pins in my cheek, and kids talked about me, you know what the teachers would say?"

Ani came up blank. "No."

"Not a damn thing."

She handed Ani the headphone. *Damn. I was hoping she'd forget.* They rode home to My Chemical Romance.

* * *

When she got home, the Audi was already in the driveway. She walked in the house and her mom was at the kitchen table, a paper with school letterhead in her hand. "What is this?"

"Uh..." Ani said. "I don't know, Mom. What is that?"

"You'd think it'd be about your face, but it can't be, because this is postmarked last Friday."

"Mom... what? You have to tell me what it is."

"Conference requests. Weller. Gursslin. Johnson." She gestured to a chair. "Sit." Ani sat. "Explain."

"Mom, my grades have slid a little." Her mom's eyebrow went up. *I hate that eyebrow.* "Not much. Nothing less than a B- minus." *I hope.*

She just sat there, staring. Ten seconds went by. Then twenty. Ani shifted in her chair, unable to look away.

"Okay," her mom said, raising a finger. "You're quitting the Lair." Ani opened her mouth, but the upraised finger stilled her tongue. "You can burn incense in your room. I'll give you a bit of an allowance, or you can sell booze to that little alcoholic boy who's always on your heels. But if you can't handle a job and your schoolwork, the job goes. You go to school, you come home, you do your homework, and then, if and when your grades improve, we can talk about another job somewhere." She dropped her hand.

"Mom, seriously, the Lair is the perfect job. No uniform, so I can stay covered up, I never have to go outside, and there's, like, zero chance of injury. It's perfect. I'll get my grades up pronto. I promise. I don't need to quit."

"Doesn't the marking period end Friday?"

"Yeah, but I can do make-up work. They'll let me. They love me." *Come on, Mom....You can't do this. You can't.*

"Tell you what, I'm going to these conferences on Friday, and we'll re-evaluate then."

* * *

Ani stayed after every day, and did a mountain of make-up and extra credit work. Friday came and went. She got her new work schedule and posted it on the fridge. Her mom said nothing.

* * *

Tuesday, November 9th was another skating party, and Ani sold refreshments with her mom again. With her new system, she didn't have to worry about getting hungry. She tapped her fingers to the beat inside her coat. She was so small, and her hands so cold, that no one ever commented on the bulky jacket she had taken to wearing all the time. It gave her a place to hide chemical hot packs, too.

With the blade in her sleeve, she could cut right in front of people and they never noticed. Tiny cuts kept the edge off, and would heal without a trace in the bath overnight. Larger cuts could wait to be mended until she got home.

But today, Dylan was stuck watching his little sister, and that put him in the gym with her. He kept creeping looks at her wrists from the corner of his eye, as if she wouldn't notice. *Couldn't you at least look at my boobs like a normal person?* She couldn't understand what motivated these death-obsessed depressives, so full of life and so empty of spirit.

She was nothing like them. Nothing. An outsider in a clique of outsiders, what popularity she enjoyed was strictly a function of Fey's favor. The big-city Jersey girl had the emo crowd wrapped around her little finger, boys and girls vying for her attention at every turn. Angry, hopeless, trapped on a dead-end street of her own making, Fey for some reason had adopted Ani as her best friend. Perhaps her only friend. *These people are such a drag.*

The opening riff to *California Girls*—Katy Perry, not the Beach Boys—set the little girls to delighted shrieking. She was more like them, full of life, full of hope for the future. *Mom will come through soon, and all this will be over. Please, God, let this be over.*

"Who died?" Dylan hollered over the music. He'd walked up while she daydreamed.

She looked up at him from behind the refreshments table. "Excuse me?" *Do you remember, Dylan? And what the heck am I supposed to do about it if you do?*

"You look like someone died," he said.

"Are you volunteering?" she asked.

He put a dollar on the table and picked up a pack of Skittles. "I'm just trying to be friendly." It must be some kind of special talent to be able to sulk while yelling.

"Sorry, I'm just grumpy," she said. Dylan wouldn't notice the *faux pas*—emo kids never apologize for negative emotions.

He dragged a folding chair across the floor and plopped it down next to her. Ani noticed with some satisfaction that his steps were small and accompanied by an occasional wince. He eased down into the chair, rested his elbows on his knees and popped a handful of candy into his mouth. "What's got you grumpy?"

Her gesture encompassed the room. His lack of response was refreshing. It was as normal as she'd ever seen him.

Unasked and unwanted, he helped Ani sell candy and soda to already-hyper children, but at every idle moment, his eyes drifted to her. He helped his sister with her skates, but as she laced up, he stared at the refreshment table. Over the course of an hour, his chair got closer and closer to hers. Her mom gave her a stern look—all she could do was shrug. Another shift, another inch, and she couldn't take it anymore.

"Jesus, what?"

He jerked back. He swallowed, hard, and looked at his feet. She waited. He leaned in so that she could feel his breath on her ear. "I need to talk to you about Halloween."

No no no no no no no. She leaned in close, too close, so that her face wouldn't betray her. He smelled clean, with the familiar undertone of blood and meat that everyone carried. "What about Halloween?" She could taste his pulse, throbbing in his neck. The urge was a little rough today, but she'd had a lot worse.

"Did I...?" His exhale was sharp even over the throbbing bass line. "Did I...? What happened?"

Huh. She pulled back so she could look in his eyes and to distance herself from his flesh. His grimace was pained, but his eyes showed nothing. "You tell me."

"I don't know. When I woke up I could smell you." *Gross.* "The incense and vanilla perfume and that medicine smell underneath, and...." He ran his hand through his Edward hair.

"And what?" *Don't say it, Dylan.* Her eyes flashed to her mom and back. *Please.*

"And I really hurt." His eyes flicked to his crotch and then to the crowd of kids.

"Good," she said, her voice flat.

"Oh, God," he said, crestfallen. "I didn't hurt you, did I? I was drunk, and I'm so sorry—"

She put a finger to her lips. "It's okay, Dylan. You didn't do anything but get in my personal space. When you didn't back up, I backed you up. Forcibly. With my knee. That's all." He didn't say anything, so she added, "No big."

He collapsed in a slump as the song ended. "So we're cool?" he asked in the relative quiet.

"Sure, Dylan, we're cool." *Really, really cool.*

* * *

Her mom let her walk home. It was only a few blocks, and delayed the inevitable bath. It was cold, and she could make out the Milky Way through the streetlights, but only just. After an evening of pounding dance music, she decided to mellow out with *Imogen Heap* on the walk home. iPod in hand, she didn't hear the Washingtons' Doberman until it was too late.

Sleek and lean, it stepped out of the hedgerow, bared teeth shining white in the moonlight. She killed the volume, wary, and kept walking. *Where's your leash, Mac?* The dog stepped forward, snarling, its breath frosting in the cold. Ani froze. *Everything runs from me. Everything.*

She sidestepped toward the street, and Mac lunged. She shrieked, flailing, as the dog hit her. Teeth closed on her right arm, tearing through her coat and crushing her wrist as she fell. Her head bounced off the asphalt as Mac gnashed inches from her throat.

She slapped at Mac to dislodge him, kicked him off with both feet. She tried to stand and he bowled into her, knocking her back to the ground. He scrambled with her, snapping at her face. Desperate, she grabbed the dog's throat with her left hand. Her fingers dug in, and Mac's snarling turned to a whine. She closed her fist and pulled. Blood gushed over her face, hot and salty. Mac collapsed on top of her, and she almost shoved the meaty handful into her mouth. She threw it to the side, and a disappointed groan erupted from her mouth.

She pushed him off and rolled to her hands and knees. She licked her lips, shuddering in horrified ecstasy. Gasping in panic, she tore up her sleeve and raked with the razor blade, slicing skin and tearing her muscle, coated with canine blood, thick and black in the streetlight. She did it again. And again. *Better. Not good, but better.*

Footsteps pounded up behind her, and she whirled, fists raised, razor still in hand. Mac's blood dripped down her face. Dylan slid to a stop three feet from her, eyes wide with shock.

Brains.

"Jesus, are you—" His face blanched. "Oh my God, Ani. You're... You... I'm sorry. I didn't know."

Hot blood. Meat. Brains.

She stared at him, fists still raised, and bared her teeth. *Calm down, Ani. That's a person.*

He put his hands up, palms outward and fingers spread wide. "Easy, Ani. It's me. Dylan. It's okay." *It's anything but okay.* "The dog's not going to hurt you."

She stared at the vein in his throat, throbbing, pulsing, pumping blood to his brain. *Brains.* She stumbled backward, fists opening in supplication.

"Get away from me, Dylan." She gasped out the words. *Closer. Please, just a little closer.* "Go." Her stomach lurched, her throat constricted. *Brains!* The world started to haze red.

He stepped toward her. "I just want to make sure—"

"*GET AWAY!*" she screamed, taking a shambling step toward him.

He backpedaled, turned, and ran.

* * *

She was a sobbing wreck when she reached the house. She'd lost her wig, and the back of her head felt soft. Stringy wisps of hair—all she had left—were matted with dog blood and hung from her face. She stumbled in the side door behind her mother.

"Took you long enough," her mom said, turning. The chair fell to the floor as she leapt to her feet, and she backed toward the living room. *And the shotgun behind the couch.* "Ani?" she asked, voice quivering. Her face was sorrow and rage.

Ani shook her head. "Mom, I'm okay. It's dog blood. Washingtons' dog. Mac. He attacked me. I—I killed him."

Her mom's mouth opened in an 'O' of concern and she rushed forward, arms open wide. Ani put out her hands. "Mom! Stop!"

She stopped, wary. "What is it, sweetie?"

"It's the blood. It's got me all wonky. I need a dose. Bad."

Her mom nodded toward the basement door. "There's one in the fridge. I'll meet you downstairs in twenty minutes. Give it time to kick in."

Ani lurched to the door and half-fell down the stairs. Her hands shook as she yanked open the fridge door, and it took her three tries to extract the liquid from the phial into the syringe. She heard furniture shift over her head. *Mom. Bloody. Delicious. Right upstairs.* She found the tiny hole in the back of her head where her mom administered injections, but the entire area was pliant and mushy. She jammed the needle in place and depressed the plunger.

* * *

Her mom stopped halfway down the stairs, shotgun in hand. "You sure you're feeling okay?"

Freshly injected with a cocktail of pituitary hormones, cerebral fluid and synthetic chemicals, Ani had rinsed her mouth with bleach and felt fifty times better.

"A hundred percent, Mom." She pointed at the gun. "No need for that."

"Don't point," her mother said, lowering the barrel. "It's rude." She came down the stairs and set the shotgun in the corner. "Now let's get you cleaned up, and you can tell me what happened."

As she cleaned up and her mom reconstructed the shattered back of her skull, Ani told her about everything. Everything but Dylan. And the cutting.

CHAPTER
10

The next day the bus was abuzz about Mac. The police and the DEC were investigating. Speculation ran from a bigger dog to a bear to a mountain lion, and parents were waiting with their children as the bus picked them up. School was worse—it was the only topic of conversation—but no one seemed to notice that Ani was back to wearing her old coat.

Dylan waited at her locker before homeroom. *Why aren't you afraid?* She walked toward him, forcing her feet to keep going. He didn't look upset, or worried, or anything, but he didn't so much as glance at Fey as she split off to avoid him.

"Hey," he said, stepping out of her way so she could open her locker. He inhaled as she cut past him, his eyes fluttering closed. *Is he smelling me?*

"What's up?" she asked. It wasn't rhetorical.

His eyes snapped open. He slid a paper bag into her locker, its top folded, his eyes not leaving hers.

"What's this?" she asked. She unfolded the top and looked inside. A blood-soaked black tangle, trapped inside a zip top plastic bag. *My wig.* She shoved the bag in her purse and glared at him. Through clenched teeth she whispered, "Where did you get that?"

"The road. I went back to make sure there was nothing to put you there." A hint of a smile graced his black lips.

"Why would you do that?"

"Why would you hide that you have cancer?"

She blinked. "Cancer."

His smile blossomed, and for a moment, he was almost handsome. "You value your privacy. I get it. I really do." She opened her mouth to reply and he cut her off. "So no one needs to know about the dog. Or your hair. Or your—"

"Hey, Cutter," Devon's voice rang out behind her. "You doing animal sacrifices now?"

Ani kept her face in her locker as Dylan disappeared from view. *Just go away, Devon.*

"Step back, freak!" Devon said. Ani turned around. Dylan had Devon backed against a wall, his face inches from hers, his hands against the wall on either side of her head, blocking her escape.

"The dog was fun," he said, "but we're starting on humans next. Girls. We're tired of cutting ourselves." He ran his tongue over his front teeth. Devon turned her head to the side, white-faced.

Ani saw Mike barreling down the hall, shouldering anyone and everyone out of his way. It was impossible not to admire his physique, and his confidence using it. "Dylan, back off," she warned. She put a hand on his shoulder.

He took a step back just as Mike checked him. He stumbled sideways and spun away, escaping down the hall as Mike turned to Ani. "What the hell was that?"

Ani's reply was acid. "That was Dylan defending me from your psycho girlfriend."

"Fuck you, Cutter!" Devon spat, stepping forward.

Ani stopped her with a glare. "Try it," she muttered. She was sick and tired of being pushed around by a soulless mannequin. What Mike saw in Devon she would never know.

Mike stepped between them. "Hey! Calm down." His body was turned toward Devon. *He's protecting* me *from* her.

Mrs. Weller stepped out of her classroom, one eyebrow raised at Devon. "Miss Holcomb, language."

Devon had the good grace to blush. "Yes, Mrs. Weller." *Always the angel in front of adults.* Mere compliance was never enough to satisfy Mrs. Weller, who ignored Mike to look at the girls.

"What's going on, ladies?" she asked. Mike took his cue and stepped back.

"Nothing," Devon said. "Nothing at all."

Mrs. Weller looked at Ani. "Ani?"

Ani didn't reply.

"It didn't sound like nothing." Nobody said anything. Finally, Mrs. Weller gave her verdict. "Devon, you have detention with me tonight—"

"I have practice!" Devon protested.

"Then you'll be late," Mrs. Weller snapped. "And unless you want more, you'll be quiet." She turned to Ani. "Ani, you have detention tomorrow." *No point in protesting.* "You girls stay away from each other, or I will make your lives rather more miserable than you can imagine." *Fat chance.* "Now get to class."

Devon mouthed, "You're dead, Cutter," before stalking off, Mike at her heels. He turned around long enough to give her an apologetic shrug.

I know it can never be me, but why her?

* * *

Sarah Romero: expert on ZV epidemiology, former cardiac surgeon, current school nurse, and mother of one. It was the first of these that took her out of town the next day and the day after. A recent ZV outbreak had been pacified by the Venezuelan military, but it had triggered a conference on modern techniques for ZV control at Strong Memorial Hospital in Rochester. This left Ani on her own during school, with no refuge to flee to. *I'm seventeen years old, dead, and I miss my mommy. Pathetic.*

Fey had a new lip ring, alternating bands of fake gold and fake emerald, and Jake couldn't keep his stoned eyes off it. Trapped together in the cafeteria, Dylan tried so hard not to look at or speak to Ani that he might as well have been screaming.

Fey dropped her fork of mashed potatoes and rolled her eyes at Jake. "Not for nothing, you're freaking me out. Just go hide for a while. Shoo." Jake recoiled, then grinned at Dylan. Fey waved him off. "I said 'shoo'. Beat it. Scram." As Jake got up from the table, she turned to Dylan, who hadn't looked up from his hands. "And you with him. Scat. It's girl time." Dylan followed Jake to the far end of the Anime nerds' table, where they were sure to get funny looks, but nothing more.

As soon as they were gone, Fey grabbed Ani's hands—they'd been in her pockets with the hot pad—and leaned in, nose to nose. "Is Dylan totally obsessed with you or what? He hasn't looked at my ass once today, and he's totally bugging. What gives?"

Ani withdrew her hands and held them up in a shrug. "I hadn't noticed." Her smile didn't even convince herself. *Please just let it go, Fey.* She knew she wouldn't.

"Yeah, sure you hadn't," Fey said through another bite of potatoes. "Spill."

Ani schooled her features and tried again. "There's nothing to spill, Fey. I have no idea what's going on in that demented little brain." *True, as far as it went.*

Fey looked in her eyes, searching. "You're a good liar, but not good enough." She leaned back. "Fine, you don't want to talk, you don't want to talk. Better you than me anyway." She shoved another fork load of potatoes into her mouth.

* * *

As weird as it was to be in school without her mom, being home without her was weirder still. After an uneventful three hours at the Lair, Ani locked herself behind familiar walls, closed the blinds, changed into her nightgown and sat at the Baby Grand in the dark. She closed her eyes. Mussorgsky's *Une Larme* flowed from her hands, through the wood and ivory and taut metal, and out into the air. Haunting and melancholy and sweet, it ended with a hint of hope. While she found no flaw in her technique, she had yet to evoke the emotion it should have, so she tried again. And again.

As she finished the third time, she heard the latch on the kitchen door jiggle, and opened her eyes. She spun off the bench and stood, then tiptoed to the couch, avoiding the creaky floorboards. She reached behind the couch, found the cherry stock, and lifted the shotgun from the cradle velcroed to the upholstery. The kitchen door opened, and she tensed.

Mom's rules were clear: no one sees the basement. Ever. A security system might scare away an intruder, but it would bring the police, too, and that was unacceptable. Hands shaking, she stepped deeper into the shadow afforded by the media center. *My heart should be racing.* It beat with mechanical precision, correct to a thousandth of a second and useless except as subterfuge.

A silhouette appeared in the doorway, lean, perhaps six feet tall. It ran its hand through its ridiculous poufy hair. *Oh, great.*

"Don't move," she said. She cocked the shotgun for effect. A cartridge pinged on the floor. *Already chambered. Go Mom.*

"Ani, it's Dylan!" the figure said.

"I know. That's why I haven't shot yet." She didn't move, didn't turn on the lights. "You want to explain what you're doing breaking into my house?"

"I... I have to talk to you."

"Ever heard of a phone call? Text? Doorbell?"

"I know. I'm sorry. I wanted to see you. I heard you practicing. I didn't want to interrupt." *That worked.*

She set the shotgun on the couch, felt along the wall and flipped the dimmer switch. He squeezed his eyes shut against the burst of light, and she used the opportunity to tighten the sash on her nightgown.

Dylan's eyes opened, then widened as he took her in. "Oh... I'm sorry, I didn't realize..." It had been a long time since someone had looked at her that way. She was way past embarrassment, and if he weren't such a creeper, she'd feel flattered. A little. He smiled. "I didn't figure you for pink."

"I didn't figure you for breaking into my house." She sat on the couch and crossed her fishy white legs as his chest puffed out a little.

"I'm full of surprises."

"You're an idiot who almost got himself shot." She nodded to the loveseat. "Take a chair." He sat, deflated.

They looked at each other for a minute. Ani forced herself to stop chewing her lip. *I stare at the inside of a refrigerator eight hours every night. I can outwait anyone.*

At long last he spoke. "Take off your wig."

Ask, much? "No," she said. *At least there was no 'bitch' this time.*

"Please?" His voice was full of the desperate intensity that was so effective at turning off Fey... and every other girl on the planet.

"I said no." *And who the hell are you to even ask?*

He scowled. "I just want to see—"

"It's not going to happen, not today, not ever. It shouldn't have happened last night. That stupid dog..." She scowled. *Poor Mac never did anything to hurt anyone. He was protecting his family from the monster.*

"You killed it with your bare hands," he said. "All that hot blood—"

She gave him a withering look. "Do you have to fill every pause in a conversation?"

He looked down, silent. She got up, scooped the shotgun shell off the floor, and set it on the piano. She turned around. Dylan's mouth was open, his head listing to one side, his eyes unfocused. *What an idiot.*

"You're stoned."

He blinked hard, then nodded. "I am. I'm trying to make sense of last night."

"Good idea," she said. "Getting high makes everything so much clearer." She leaned back against the piano.

He nodded. She put her hand to her forehead. *Yeah, I really meant that literally.*

When she removed her hand, he was inches from her face. She froze. He ran a warm fingertip down her safety-pinned cheek, his eyes on her lips. He started to pucker, and she straight-armed him in the chest.

His ankle hit the corner of the coffee table and he tumbled backward, arms spiraling. He landed hard on his tailbone and tears sprang to his eyes. He clutched his left hand to his chest, his face twisted in pain.

"I like you, Dylan." *I don't. You're creepy and pathetic and full of meanness and hate.* "But not that way." *And besides, I'm not who you think I am.* "Go home."

Tears flowing, he bolted for the kitchen door.

She watched him lope across the lawn and hop the fence, then she re-locked the door. *Lot of good that lock does.*

A few minutes later, tires squealed in the darkness.

CHAPTER
11

It felt weird to have a Thursday off school. Ani's mom had called to let her know that she'd be home around noon—because it was Veteran's Day, she was skipping the last half-day of the conference in order to get some research done. Ani spent the morning painting landscapes and tidying up around the house.

She heard the lock in the door and sighed in relief. As her mom walked in, Ani grunted in surprise. A cute pixie cut had removed most of her hair, and she was wearing a pink business suit Ani had never seen before.

"Do you like it?" her mom asked. She kicked off her heels and Ani noticed that she was showing a little cleavage and a red lace bra. *Oh, God, that's going to take some getting used to.*

"It's cute," Ani said. "It looks really nice. Midlife crisis?" *Mental breakdown? Late-onset sluttiness?*

The spark in her mom's eye faded a little, but her smile widened. "Something like that. Here." She held out the bags. *Okay, let's not talk about it. Whatever "it" is....*

Ani smiled back and helped her with her bags, two from the conference and two full of new clothes. Her mom changed into scrubs, used the bathroom, ate a light lunch, then clapped her hands together. "Are you ready?"

Ani smiled, the safety pins in her cheek pulling it lopsided. Her mom was at her most animated when doing research, and she loved to see her so happy. "Let's do it!" The bookcase was on Teflon sliders. Ani slid it out of the way, exposing the basement door as her mother got the key to the padlock.

*   *   *

Ani spent the next several hours being poked, prodded, cut, injected, extracted, and implanted. Cells were removed from her body, subjected to chemical concoctions, and examined under microscopes. In its own way, it was kind of fun. It was almost eight o'clock—they'd worked through dinner—when her mother gave her a sad smile. "Sweetie, I have a new serum I want to try tonight."

"Okay," Ani said. "I'll go get some audiobooks." She went upstairs, and returned a few minutes later with the old CD changer and a stack of Amy Glenn Vega's *Nursing Novellas*. She programmed the CD player while her mom watched her, a tear in her eye. *All this crying is starting to freak me out.* "What?" she asked.

"Nothing." She wiped it away. "I hate putting my baby in there. And I hate what might happen if things go wrong." *We've done it a million times.*

"I know, Mom. But we have to try, and we have to be safe." She opened the steel door in the wall, revealing a tiny room—it used to be an industrial coal furnace—equipped with a steel-reinforced recliner. As her mom shackled her in, she tried not to let her eyes wander to the propane tubes in the wall, or the asbestos-lined steel chimney above her.

"Are they tight enough, honey?" her mom asked. Ani tried to sit up, lean forward, reach with her arms. She had no more than two inches of freedom in any direction. *Perfect.*

"Yup."

"Okay." Her mom inserted the steel bite-guard into Ani's mouth, then moved around behind her and pulled the leather straps tight. "Good?"

Ani nodded, and her mom switched on the digital video camera and shifted into doctor mode. She moved out of sight behind Ani.

"November eleventh, eight-twelve p.m. ZV-counteractive

gamma-four trial one. Subject is female, seventeen years old, animate two years. Current success with beta-four excellent but dropping. Administering two hundred cc's gamma-four via injection into the anterior cerebellum."

No matter how many times it happened, Ani never got used to the feeling of needles entering her brain. The prick through the skin, the push through the bone, and then... nothing. It didn't feel like anything at all. The needle pulled out, and a moment later, her mom appeared in front of her, surgical mask over her face, eyes searching.

"How do you feel, honey?" Ani shrugged. "Any discomfort?" She shook her head. "Intoxication? Trouble thinking?" She shook her head again, and her mom turned to the camera. "No dilation, no visible response. Cognition appears to be human-normal." She turned back. "Good night, sweetie. I love you. I'll monitor your condition from upstairs."

Ani mumbled "I love you, Mom" through the bite-guard. It might have sounded like English. The steel door closed, and she heard the bar fall into place. Words flooded through the speaker in the wall, and she tried to lose herself in the fiction.

* * *

At four-thirty a.m. her mom came in wearing a new nightgown, sheer cream-colored cotton and lace. She ran a battery of tests, then removed the bite guard and asked Ani questions. No, she wasn't hungry. Yes, she felt good—fantastic, in fact. She lived in Ohneka Falls, New York, was seventeen, a junior in high school. She knew the year, the president, blah blah blah. Satisfied, her mother unshackled her so she could get ready for school.

* * *

Dylan skipped school on Friday, which was awesome. He wasn't there Monday or Tuesday, either. Jake said he was sick and would be out for a week. *Super-awesome.*

Ani got on the bus Wednesday morning and found Mike sitting in her seat, staring up at her with those beautiful green eyes. She tried not to smile, and failed. "Uh, you're in my seat."

He grinned at her, stood, and let her past him so she could sit down. She brushed against him as she slid by, felt the taut muscle and tried to keep her wits about her. She sat, and he sat next to her, filling the seat with his solid, masculine frame.

"Now you're in Fey's seat," she said. *Please don't move.* Her eyes drifted down his body, then back up to his eyes.

He shrugged. "She'll get over it. It's just today anyway."

She raised an eyebrow. "No Devon today?" She tamped down a spike of anger.

He shook his head. "Nope. College visit. She went to Potsdam with her mom." *Super, duper, duper-awesome.* Then it hit her. Devon would be going to college next year. College.

"Is she applying anywhere local?" she asked. Mike had a strong jaw-line, square and masculine and dusted with a tiny hint of blond stubble. *What the hell is wrong with me?*

"Closest is Geneseo. That's like an hour away." *And she probably wouldn't get in, which means even farther.*

"That sucks," she said. *For Devon. It's great for me. For us.*

"Hey, meatloaf," Fey said from the aisle. "You're in my seat. Scram." Ani hadn't even realized the bus had stopped again. Fey gave Mike her best "and if you could die while you're at it, that'd be great" look.

Mike smiled at her. "We're talking. There are other seats." He turned back to Ani. Fey widened her eyes at Ani. Ani looked at Fey, then Mike, then back at Fey.

"Just give us a minute, Fey."

Fey scoffed, rolled her eyes, and disappeared from view.

Mike shifted closer, and Ani was enveloped by his presence. They talked about college dreams and absent dads, days gone by, and trigonometry. She felt warm, dangerous, protected. On a precipice. Alive. In love.

The bus stopped in front of the school, and the brakes

engaged with a sharp hiss. Mike stood and said, "Well, have a good day. See you in trig." He disappeared into the school, and her heart went with him. By habit, she inhaled a bit of water from her bottle before following him out into the cold.

Ani expected Fey to be furious for blowing her off. She wasn't. She looked worried.

"Not for nothing, but you're going to die when Devon gets back."

Ani felt herself blush. *Blush? How?* "Why, who's telling?" She pulled out her compact and looked at herself in the mirror, pretending to check her lipstick. Same pale face, same dead eyes. It *felt* like a blush.

Fey rolled her eyes. "Oh, probably the whole bus. On top of the Dylan thing, you're getting quite the reputation."

"We were only—wait, what 'Dylan thing'?"

Fey's lip curled up, more sneer than smile. "Dylan told Jake what happened at your house while your mom was out of town, and Jake told, well, everyone." Fey turned to leave, and Ani grabbed her arm and spun her back.

"Ow! Jesus!" Fey pulled away, rubbing her arm.

"Sorry," Ani said, wincing. "Just what exactly is Dylan telling people happened?"

Fey's eyes widened. "Oh..." She looked toward the school, as if to escape. She fiddled her lip ring with her tongue. "Even I thought it was true."

Now how could I be hyperventilating without a functional respiratory system? She forced herself to calm down. She closed her eyes and matched her breathing to her heart rate. *In for four beats, out for four beats.* She opened her eyes. Fey was still there.

"You thought what was true?" Ani asked.

Fey looked at the door again. "Shit. Ani. He said... that you and he...." She held up her left hand in the shape of an 'o', and put her right index finger through it several times.

Is that why Mike was being so nice? Or was it coincidence?

Ani growled and stepped toward the doors. Fey grabbed her

shoulders. She focused on Fey's eyes, and steadied herself. "I'm calm. I'm okay. I won't do anything stupid. I'm just going to go into school, find Dylan, and break his neck."

"Sweet," Fey said. "Dibs on his stash."

But Dylan was absent again.

* * *

At eleven o'clock, she went to the nurse's office and dropped into a chair at her mom's desk. In hushed tones, she told her about Dylan's lie—leaving out that he was in their house—about her physical response to Mike on the bus, and about the blush. "I feel great, Mom, but I'm kind of freaking out."

"Well, honey," her mom said, "you're not used to this anymore." She flipped on a penlight and looked into Ani's eyes, nodded to herself, and turned it off. "On the bright side the new serum seems to be working great. That means we're going in the right direction. A very positive sign."

Ani nodded. "Yeah, it's great, Mom, but can I get a note to go home for the afternoon? So I don't do anything stupid? I'll hand in my homework before I go, get my assignments."

Her mom spoke up for the benefit of the secretary, diagnosing Ani with a low-grade fever and signing an excuse for her to go home for the afternoon. The day had warmed up into the mid-forties, and home wasn't far, so she walked.

* * *

Ani didn't realize she was going to Dylan's house until she was halfway there. She wasn't sure what she was going to say, but they had to have a talk. *Had* to. The TV flickered through the living room window as she stalked up the sidewalk. She rang the doorbell, then pounded on the door.

Dylan opened it, shirtless and surprised. "Ani!" He looked funny without his makeup, almost normal. She pushed past him into his living room, noting the cold pizza, the litter of Coke cans on

the coffee table, and the paused X-box. He followed her in. "Hey."
Like nothing's wrong.

"Are you home alone?" she asked. She didn't hear anything but the bubbling of the fish tank.

His smile was self-satisfied under his thousand-yard stare. "Mom's in Buffalo for the week, and she took my sister, so I figured a few days off school would do me some good. What's up?" *This scrawny little jerk is telling people I slept with him?*

He gasped in surprise as she grabbed his chin with her left hand and forced him backward. He clutched at her wrist to dislodge it, but he didn't have the strength. The wall shuddered as his head hit it, and he groaned in pain.

She spoke through clenched teeth. "We need to have a little conversation."

He swallowed. "Ani, you're hurting me." He slapped at her arm.

"I know." She lifted. His feet left the ground as he pried at her fingers, his knuckles white.

"You going to kill me, Ani?" he said, his breath hot on her fingers. "Do it. I want you to." His voice enticed, but his eyes cowered.

She slammed his head back, and he gasped in pain. "I'm not bluffing," she snarled. His heels banged against the wall as she schooled her voice. "You're going to go to school tomorrow. No piercings, no makeup, no black clothes. You're going to find new friends, and you're never going to talk to or about me to anyone, ever again. Because if you do..." She twisted her hand and his head bent to the side. She smelled urine, and a stain spread on his shorts. She lowered him to eye level, his legs dangling against the floor, and leaned in so that her lips touched his ear. "If you do, I am going to kill you."

She left him sobbing in the fetal position on the floor.

* * *

Her hands shook so much that it took her four tries to get the key into the lock. *I almost killed him. I really almost killed him.* Once inside, she slid down against the door, held the world at bay, and sobbed without tears.

CHAPTER
12

Dylan came to school in a Dragonball Z shirt, his hair bleached blond. Ani didn't see him until lunch but had heard all about it from Fey. He hadn't said a word to her, or Jake, or any of the other emos. *Perfect.*

"Look at him," Fey said around a mouthful of lukewarm goulash. "Sitting over there with his new friends like he's the shit." From the uncomfortable looks the other kids at the anime table gave him, Ani wasn't sure how friendly they all were. "Where the hell does he get off, thinking he's too good for us?"

Jake blinked at Ani, then looked sidelong at Fey. "I thought you wanted him to leave you alone."

Fey poked her fork toward him. "You don't get it. He's disrespecting us." She looked at Ani. "Am I right? It's disrespectful."

Ani shrugged. "Sure, Fey. But who cares?"

"Yeah," Fey said. "Screw him."

* * *

Ani took the next two weeks as they came. Dylan turned his thousand-yard stare on his new clique, and from what she heard was sprinkling Japanese into his conversations. They didn't accept him—several complained about how unnerving he was—but they had little recourse once he decided to force himself among them. He avoided the emo crowd like they were lepers. Jake was more depressed than usual. Ani thought he might have had a thing for Dylan. After she got over herself a bit, Fey called it good riddance, and if she'd connected the dots to Ani, she didn't say so.

Mike was his usual self, which meant he was nice when Devon wasn't around, and ignored her when she was. Keegan tried to strike up a conversation with her a few times, but they had nothing to talk about, nothing whatsoever in common. All he knew was sports, while she had to feign ignorance on the topic. And she hadn't forgotten the apple to the head on Halloween, his car speeding off into the night.

Devon ignored her, but as Thanksgiving approached, she got clingier and clingier with Mike, to the point that she was always on his arm. She started to freak at him if he so much as talked to another girl, even Leah and Rose.

After witnessing one of her psychotic tirades outside the gym, Ani leaned over to Fey. "Do you know what that's all about?"

Fey rolled her eyes. "You need a life, that's what it's about. I might have one in my purse—I'll trade you for some smokes."

"I'm serious."

Fey raised her eyebrows. "You really want to know?"

Ani nodded.

She leaned in and whispered. "Well, Mary—you know Mary Forsythe?" Ani nodded. "Mary tells me she was at a party last week up at Alfred, and she sees Devon there. But not Mike. Devon gets all drunk and she's dancing and shit, and then she goes into a bedroom with a guy, doesn't come home at all that night. Now she's all afraid he'll return the favor." Ani's mouth hung open.

"Does Mike know?"

Fey snorted. "Who cares?"

* * *

The day before Thanksgiving was the first real snow of the season. Maybe four inches blanketed the town, but it was supposed to melt off by evening. Ani loved the snow, so she took a dawn walk, pepper spray in her pocket and good boots on her feet. She told her mom she'd be back by nine so they could do more tests.

Most people skipped town for the weekend, so the streets were deserted. A splash of red in a leafless maple caught her eye. The cardinal chirped an alarm and fled to a higher branch. Chickadees scattered from a hedgerow as she walked by. Deer froze in Baker's lawn, then bolted for the copse of trees behind the house. The world was silent and peaceful under a cold blue sky.

She'd been walking for a half-hour when she heard rapid footsteps, muffled by the snow, coming up behind her. She turned, her hand on the pepper spray.

Mike jogged up behind her, glorious even in jogging sweats. He smiled, and it lit up his face. "Ani, hey. Taking a walk?"

She suppressed the urge to make a *Here's your sign* joke. "Yeah. I love how everything looks in the snow, and it's not going to last."

He slowed down to walk next to her. He looked around, a mock-sneer on his face. "There'll be plenty more where this came from. Wait until February."

"I know, but I can't help it." She looked up and down the street. "Aren't you going to take shit for talking to me?"

He shrugged. "Devon's in Georgia for Turkey Day. Besides, her insecurities are her problem."

She chuckled. "They seem to be my problem, too."

"Yeah," he said. "Sorry about that. I don't know why she hates you so much." *Are boys really that dumb, Mike? Are you?* "Not that you do yourself any favors."

She stopped. "What's that supposed to mean?"

He glowered for effect. "Said the girl with a billion piercings in her face." His grin softened the blow, but it still hurt.

She looked at her feet and started walking again. "I'm the same girl you used to know, Mike."

She saw the headshake in his shadow. "No, you're not. You're dark, moody, standoffish. You almost never smile, and you hang out with depressing losers." A crow cawed at her from a telephone line. She looked at it and it fled, squawking. She turned her gaze to Mike.

"Those 'depressing losers' are my friends." *Sort of.*

He shrugged. "Friends are supposed to make you happy. Are you happy, Ani?"

She stopped again and turned to look at him. She shook her head.

"Then why are you doing this?" *Mom's rules. Survival.*

"I'm just being myself." *And driving you away.* It was so much harder than it used to be.

"'Yourself' is Tiffany's toady?"

"I don't badmouth your friends." She turned away from him and started walking again, each footstep marring the perfect blanket of snow. "Fey's good people, in her own way. And she doesn't like it when people call her Tiffany."

"That's what I mean. She's kind of a bitch," Mike said.

"I should hope so, given what she's been through. She's had it pretty rough."

"What about you?" Mike asked. "How rough have you had it?"

Oh, the usual... I've been dead for two years because my dad was infected when he knocked up my mom. I have to pretend to hate everything I love so they don't burn me. I cut myself to avoid eating people. She gave him a sad smile. "Aren't you supposed to be with your dad this weekend?" She bit her lip.

He shrugged, but his eyes narrowed. "Uh-huh. He ditched me again."

"At least you know him. My dad abandoned us when I was an infant." *But not before he went cannibal and Mom blew his head off.*

"I know. And that sucks... But you can't let it eat you up inside. You squeeze what good you can out of life. Good choices lead to good places."

You've been drinking the Guidance Department Kool-Aid. "You mean like abandoning your childhood friend when she's no longer one of the cool kids? That kind of good choice?"

Mike stiffened. "You know what? I don't need this. I was trying to help." He took off at a jog, leaving her behind.

"I DON'T NEED YOUR GODDAMN HELP!" she screamed.

I need a cure, dammit.

* * *

When she got home, her mom had left a note that she'd gone to the store. She came back loaded with produce and a bag full of Boston Market.

"What's that, Mom?" Ani grabbed the Boston Market bag and put it on the counter.

"Tomorrow's dinner. No point in cooking a whole turkey just for me."

Ani looked at her mom, then at the bag, and then at the floor. "That sucks."

Her mom smiled. "Hey, one day, when you can eat without having to manually flush out your system afterward, we'll cook an outright Thanksgiving feast and gorge ourselves until we burst."

"Sounds appealing," she said, putting the bananas on the counter and the rest of the food in the fridge.

"It'll be great. In the meantime, why don't we get some work done in the basement?"

Thanksgiving agenda: piss off the only boy you like, perform medical experiments on yourself, sleep in a furnace. Awesome.

They worked until bedtime but weren't quite ready for the next serum, so Ani slept in the bath. They got to work at dawn and took a break for the parade and lunch. The serum was ready by five, and so Ani found herself chained to the recliner, listening to the audio book of *Cassandra French's Finishing School for Boys* on MP3.

The clock read one-twelve a.m. when she heard rustling behind the steel door. The clink of glass being moved, the click of cupboards being opened and closed. She heard her mom's voice, clinical and dispassionate, and realized it was a recording of previous serum tests. *Mom must be restless.*

She put it out of her mind until two-oh-five, when the door opened. Dylan stood there, dressed in black, his head brush-cut. His face was wet with tears, and in his gloved hands, he held her mom's shotgun. He stepped forward and hit 'stop' on the video camera. Ani didn't bother trying to struggle or to talk. That was the whole point of this setup. The best she could do was plead with her eyes.

He stepped inside, eyes wide, pupils huge, and took in the room—the fuel tubes, the chimney. "So that's what the big red button is for," he whispered. He stepped forward and hit 'stop' on the MP3 player, then raised the shotgun. The hole in front of the barrel dominated her vision, a yawning black chasm ready to swallow her, to drag her into oblivion. *Can zombies go to heaven? Is there heaven?*

He stood over her and pressed the barrel against her forehead, right between her eyes. The metal was cold against her skin. "Isn't this what we're supposed to do, Ani? With zombies?" His finger found the trigger.

Please, Mom. Please. She moaned.

He pulled the gun back, knelt, and set it on the floor. He looked at her, and his eyes were blazing, crazy. "I knew," he said. "I knew it." He shuffled forward to hover over her, and ran a finger down her cheek. "You're so beautiful, Ani. So beautiful."

He leaned forward and she closed her eyes. His lips were warm and soft on her forehead where he had pressed the gun barrel. He kissed her eyelids, her cheek, her neck. She shuddered.

"Shhh," he said. "I know. I know." He ran his finger along her lips, dry and cold around the bite guard. "I can't kiss you there, can I? One kiss and that would be it, the end. For me. For you. For Ohneka Falls. Quarantine and fire. Blood and death." He leaned in, his lips an inch from hers. Half an inch. His entire body quivered. She tried to pull away, but the chains held her fast. He pulled back, just.

"We all pretend like we're embracing death, but you... You *are* death. Waking, breathing *death*." He put his forehead against hers, closed his eyes, and breathed her in. "So cold... So impossible... So perfect." His hand moved down, brushing over her breast, to the sash of her nightgown. "So very perfect." His fingers lingered on the knot, then his eyes snapped open. "I love you, Ani." He leapt back, spun around, and stumbled out the door. He didn't close it behind him.

She heard him go up the steps, and then nothing.

* * *

"Ani?" Her mom's anxious voice flooded her with relief. *She's okay!*

Mom stumbled down the stairs in a panic. "Oh, my baby, my sweet baby, are you okay?" She covered Ani's face in kisses, then hugged her.

"Can you let me out, Mom?" It might have been understandable through the bite guard.

She squeezed harder. "In just a minute. I want to hold my baby." They sat like that for a minute, Ani half-suffocated if she had needed to breathe, before her mom pulled herself back. She undid the clasp on the bite guard and started on the other restraints. "Tell me what happened."

She did.

Her mom, of course, freaked, no matter how much she downplayed it. Dylan wouldn't tell anyone, and no one would believe him if he did. It wasn't good enough.

Their options were limited. They couldn't go to the cops—any police involvement would be more dangerous to Ani than Dylan could ever be. They couldn't go to Dylan's mom. They couldn't just make him disappear—her mom broached the topic, and Ani vetoed it—and he wasn't going to disappear on his own. Sometimes "not good enough" was all you had.

* * *

Monday, third period, she opened her locker and a dozen dead roses fell out, scattering brittle petals across the floor.

"Where'd those come from?" Fey asked.

Ani looked around. *No one there.* "I have no idea." She pulled a cigarette out of her band folder and handed it to Fey, who tucked it into her cleavage.

"You're a doll, Ani." Fey kicked the roses over to the garbage can and left them on the floor. "See ya."

When she was gone, Ani closed her eyes. "What do you want, Dylan?"

Dylan stepped out of Mrs. Weller's doorway, all in black. "How did you know I was here?"

"Who else would it be?" *And of course you'd be watching.*

He walked up to her with his crazy smile. "You're right. Nobody else knows your secret. Our secret."

"I told you if you talked to me again I'd kill you."

"Would you?" he asked. Insane eyes, insane smile. He put his hands at his side and tilted his head back, baring his bruised throat. He sighed. "Do it. Like the dog. I am a dog. Your dog. Do it, and we can be together, forever."

She shut her locker and walked away.

*   *   *

Dylan stared at her through band. And lunch. And art. His car followed her bus home. When she left the Lair—thank God he was still banned—his car was in the CVS parking lot across the street. Her mom drove her home, and if he followed, they couldn't tell.

Her mom wired up a private security system in the house. *It's not like we could get a dog.* Ani was forbidden from walking to or from anywhere. Her mom watched from the house as she got on the bus, and drove her home every day.

A week passed, then two, in near-normalcy. She found more creepy gifts in her locker—more dead flowers; an ankh; a desiccated bat, shriveled and sad; a bow of human hair, dyed black—and Dylan stared at her three periods a day. Quiet in the first place, he stopped speaking to anyone. He'd answer questions in class if asked, but that was all. He didn't defend himself when the bullies found him an easy target, didn't even react, and they got bored of trying. Already lean, he lost weight, and his eyes developed sunken, black rings that were not makeup.

But he never spoke to her, and he never broke into her house. *If he did, we could shoot him.* Even her mom agreed with that thought, whether it got the police involved or not.

In the end, he became one more reason for people to avoid Ani. Nobody wanted to be subject to that vacant, haunted gaze. Nobody but Fey and Jake—they claimed not to care.

*   *   *

Her first quarter grades sucked—only band and art were A's, and everything else C's. Her mother let it go.

CHAPTER
13

The skating party on the fourteenth was Christmas-themed, festive with red, white and green decorations. *Jingle Bell Rock* made the mix, as did *Santa Baby*. The energy was high, the kids had a blast, and if Dylan sat in the corner, staring at her from the darkness, so what?

The new serum was fantastic, now that she was more used to it. She felt more normal with every passing day and she didn't have to cut, not even with all the kids around her. She doled out candy and soda, and something she hadn't been able to do for over a year—hugs. She half-expected to start breathing again.

Ani and her mom walked out of the gym to the parking lot, singing *Feliz Navidad* at inappropriate volumes. Her mom frowned at their car, and Ani looked. The decapitated head of a lawn Rudolph sat propped on the windshield wipers, red nose dull under the yellow halogen lights. Ani clutched the ever-present pepper spray in her pocket.

Her mom *tsk*-ed and knocked the head off the car. "That boy needs a mental examination, but I'll be damned if I'm recommending one." They got in and headed home, Rudolph's dead eyes gazed after them from the parking lot.

* * *

That Friday afternoon was the Winter Carnival, and Ani was again painting faces. Little kids got snowflakes, polar bears, Santa hats, and presents. One precocious little boy got a teddy bear with fangs by request, proudly showed it to his mother, and was ushered crying to the bathroom to wash it off. *Ho, ho, freakin' ho, lady.*

Ani was in the bathroom scrubbing paint off her hands when Devon walked in. Ani watched her sidelong through the mirror but said nothing. Devon didn't go to a stall; instead, she walked up next to Ani and started futzing with her makeup. She looked almost flawless.

"Can I ask you something?" Devon asked. Her voice was neutral, without a hint of spite or false friendship.

Ani snorted. "Only if you call me Cutter."

Devon put her mascara away and turned to face her. "Seriously."

Ani turned off the water and dried her hands on a paper towel. "Sure, Devon, ask me whatever you want."

She twirled a lock of light brown hair around her index finger, then licked her lips. "What does Mike see in you?" Devon might as well have slapped her.

"In me?" She thought about it for a moment. *Compared to you? Actual thoughts. A personality. A brain.* "I don't know. We grew up on the same street, spent a lot of time together in elementary school. We were friends for a long time."

"Were," Devon said.

Ani sighed. "Yes. Were. I talk to him maybe once a week, sometimes twice, and then for maybe a minute or two. Jocks don't hang with emo kids."

"Fey was with Keegan last summer."

"For a weekend," Ani said. "Then she regained her sanity."

"What's wrong with Keegan?" Devon asked.

"Nothing. Everything. It's the wrong question."

Devon leaned against the sink and waited for her to continue.

"What's right with Keegan? For her I mean. Keeg's an okay guy, but what do they have in common besides hormones?"

Devon's face darkened. *Maybe I hit a nerve.* Devon fixed her hair in the mirror, plastered a fake smile on her face, and walked out the door. "See you at school, Cutter."

Fey rushed in an instant later. "What the hell was that?" she asked.

"I have no idea," Ani said, staring out the door. She shook it off and looked at Fey's shirt, a dead tree clawing at a gray sky. "I wouldn't have pegged you for a Winter Carnival type. What are you doing here?"

"Looking for you."

Ani smiled. "You found me. What's up?"

"I think you need another job. The Dragon's Lair is gone."

"What do you mean, gone?"

She flicked her hands at Ani. "Poof. Fire."

"Bullshit. What the hell are you talking about?" Ani asked.

"No, I'm serious. Heard it on my step-dad's scanner. Drove by on my way here. Leveled, there's nothing left but foundation. I thought you might want to swing by, check it out before the concert."

"Travis?" Ani asked.

"He was outside, covered in black. Stan said the whole place stank like gas. They think it's arson."

"Dylan," Ani said.

Fey rolled her eyes. "That kid's a nutcase, but he wouldn't do something like that."

Oh yes he would. "He burned down that bike shed last year. To impress you."

Fey smiled. "Lot of good it did him. And still, it's a big step from an abandoned shed to a store. He's all show."

"It was him," Ani said. "I'm sure of it."

"You got Dylan on the brain, Miss CSI. Travis probably did it for insurance money or something. Happened all the time back home."

"Fey, you've lived here for eight years. This is back home."

"Well, shit."

*　*　*

Fey's rusty El Camino smelled like vanilla and cigarettes. Mercifully, the radio didn't work, so they rode in relative silence to check out the remains of the Dragon's Lair. By the time they got there, the fire trucks were gone, and the area was sectioned off with 'DO NOT CROSS' tape.

The Lair was a ruin. A few black timbers smoldered in the falling snow above a congealed pool of soggy ashes. The siding on the diner next door had melted, exposing primed plywood beneath, but other than that, the fire appeared to have been contained to the one building.

"Is that cool or what?" Fey asked.

"Man..." Ani replied. *What is wrong with your demented little brain?* "Any idea where Travis is staying?"

Fey shrugged. "I don't keep tabs on the guy. Hope he had insurance."

I hope there's enough evidence to land Dylan in jail.

* * *

Ani sat at the grand piano in a full-sleeved black dress that covered her from neck to ankle. *Thank God I don't have to wear a costume.* Two years ago her mother had forged a diagnosis of *erythropoietic protoporphyria*—extreme sensitivity to sunlight. It got her out of outdoor activities in Phys Ed, it explained the discoloration of her skin, and it had the side benefit that Mr. Bariteau let her wear whatever she wanted to concerts, as long as it was "classy." How a man concerned with class could require elf costumes she would never know. Mr. Classy was, of course, dressed as Santa, complete with a fake beard and bushy eyebrows.

Devon was first flute, and, while she had given Ani a look when she walked in, it was more appraising than hostile. Mike sat with the baritones on the chorus risers, and her mom sat in the back of the auditorium, as usual. Fey didn't come—too cheery—and Jake wouldn't be caught dead there. There was no sign of Dylan, who should have been sitting with the tenor saxophones.

The band was first. They played several pop standards—*Winter Wonderland, White Christmas, Sleigh Bells*—as well as some lesser-known works such as James Curnow's *Christmas Troika*. As an interlude between the band and the chorus, Ani got to show off a little with Tchaikovsky's *The Seasons: December-Christmas*. It was the only thing on the docket that required any real skill, and it was light and upbeat and happy.

She closed her eyes and launched into it, her fingers frolicking across the keys. The acoustics in the auditorium were acceptable but not great. She thought of sledding and cozy fires and happy children, concentrating on getting the emotion of the piece correct. The notes would take care of themselves.

She was two-thirds through and proud of her performance when someone shrieked. Her eyes came open as her mother screamed her name. Mike sprinted at her from the left, his face twisted in hate. She cringed over the keys as he dove, arms wide in a grapple. As he flew over her, his foot caught her shoulder, spinning her from her seat.

She fell to the floor, too stunned to move. Dylan scrambled from under Mike and bolted for the front exit, sobbing. People scattered out of his way. Mr. Clark blocked the door, then raised his hands and stepped out of the way. Dylan swung a pistol toward the crowd, backing them up, and then bolted out of the auditorium. Children wailed.

Ani crawled over to Mike, who lay on his side. She saw the blood pooling on the floor, and screamed, "MOM!" He reached for her face. She slapped his hand away and tore his shirt, exposing a deep gash on his abdomen. A kitchen knife lay under him.

His voice was thick, confused. "Ani?"

Devon knelt next to her as she pressed her hands over the wound, Mike's hot blood flowing through her fingers. It smelled like iron and steak, and she felt her salivary glands pump what little fluid existed into her mouth. She looked down at him, hungry for the first time in weeks, and drowned in his eyes.

"Ani... I thought he was... I couldn't let..."

She heard Mr. Bariteau on the phone with 911.

"Shhh..." she said. "You'll be okay, Mike."

Her mother body-checked her out of the way, latex gloves already on her hands. Ani almost face-planted on the stage floor as her hands slipped in the blood. "Go wash up," her mother said. She looked at Ani, her brow streaked with worry. "Now."

She was escorted to the bathroom by a throng of concerned adults and students on nervous lookout for Dylan. As she scrubbed the blood from her hands, careful to get every trace from under her fingernails, she got them to back off as they told her what happened. The hunger faded to an ember's glow, lingering in the background but under control.

Dylan had come from nowhere. He leaped out of the orchestra pit with a knife in his hand, raised over his head, point down, ready to do... something. Kill her. Kill himself. Nobody was sure.

At last the water in the drain ran clear, and she returned to the stage. The sight of blood spiked her hunger, but it was a distant thing, lurking without strength in her gut. Mike was on a stretcher from the nurse's office, his side wrapped in bandages. Devon covered his face with soft kisses as he murmured to her, and Ani strangled a spike of jealousy. Her mom finished setting up a saline drip, then turned to Ani.

"It's superficial," she said, drawing Ani's gaze from Mike, her face in full-on doctor mode. "Painful, but a few stitches and he'll be fine." She lifted Ani's hands one at a time, examined them, and then let them go. "How are you?"

"I'm okay, Mom. Just a little shaken up." Her mom held her gaze. "I'm fine. Really."

"Okay," she said, and pulled Ani to her chest, squeezing tight. Ani's stomach lurched at the proximity, but she held strong. "We'll get him, Ani. The police will find him, and they'll lock him in a padded room forever."

CHAPTER
14

They stitched up Mike, held him for observation, and released him the next morning with a prescription for painkillers and bed-rest. Whatever connection Ani thought she might have made with Devon had disappeared, killed and eaten by psychotic, hormone-crazed jealousy. Ani avoided her when she could and used Fey for cover when she couldn't.

That night the phone rang, interrupting her mom's dinner. Ani didn't recognize the number, but it was local. Her mom was mid-chew, so Ani hit 'Send' and put it to her ear.

"Hello?"

"Hi, Sarah?" The voice was female but she didn't recognize it.

"It's Ani. Let me get—"

"Oh, Ani, thank God you're alright! This is Mrs. Johnson. Dylan's mom." Ani's bugged out eyes glared at her mom, who was eavesdropping. "I'm so, so sorry. I don't know what came over my little boy." She started to sob.

Ani held the phone and waited, with no idea what to say. *It's okay? I hope the cops catch him soon?*

"Are you there?"

"Yeah, I'm here," Ani said.

Mrs. Johnson sniffled. "Well I just wanted to say I'm sorry for everything."

"Okay," Ani said. "Thank you for calling." She hit 'End' and set the phone down. Her mom took another bite of mashed potatoes. "That was weird."

Mrs. Johnson called again the next day, and the day after that she stopped by with a plate of cookies.

* * *

Aside from nervous waiting for some word from the police, the only excitement was when Ani's five-week grades came out on the 23rd—and it wasn't the good kind of excitement. Even though she had done all of her work, her test scores were a shambles. It was hard to concentrate with the thought of Dylan appearing behind her, knife in hand. Even moving her seat to the back of the classroom, where she had a full view of the door and windows, didn't help. Her mother remained firm—she was grounded. Not that she had a job or a life, or was allowed to go see anyone in the first place. *Like grounding a houseplant.*

Still, come Christmas Eve the house smelled like cinnamon and nutmeg and the pine wreath over the mantle, Bing Crosby crooned on the stereo, and their fake plastic tree twinkled with colored lights and ornaments. *Things could be a lot worse.*

The doorbell rang.

Ani looked at her mom. "I got it," she said. "Maybe it's the police." Her mom moved over to the couch as Ani checked the peep-hole. "It's Mike!"

Her mom *tsk*-ed and moved back to her desk. Ani schooled her face blank, then undid the double deadbolts and opened the door.

"Merry Christmas," she said. "Come on in."

She stepped aside so he could do just that, shut the door behind him, and re-set the locks.

"Merry Christmas, Ani." He handed her a small box wrapped in gold paper. "Merry Christmas, Mrs. Romero."

"Miss. Or Doctor." She smiled at him. "Merry Christmas to you, too. Make yourself at home."

Ani set the gift on the piano while Mike removed his boots.

"Do you want something to drink?" she asked. He shook his head.

"No, I'm good," he said. She sat on the couch, and he sat next to her, then glanced at the present.

"I didn't get you anything," she said. *Dammit, dammit, dammit.*

"That's okay," he replied. "I wasn't expecting anything." *Neither was I, but I should have gotten you something anyway.*

They sat in awkward silence, thighs touching, him staring at the floor while she stared at the shuttered window. Her mom scribbled in a notebook, and the pencil scratching across the paper was the loudest thing in the room.

Mike cleared his throat. "Hey, I got my mom a keyboard, a Yamaha DGX-530. Got it used on Craigslist."

Ani smiled, trying not to stare at him. "Wow. That's a nice machine." *Expensive.* "I didn't know she plays."

Mike returned her smile. *Why is it so hard to breathe when I don't even have to?* "She doesn't, but she's always wanted to. I was hoping you'd give her some lessons."

"Uh..." Ani said. Her mom frowned at her from across the room. "Um..." Her mom shook her head. She looked at Mike. *I can't say no to those eyes.* She held up a finger. "Don't go anywhere. I'll be right back."

She rushed to the study, pulled a Christmas card from the file, and wrote in it. *This card good for ten hours of lessons at Ani's house.* She popped it into an envelope, sealed it, walked back to the couch and held it out to Mike. "Give her that."

He took the envelope, looked at it, then looked at Ani. "Okay, thanks." She stood in front of him, and they stared at each other. He looked at his knees. "Um, I got to get going." She took a step back as he stood. She noticed him wince as he got to his feet.

"Thanks again, Mike. For everything."

He hugged her, and held it for a bit longer than was proper for a boy with a girlfriend. His whisper in her ear was fierce. "They'll catch him, Ani." He stepped back, put on his boots, and was gone.

The moment the door closed her mother slammed the notebook shut. "You are not going to that boy's house for piano lessons."

Ani suppressed the urge to roll her eyes. "I know, Mom. I'm giving her ten hours of lessons here. I had to do something." *I wanted to do something.*

Her mom frowned at the door. "Yes. I suppose you did."

Ani approached the gold-wrapped box like it was a rattlesnake. She picked it up, bit her bottom lip, and looked at her mom. It was light and made no noise when she shook it.

"Oh, sweetie, you're a basket case. Christmas Eve is close enough."

She tore off the wrapping paper, revealing a white box. She pulled off the lid and a card fell to the floor. Underneath was a pewter ring of tiny skulls with red glass for eyes. Engraved on the inside it said, *For Ani. Forever your friend. Mike.* She put it on her middle finger and held it out to her mom, who smiled up at her.

"It's vile," Ani said. "I love it." She put a hand to her mouth, reached down and picked up the envelope. Inside was a handwritten note on plain stationery.

* * *

Dear Ani,

I didn't realize how much you still meant to me until last week. I'm so sorry I couldn't hold on to him. I'm sorry that I pushed you away. I'll call you tomorrow. Please don't show this to anyone.

Forever your friend,
Mike.

* * *

Her mom held out her hand, and Ani handed her the note. Her eyes scanned it twice, three, four times. Finally, she looked up. "I know that look, Ani. Be smart."

Ani swallowed. "I will, Mom."

"I mean it."

"So do I." She almost believed herself.

* * *

Christmas morning, her mom unwrapped her presents. She seemed to enjoy the sweater and the earrings Ani had made in art class. *How do you shop for someone whose only hobby is cutting off parts of her daughter's flesh and performing experiments?*

Ani shredded the pink wrapping paper on her gift from her mother and pulled the top off the cardboard garment box. Inside was a strapless mini-dress in her favorite color: Barbie Dream-House Pink. She ran her hands down the smooth satin, then lifted it out of the box.

"What's this?"

Her mom's smile was fierce. "That is a promise, from me to you. You will be able to wear that dress to graduation, in front of everyone, because you will be beautiful, you will be confident, and you will be symptom-free."

* * *

Mike didn't call on Christmas day. Or the next day. Or the next. A quick walk by his house—with Fey, Jake, and pepper spray in her pocket, and a promise to her mother that she wouldn't be gone more than an hour, and all of this after an hour of begging that she was going crazy and just needed to get outside for a while—revealed Devon's car in the driveway, but not his mom's car. Ani didn't think Fey noticed her looking.

* * *

She got home and moped in her room while her mom ran to the store. *He said he'd call.* She picked up the phone, dialed his number, and hit END. She put the phone back in the cradle and went back to reading. *More like holding a book and sulking.* She gave up after a half-hour. She looked at the phone. *Maybe I'll paint.*

She grabbed her brushes, easel, and canvas, tucked her box of paints into her right elbow, and walked out into the hall.

Her head rang.

The world slowed, smeared.

Paint brushes like spilled spaghetti onto the floor, beautiful in their simplicity. Tiny paint cans bumbled and bustled their way over the railing, a suicide of color trapped in chrome.

The world hazed red, and she crumpled to the floor.

Something grabbed her shoulder and rolled her onto her back. Several figures in black stood above her, looking down, swimming in and out of each other. As they knelt, they resolved themselves into a single shape.

Dylan.

His hair was black again, but his chin was coated with downy blond peach fuzz. Black turtleneck, black jeans, white makeup. He wore his stupid silver bracelet. She tried to speak, but her tongue was thick and syrupy in her mouth.

"Shhh," he said, raising his right hand. He held a pistol, the grip wrapped in black electrical tape. "I don't want to hit you again, but I will if you force me to." He straddled her and brushed her cheek with the back of his left hand. He sucked in a breath, held it, and let it out, shuddering.

She struggled, but her arms were pinned by his legs. She was strong, stronger than any normal human girl could be, but she had no leverage, and he was twice her size. He shook his head, his frown almost sad.

"Ani. Stop. It doesn't have to be like this." She kicked. His legs tightened, and the barrel of the pistol tilted down to her face. All emotion left his voice, and his face went slack. "I said stop."

She froze.

He leaned forward and put his elbow on the floor, the pistol cold against her temple. "Don't move. Don't even breathe." He shifted so that he lay half on top of her, interposing his leg between hers, and his left hand slid down her body, nestling between her legs. He gasped and leaned in close, his eyes flat, mouth open in ecstasy as he felt her through her jeans. She forced herself not to react.

"See? We can be—"

Ani lunged and bit down, then wrenched her head to the side.

His cheek tore from his face as the pistol went off beneath her head. Crimson gore showered her as he screamed, recoiling. She grabbed his thigh with her right hand and heaved, half-standing as he crashed through the railing. He grabbed her arm and yanked her off her feet. They fell in a shower of splintered wood.

Dylan hit the floor headfirst with a sickening thud. Ani landed on her side and heard a crack as pain blossomed in her hip. She sat up and felt bone grinding in her pelvis, a numb inferno wracking her body. Gritting her teeth against it, she looked at Dylan.

His eyes were half-open, and she could see bone through the ruin of his cheek. He wasn't moving. His chest rose, then fell. Rose, then fell. He looked delicious, but the pain in her hip obliterated thoughts of food. Without taking her eyes off him, she clawed her way up the couch, then used the armrest to stand.

She took a step and cried out, a hot iron stabbing into her hip. *Oh, God.* She slid her right foot forward and put weight on it, gasping. *I can't do it.* Then her left foot. *It's too much.* She gritted her teeth and shambled to her mom's desk, one foot at a time.

She grabbed the phone off the cradle and lowered herself into the loveseat. Sitting was almost as bad. She dialed her mother's cell phone.

She picked up on the first ring. "This is Sarah."

"Mom, you have to come home right now." The calm of her own voice surprised her.

"I'm at the bank. It'll be—"

"It's an emergency."

A brief pause, then, "Two minutes."

It took her three.

Her mom strode into the room, took stock of the situation, and took charge. "Ani, get yourself cleaned up. *Now.* I'll take care of Dylan."

"What are you—" Her mom held up a finger, then used it to point at the bathroom. Ani pulled herself to her feet and shuffled into the bathroom to wash up, each step an agony. She scrubbed the blood from her face and hands, using a makeup mirror to ensure that she got it all. She heard the front door open, and voices murmured as she brushed her teeth.

By the time she came back out, Mr. Washington was there. So were the police, a pair of mustached officers in blue uniforms. Before Ani could do anything, her mom rushed forward and pulled her into a hug, rocking her back and forth. "Oh, Ani, I'm so glad you're all right!" Then she whispered. "*Mrs. Washington called 911 when they heard the gunshot. He's in a coma. I gave him a shot of serum.*" Ani felt the sting of a needle enter the base of her skull, then pull away.

"*He attacked you,*" her mom whispered. "*You pushed him through the railing. That's it. You don't remember anything else.*"

"*Mom, I bit him,*" she whispered back, trying not to move her lips. "*They're going to test me.*"

Her mom squeezed tighter. "*No they won't. Trust me. Try not to limp too much. We can't have you going to the hospital.*"

"Ma'am?" one of the policemen said. "Can we ask your daughter some questions?"

Her mother pulled away, then helped Ani to a chair. "Certainly, officer."

The interrogation took twenty minutes. They asked her the same questions over and over again, but she kept saying she didn't know. Finally, they left.

* * *

They stayed up all night so that her mom could pin her fractured hip and forge documentation from the nonexistent doctor Ani had been seeing for two years. The pin helped a lot, but it wasn't her mother's area of expertise, and Ani's left foot dragged a little as she walked. Her mom assured her it would get better with time and regenerative therapy. She'd always been a bad liar.

Her mom assured her that she had made the cheek wound look like it was caused by the railing and that the hospital staff wouldn't even question the story. They never found the missing hunk of flesh.

"Won't he turn into a zombie now?" Ani asked.

"No. Your saliva hasn't been contagious since you went on the new serum."

"Are you sure?"

Her mom thought about it, then nodded. "It doesn't infect human flesh in a Petri dish. There's no reason to think it would infect Dylan. He's under full psychiatric restraints, anyway, just in case he wakes up."

They ran a fresh test, just to be sure. It came back clean.

Mike called the next morning, but her mother intercepted it. "She's fine; she's resting. You can talk to her at school." Then everyone else called. They spent the next three days fending off reporters, well-wishers, gossip-seekers, and ambulance-chasers. Dylan's mom brought Ani flowers and tried to convince them not to press charges. Ani was banished to her room when talk of lawyers came up.

* * *

The medical equipment chirped and hissed everywhere in the brain trauma unit. "We shouldn't be here," Ani's mom said without conviction. The sterile white sheets rose and fell in time with Dylan's chest. His face was a greenish-gray, his slack jaw propped to accommodate the feeding tube. An IV trickled life-giving fluids into his arm.

"I know," Ani said, eyeing the armed policeman on guard outside the room. "But I had to see him, know that he's..."

"Asleep?" her mom asked. *Not a mindless, brain-eating monster.*

"That, too," Ani said.

"You can't blame yourself," her mom said, putting a hand on her shoulder. "He attacked you."

"I know," Ani said. *And he tried to rape me. But he's here because of what I am.* "But what happens when he wakes up?" *If he wakes up.*

Her mom looked at the policeman, then back at Dylan. "When he wakes up he goes to jail and then to trial. I've already spoken to Judge Green, and there's no way he'll be getting bail."

"But what—"

"Hush," her mom said. "We've seen enough." She kissed Ani on the forehead. "Okay, sweetie?"

Dylan looked so pathetic and sad and small. "Yeah." Ani averted her eyes. "Okay."

* * *

Fey called on New Year's Eve.

"Ani, party tonight. Boys, booze, bouncing. You in?"

Oh, God, no. "I'm not up for bouncing." *Or boys. Or booze.* "Anyway, I'd have to ask my mom."

She could almost hear the smile in Fey's voice. "Not for nothing, but you're an idiot. Like I'm going to a New Year's party. For real, I scored a couple bottles of Asti and some ox. We're going to hang out at the gravel pit and launch firecrackers. See you at ten?"

"Hold on a sec." She set the phone on the table and shambled over to her mom. She told her what they'd be doing, and her mom said yes.

As she put the phone back to her ear, her mom raised her voice. "You'll be at Fey's the entire time? No sneaking out? No stupid stuff?"

"Mom..." Ani said. *It's hard to whine while smiling.* "If you can't trust me now, you'll never be able to."

Her mom paused for effect, then said, "Okay, but you're in this house by twelve-thirty. And not a minute later."

"Heard it," Fey said and hung up.

She gave the phone to her mom and pecked her cheek.

"Be home by one. And when you get here," her mother said, "you get straight in the bath."

* * *

It was freezing at the gravel pit, and ice-rime coated everything. Jake's car was already there, the windows fogged, Halestorm blaring on the stereo. They knocked on the window and let themselves in, with Fey taking shotgun. The car wasn't much warmer than outside.

"Can we listen to real music?" Fey asked. *Like Chopin?* She pulled Jake's CDs from under the passenger seat and flipped through them with shaking hands. "It's freezing in here."

Ani handed Jake two bottles of vodka, one half-empty. "Sweet," he said. He popped out of the car and put them in the trunk, under the spare tire.

Fey settled on Evanescence's first album, struggled to put the CD into the player, then rubbed her hands together. "Screw this." She got out of the car and into the back seat, bumping Ani to the middle. Jake joined them, and they huddled under his emergency blanket. The hot pads hidden in Ani's coat helped, and after a while, Fey's teeth stopped chattering.

They passed the champagne back and forth, with Jake drinking more than half of it himself, and with no more than a few swallows left he pulled out a couple of small white pills. *Oxycodone?* "Yes, please!" Fey said, and plucked one out of his offered hand. Ani declined. They washed them down with the last of the champagne. Fey had one. Jake had three.

"So where are the fireworks?" Fey asked. "It ain't New Year's without fireworks."

Jake reached into the front seat and popped the glove box, revealing all of six bottle rockets and a pack of jumping jacks. He lit the jumping jacks one at a time with the cigarette lighter and popped them out the door, blasting the car with cold every time. He went outside to fire the bottle rockets, "wowing" at the crystal-clear sky every time he looked up. Twenty minutes after they were gone, he was curled up against Fey, semi-fetal, eyes closed, and snoring.

Ani and Fey listened to Trent Reznor's bass-driven, violence-porn almost-music, complained about life, and counted drunk drivers.

It felt so good to be out of the house. Free.

CHAPTER
15

Travis had a meeting with the insurance adjuster that coming Monday, so Ani spent both New Year's Day and Sunday helping him reconstruct his inventory. All receipts and records had been lost in the fire so they had to do it from memory, but after sixteen hours, they had a good approximation of what was in the store at the time. He paid her a hundred and forty dollars, cash, under the table.

Unfortunately, he also took her to lunch both days. This meant drinking digestive enzymes when she got home, followed by needles in her stomach to excavate the dissolved food the next morning. And breath mints. Oodles of breath mints.

* * *

Monday was back to school, where, for the first time, she truly understood the curse of celebrity. Everyone pestered her to tell the story. Even teachers asked. Each time, she gave the same answer. "The police told me not to talk about it." It wasn't true, but it got them off her back. Mostly.

She barely saw Mike, and they would never be alone anyway. Between the people harassing her for details and Devon's constant presence on his arm, they had no opportunity to talk. He didn't even try.

Fey saw her looking at him and rolled her eyes. "Not for nothing, but if you weren't the only person on the planet without a cell phone you could text him instead of just staring lovey-dovey at him."

"Mom won't let me."

"*Mom won't let me,*" Fey mocked. "You're seventeen freaking years old. Buy a prepaid and don't tell her."

Ani shook her head. "Yeah... That's... I... I'm not going to do that."

"Why the hell not?" *Because it's one of the rules. No secrets, no chance for secrets, no social life except what is expressly approved.*

"Because she'd kill me. Literally."

"Whatever," Fey said. As she walked away, more busybodies took her place. Ani did her best to blow them off. *If I got a prepaid, where could I hide it that Mom wouldn't find?* Nowhere came to mind.

* * *

She walked home, shielded from the sun by her coat and hat. The day had turned bitter cold under the cloudless sky, and her damaged gait left weird, lopsided footprints behind her, but she didn't mind. She was outside; she wore heated gloves and leggings, and protected her face with a scarf. *It's not like I have to worry about hypothermia.*

As she turned the corner to her street, Devon's car passed. It stopped at Mike's house, idling at the bottom of the driveway. He got out of the passenger's side, and it drove away. Ani waved at him. He hesitated, then gave a half-wave before going inside.

What the heck was that?

She was in a foul mood by the time she got in the house and fuming when her mom got home. She painted to hide her agitation—she'd betray herself pounding on the piano—but didn't manage more than some angry impressionistic brush strokes before she gave up and went to her room.

She lay back on the bed and stared at the ceiling. A normal girl would have gone to sleep in a depressed funk, but that was one more thing her dead body couldn't do.

* * *

Wednesday was "Shadowing Day." Each willing and unwilling

eleventh grader was assigned an eighth grader from the Lower School, who followed them from class to class and made any real social interaction impossible. Ani and Fey had been saddled with twin sisters, up-and-comers on the emo scene, full of angst and malaise. They spent most of the day not talking. *Now this is a reason to hate life, girls.*

There was a small spot of drama before lunch, when Mrs. Weller saw Jake selling oranges to the noobs for five bucks a piece. *Serves him right. They're jaded, not stupid.* The oranges were confiscated, and Jake was marched off to the principal's office.

Ani had just survived another period of polyhedron proofs and was working on her homework when the announcement hit that all eighth graders were to report to their busses. As Suicide Twin #1 said her goodbyes, Ani caught Mike's eye and smiled. His eyes flicked away. *I thought....*

Feeling like a plague victim, she went back to her homework. A few minutes later, Mr. Gursslin's phone rang. "Yes?" A pause. "She is. I'll send her right down." He hung up the phone. "Ani? You're wanted in the office." Everyone looked at her. Everyone except Mike.

Why would they want me?

"Why?" she asked.

Mr. Gursslin shrugged. "They didn't say. There's only a minute left. Go ahead and take your books." She packed up her stuff and limped out of the room, left foot dragging across the tile where she couldn't quite lift it.

When she got to the main office the secretary told her to sit. "Mr. Bastian will be with you in a moment." The bell rang, and she endured the curious stares of walkers-by, student and teacher alike. She'd never been inside the principal's office. Her stomach erupted in butterflies.

A few minutes later Mr. Bastian's door opened. Jake emerged, red-faced, his mother right behind him. He kept his head down as she badgered him with whispers, and if he noticed Ani he made no effort to communicate. *Oh, shit.*

Mr. Bastian stood at the door in a blue, single-breasted suit. Five-eight or so, he was lean, clean-shaven and almost bald even though he couldn't be more than forty. She usually saw him smiling, and his current guarded expression was unnerving.

"Miss Romero, my office, please."

Her mind raced. *I don't know what you're talking about.* She got to her feet slower than she had to and dragged her foot more than necessary. *It wasn't me. He's lying.* Step, drag. *I'm in pain and under stress and made a bad decision.* Step, drag. *Yeah. That last one is pretty good.* She got to the doorway and looked into the eyes of her mother, red-faced and furious, at the principal's conference table. The butterflies grew claws and teeth. *I'm doomed.*

As Mr. Bastian turned to escort her to the table, her mom gave her a wink. *Or not.* He pulled out a chair and she sat down, feeling better already. She winced as she scooted forward and let out a tiny grunt of discomfort.

"Miss Romero," he began. "Do you know why you're here?" *Because my friends are idiots?*

She looked at her mom, who gave her the barest of nods, and crossed her arms for effect.

"Am I in trouble?"

He glanced at her mom, then back to her. "Yes. Do you know why?"

"Does it have something to do with Jake?" She didn't have to fake a scowl. *That jerk ratted me out.*

"Yes, it does. If you tell the truth, it will speak well for you." *And if I could lie with a straight face I'd deny everything.*

She locked her eyes on her mom. *Maybe he'll think I'm afraid of looking at him.* She let out a huge sigh, put her head in her hands, and mumbled.

"Last week Jake asked if I could score him some booze. I took two bottles of vodka from the liquor cabinet and gave them to him."

Her mom uttered a disappointed "Oh, honey!" that she had to admire.

"Jake is an idiot and brought vodka-soaked oranges to school today. Mrs. Weller caught him, you put two and two together, and here I am."

"That's correct," he said. *Duh.* He touched her hand to get her attention, and she jerked it out of his grip. "Do you know that distributing alcohol on school grounds is a felony?"

She crossed her arms again, trying to look as sullen as possible while her mom glared at her. "Sucks for Jake." *That wasn't a lie.*

"I wasn't talking about Jake," he said. "Anyone involved could face expulsion as well as jail time."

Her eyes widened and she looked at her mom, then at him. "Whoa, whoa, whoa—I didn't bring anything onto school grounds. I gave those bottles to him at the gravel pit. Ask him. Ask Fey—Tiffany." She winced. *Oh, shit. Don't kill me, Fey.*

Her mom jumped to her rescue. "You have no evidence that my daughter had anything to do with that alcohol coming to school." *Go, Mom!*

He frowned at her. "Sarah, she gave alcohol to a minor—"

"Who's older than I am!" Ani retorted.

"—which is also a felony." He looked at Ani. "Ani, will you excuse us for a moment?"

Her mom's lips tightened as Ani got up and lurched out of the room. A boy sat on the bench next to the secretary's desk, mumbling to himself. Mr. Bastian closed the door behind her.

Her mom's voice was muffled but audible. "I'm on-board with reasonable disciplinary measures for this, Geoff, but if you try to have my daughter prosecuted things will go very, very badly for you."

"Have you forgotten that I'm your boss?"

"Have you forgotten basketball sectionals last year? Prescription narcotics? A directive not to report it? 'It would be bad for school morale if this got out.' That's what you said, wasn't it?"

The boy looked at Ani, his eyes wide.

Ani had to strain to hear Mr. Bastian's reply. "You're treading on dangerous ground, Sarah. You have no evidence that conversation ever took place."

There was a pause. "I carry this with me everywhere I go. Would you like me to play it back to you?" If he replied, Ani didn't hear it. "I will accept five days of in-school suspension, and no police. It's reasonable." *Especially since I didn't do anything even vaguely in the jurisdiction of the school.* Pretending misery got easier every day.

"Five days out of school," he countered. "All drug and alcohol cases get out of school suspension." *Except sports teams, apparently.*

"No superintendent's hearing, no cops, and I stay home to

supervise my daughter, who has been through so much lately. And it doesn't count as personal time."

"It's a deal. Now get out of my office."

* * *

"Oh, my God that was incredible!" Ani said as she got in the car.

"Don't smile," her mom said. "People can see us."

She stared at her feet and concentrated on the pain in her hip. "I can't believe you let the basketball team off the hook for being high."

"I was ordered to, and besides, it gave me ammunition I might someday have to use." She started the car but left it in park. She turned ferocious eyes on Ani. "You're my baby girl."

"I know, Mom." She looked back down at the floor and tried not to smile. "It's a good thing you recorded that conversation."

Her mom scowled as she put the car in gear. "It's a good thing he doesn't know I didn't."

CHAPTER
16

Five days of out-of-school suspension plus the weekend gave them seven and a half days of research time. They stocked up on groceries to minimize interruptions and headed to the basement. Her mom was focused on something "promising"—it was Ani's job to fetch equipment, turn dials, and of course donate skin, muscle, and whatever other cells were required. Her hip bothered her, and she felt like Igor, shuffling about the laboratory to fulfill the whims of Doctor Frankenmom.

She spent the night in the bath, got up, and went right back to work. Ani got a lot of reading done as her mom prepared solutions, fiddled with tissue plastic and glass plates coated with agar or collagen or something called Matrigel, tinkered with settings, and looked through microscopes. The printer spat out images from the electron microscope, viruses attacking cells and cells regenerating under chemical treatment. Used samples went into the biohazard incinerator. Her mom spoke into the recorder, and Ani transcribed the notes onto the computer—even if she didn't understand half of what she typed.

The next night they were testing another serum with the same appetite suppression, but with better healing power. Her mom thought it might be enough to repair some of her more delicate tissues—sweat glands, tear ducts, salivary glands. "If this works, you might be able to cut down on baths to once, maybe twice a week," her mom said.

Ani beamed. "Oh, man, that'd be awesome." She lurched her way upstairs for some audio books. When she got back, the 'just in case' room was prepped. She looked at the recliner, the leather and metal straps, and she started to shake. *Dylan's lips were warm and soft on her forehead where he had pressed the gun barrel. He kissed her eyelids, her cheek, her neck.*

Arms wrapped her from behind, warm and comforting. "It'll be okay, sweetie. He can't hurt you now." The reassurances didn't help. At last, her mother sighed. "I'll bring the cot down, sleep right outside the door. Would that help?"

Ani leaned her head into her mother's arm and smiled. "I love you, Mom."

"I love you too, sweetie. Now get in the chair, please."

Ani shuffled forward, each step harder than the last, but she made it. Once Ani was strapped in and gagged, her mother injected her with the serum, a sharp pinch followed by nothing. A warm glow suffused her, enveloping her in its comforting softness. Her mom, fuzzy and indistinct, asked her the same questions she always asked.

"How do you feel, honey?" Ani widened her eyes and lolled her head back and forth.

Her mom spoke for the camera. "Subject is experiencing intoxication." Her voice sounded too deep by an octave and too slow by half.

"Any discomfort?" Ani shook her head, setting the world to swimming. She couldn't even feel her hip.

"Trouble thinking?" She nodded, rocking the planet, and her mom turned to the camera.

Her stomach lurched. A stabbing pain wracked her abdomen, shattered through her body. The world drowned in blood, and she drooled at the meat in front of her. *Right there. Closer. Closer.* There was something in her mouth. She chewed at it, pushed it with her tongue, but it wouldn't dislodge. She moaned in frustration.

The meat came closer, and she could smell something more, something better. *Brains. Delicious brains.* She snapped and struggled but couldn't move. Couldn't eat. She howled in rage and despair as the meat moved behind her. She could smell it, almost taste it, so close. *So close.* But not close enough.

She pulled, her muscles straining against the metal cutting into her skin. *Brains!* Choking on her own saliva, she screamed against the gag. There was a prick at the back of her neck, and the world faded to red, and then to black. And then silence.

* * *

Her eyes fluttered open. *Where am I?* She looked around. Propane tubes, brick walls, an IV in both arms. She looked up at the hole in the ceiling, black and forbidding, and then out through the tiny window in the door. She craned her neck for a better look and felt a pinch in her spine just below her skull. *Auto-injector.*

Out in the lab her mom was on her knees, her head in her hands, shaking. Broken glass littered the floor beside the overturned table. Her notebooks lay scattered.

Ani heard a hiss behind her and felt a warm rush as fluids injected into her brain. She tried to fight her eyelids, but they closed anyway.

* * *

When she came to, her mom sat in front of her, reading a book. The door was open, and there was no sign that the lab had been trashed. Everything was neat, tidy, labeled.

"Hi, Mom." It came out a wordless mumble through the bite guard.

Her mom looked up and smiled. "Hey, honey. Welcome back." She closed her book. "How do you feel?"

She thought about it. *Alone. Sad. My hip hurts. Disappointed. Not hungry, though.* She shrugged.

"Any discomfort? Trouble thinking?"

She shook her head.

"Hunger?"

She shook her head again. *A little sick to my stomach, but that's just nerves.* Her mom got up, moved behind her, and undid the strap on the gag. She pushed it out of her mouth with her tongue.

"Ugh. My jaw hurts."

"I'm not surprised," her mom said behind her. "You spent the past forty hours trying to chew through steel-reinforced leather."

Ow. "What happened?"

Her mom stepped back in front of her, shined a penlight into first one eye, then the next. "You had a bad reaction. I flushed your system and started you back on gamma-seven. How do you feel?"

"Pretty normal, I guess."

"Good. Now open your mouth."

She opened her mouth and her mom swabbed her cheek with a Q-Tip, placed it into a receptacle, and walked back into the lab. She spoke over her shoulder. "We're going to leave you strapped down another twelve hours or so, just to be sure. That should give me time to check your saliva, make sure you're still not contagious. Music?"

"Sure, Mom."

"What do you want?" she asked, sitting at the perfectly-arranged and organized lab table.

"How about Billy Joel?"

"Billy Joel it is."

* * *

She didn't realize that they'd missed the January roller-skating party until she was waiting for the bus. *Damn.* It felt weird going back to school on a Thursday. She got on the bus, expecting stares, and was surprised by the complete lack of reaction. Nobody seemed to care that she was a miscreant, a criminal given the harshest sentence a principal can hand out. It was almost disappointing.

The bus pulled up to Fey's house as Fey argued with her mother. She stormed aboard, saw Ani, glared at her, then sat in the front. Ani grunted. *I guess I deserve that.*

By the time she got off the bus, Fey was gone. Ani went to her locker but Fey wasn't there either. Jake was, with an apologetic shrug and downcast eyes.

"Ani, look," he said as she grabbed the handle to her locker and kicked the bottom to pop it open. "I didn't have a choice. I told them I stole it from the liquor store—what's a misdemeanor on top of a felony, right?—so they drag me down there. The guy says, 'I'm not missing any vodka,' so they know I'm lying. I didn't have a choice."

Ani nibbled her bottom lip. "So you just want me to forgive you." She snapped her fingers. "Like that."

His eyes pled his case. "Yeah. Are we cool?"

She punched him in the arm. "No, we're freaks and rejects. But I forgive you. The unexpected vacation was quite nice, what with Christmas being so... eventful." They stood in awkward silence for a moment. "You know you've lost your supplier."

He nodded. "Yeah. I'll figure something out."

"Meantime, what do we do about Fey?"

Jake grinned. "Oh, don't worry about Fey. She'll come around once she realizes nobody else likes her."

Ani wasn't sure.

* * *

As she sat next to Fey at lunch, Fey grabbed her tray and started to stand. Ani grabbed her wrist. "Fey, wait. Please."

Fey set the tray down and sank back to her seat. "Why? We've got nothing to say to each other."

"I'm sorry. I didn't even mean to say your name. It just popped out. And you didn't do anything wrong except be there." A tray plopped down to Ani's right. She looked up as Jake sat down. *Next to me, not her.*

Fey rolled her eyes. "You guys don't understand. I'm eighteen. You guys aren't. You know what that means?"

Ani shook her head. *Trouble?*

"It means if they find out about the ox, or even the champagne, I'm screwed."

Ani's eyes widened. "I didn't say anything—"

"Me neith—"

Fey held up a hand. "But both of you let slip I was there. Not for nothing, but you need to watch your mouths. The last thing I need is a rap sheet."

"Won't happen from me, ever again." Jake crossed his heart.

Ani patted Fey's hand. "The liquor cabinet is under lock and key, now. I couldn't do it again if I tried."

Fey stood with her tray. "Yeah, well, keep your damn mouths shut." She stalked out of the cafeteria and was accosted by a hall monitor. *No food outside the cafeteria, Fey.* Scowling, she came back in, badgered an AV kid out of his seat, set down her tray, and ate.

* * *

Two days of school, then a three-day weekend for Martin Luther King Day. She got home from school on Friday, having stayed after to catch up on the work she had missed, and saw her mother standing in the bathroom wearing makeup, a long blue dress, and pearls. Her face was haggard and tired—these days it was always haggard and tired—but it held a tension that Ani didn't recognize.

"Is everything okay, Mom?" Ani asked, worried.

"Yes," her mother said. Her hands shook. "No. I...."

Ani grabbed her hands. She searched her eyes and saw panic. "What, Mom? You can tell me."

"I have a date."

Ani blinked. "A what?"

Her mom smiled. "You know, a date. Where a man and a woman go out and have a nice time, perhaps to a movie or the theater, to get to know one another better. A date."

Ani couldn't suppress a bemused grin. "I... You... You've never... With who?"

"None of your business," she snapped, and let go of Ani's hands. Then she smiled. "A man I bumped into in the grocery store. He seems very nice." She paused to put on her heels. "His name is Mike."

That sucks. "Is he cute?"

"Sure," she said, turning to look at herself in the mirror.

"Mom, you're blushing!"

Her mother whirled around and raised a finger. "I will be gone until midnight or one. You will have no one over, you will go nowhere, and you will be in the bath by eleven. We can't take any chances until we're certain that you are one hundred percent." She grabbed Ani and pulled her in to kiss her forehead. "I love you, my baby girl." She pushed her out to arm's length. "How do I look?"

Tired. Anxious. Nervous. "You look great."

* * *

The phone rang as her mom pulled out of the driveway. The caller ID said "Daniels." She picked up the phone.

"Hey, Fey, what's up?"

"I'm coming over. Stan and Mom have been bitching at each other for hours. I got to get out of here before I kill myself."

Ani watched as the Audi turned the corner toward town. "Mom says nobody comes over when she's not home."

"She just took off dressed like the First Lady. She won't be back for a few hours. She won't know." Fey Said.

Ani took a deep breath, held it, and let it out. "She always knows. With the suspension and everything, I've got to be careful."

There was a pregnant pause. "You owe me."

"I do, I really do, but I can't have you over tonight. My mom's like a CSI. She'll pick up on the tiniest detail, and she'll kill me."

"So we'll hang out outside."

"Fey, it's five below zero. You'd be dead in ten minutes."

"So we'll go to Jakes."

"He's grounded."

"Jesus, Ani, if you don't want to hang out with me, just say so."

"I—"

Fey hung up. *Dammit.*

CHAPTER 17

Her mom spilled no details about her date, save that it was nice, and so was the play. They'd gone to see *Over the Tavern* at the city theater, then out for a late bite. Her mom had gotten home around three a.m. She went out again Saturday night, not quite as dressed up. This time Fey didn't call.

Tuesday, Fey got on the bus and passed her the headphone, like nothing was amiss. She took it and put it in her ear. "Sorry about Friday."

"Don't worry about it," Fey said. "I'm a big girl." They sat in silence for a moment, but it was comfortable. "Your mom's a bit of a tyrant, isn't she?"

Ani bit her lip. "Um, you could say that." *You have no idea. None.*

"She seems nice at school. No-nonsense, but nice."

"She's like that at home, too, until you break the rules. Then she locks you in the coal cellar and throws away the key."

Fey cranked the iPod by way of a reply, and they rode the rest of the way to school serenaded by Dashboard Confessional.

Ani was reading in study hall—she'd cut the cover off of *New Moon* and glued it on to Stephanie Rowe's *Unbecoming Behavior*—when a shadow loomed over the page.

"*Twilight* again?" Keegan asked, leaning on her desk. "How many times have you read that?"

She snapped the book closed. "Some things are timeless," she said. Then she looked up at him. "Other things get old real fast."

She expected him to walk away. Instead, he leaned closer and whispered. "Ask to go to the bathroom once Mike's out of the room. He wants to talk to you without"—he jerked his head toward Devon—"some people catching on."

Her heart skipped a beat. Or it would have, if it were not for electrical stimulation. *Mike wants to talk to me? What for? He's been avoiding me for weeks.*

When Mike left the room, she gave it forty-five seconds and then shot up her hand.

Mr. Betrus raised his eyebrows. "Yes, Miss Romero?"

"Can I go to the bathroom?"

He shook his head and looked back down at his paperwork. "Only two people out at once."

"But...."

He raised his gaze, so she tried to look as nervous as possible.

"It's female issues. It can't wait." She looked at the door, then back at him, chewing furiously on her lip.

He jerked his chin toward the door. "Go."

She hurried out of the room. Mike was at his locker, thirty feet away. She shambled over to him, cursing her dragging foot. "How was your weekend, Mike?"

He shrugged. "Same as usual. Mom was bitchy; Dad was unavailable."

"Speaking of your mom, when is she going to call me for lessons? I haven't heard a peep."

"She sold the keyboard and bought clothes."

"That sucks," Ani said. Even grumpy, his proximity intoxicated her, and she tried not to look in his eyes. "Mom's been riding my ass since I got suspended. She's merciless."

"She was so nice growing up." He looked at her, and she couldn't help it. She raised her eyes to his and drowned in a sea of green. "I guess she kind of changed..." He looked away, and the spell was broken. "When you did."

Ani self-consciously raised her hand to the safety pins in her cheek. They were no longer necessary, but she'd gotten used to them. "I guess so, but I don't think it's me. I think it's this job. She hates it here. More than I do."

Mike looked up and down the hall. "High School's not so bad."

Yeah, if you're popular. Or not a decaying freak.

"So anyway, Keegs said you wanted to talk to me?"

He brought his dazzling attention back on her, and she had to remember to breathe. "Yeah. I was wondering if you could do me a favor. A really big favor."

Anything. Everything. "You ignore me for a month and then ask for a favor?"

"Yeah, I'm sorry. Devon's under a lot of stress. She's got the Algebra II Regents next week, and she's been a real bitch. And she's jealous that I took a knife for you. Really jealous."

Ani scowled. *Why is it that when a girl gets bitchy she's a bitch, but when a guy's an asshole nobody even comments?* "Well, since you saved my life... Maybe. It depends on the favor."

"I need you to go to the Valentine's Banquet and Dance with Keegan."

She choked. "Excuse me?"

"He's already agreed, if you'll do it. It's just to get Devon off my back. No romance. She'll calm down if she sees you're interested in someone else."

Are you freaking KIDDING ME? She throttled the shrieking harridan in her head enough so that she could formulate a reply. "So let me get this straight. Instead of acting like a grownup, you want me to go to a dance with a guy I don't like and who doesn't like me so that your psycho girlfriend stops being irrationally jealous of a social outcast you almost never talk to." She looked him in the eyes, too furious to fall prey to them.

He returned the stare and nodded. "Yeah. That's the favor."

Not in a million years. "Five hundred dollars."

He rolled not only his eyes but his whole head. "I saved your life."

"True. Okay, three hundred dollars. And if Keegan tries to kiss or grope me it goes back to five hundred."

He opened his mouth and closed it several times. Finally, he forced the words out. "Two hundred. And Keegan won't try to kiss or grope you."

"This isn't a negotiation. Three hundred dollars and I will stoop to this disgusting, filthy level for you, but only because you're my friend and you saved my life. Take it or shove it."

"Deal." *Shit shit shit shit shit shit shit!*

* * *

It took her over a week to scrape up the courage to tell her mom. It helped that she could soften the blow with a report card of mostly A's and B's. She walked into the nurse's office at lunchtime and sat on the bed nearest the door. It felt like death row.

Her mom was up from her desk and across the room in a flash. Her shirt was a little low cut for a school nurse. *Is that a new bra?* "What's wrong, sweetie?"

Ani waved her off. "No, nothing like that. I just need to tell you something." She cringed.

"This doesn't sound good."

It all rushed out of her mouth at once. "Mike paid me three hundred bucks to go to the banquet and dance with Keegan so Devon won't be jealous anymore."

Her mom sat back with a grunt. "Is this a joke?" *Ha ha, right? He was supposed to say "no" when I asked for money.*

She shook her head. "I know I'm supposed to ask first, and I know you said no boys, but Keegan and I don't even like each other. There is zero chance that he'd try anything."

Her mom developed that calculated scowl that almost never meant fun times.

Ani looked at the floor and didn't move.

Finally her mom spoke. "Look, sweetie, you'll be on your own. I can't chaperone either one."

Ani opened her mouth but her mom raised a finger so she closed it.

"I was going to tell you tonight. Mike surprised me with plane tickets." Her shrug was too casual by half. "What was I going to say? We're leaving Friday and won't be back until Tuesday." *What? Where... um... you're abandoning me for a guy? And will you please for the love of all that is holy stop dating a man named Mike?* "But of more concern to me is that you'd be willing to compromise your integrity like this. Going somewhere with a boy for money is just... sleazy." She lowered her finger.

"But I'm not doing it for Keegan. We're both doing Mike a favor." *And you're supposed to be here for me.*

"Unless you're wrong. Keegan had a crush on you in middle school, if I remember correctly."

"Middle school was a long time ago, Mom. A lot has happened since then."

She leaned in close, exposing too much cleavage. "True, but boys don't change much from twelve to eighty, and they'll take what they can get when they can get it." She leaned back with a self-satisfied smirk.

"Mom, don't be gross!" *And please, please turn back into my mom. This weepy cougar thing is freaking me out.*

She frowned. "You'll learn."

Ani changed the subject. "So where are you going? This sounds exciting!" *Too exciting.*

Her mom smiled, but it didn't touch her eyes. "We're going to Key West. Mike rented a villa there, so I took three days off." The smile faded to sadness. "You're going to have to learn to be on your own, take care of yourself." *What the heck is that supposed to mean?*

Ani hugged her. "You gave up so much for me, Mom. It's okay. I'll be fine. Go have fun." *What's happening to you? And why now?*

She widened her eyes. "I'm planning on it."

Eeeeeeeeeeeeeeeeeeeew!

* * *

The approaching dance filled Ani with certain dread. Keegan stopped to talk to her for the millionth time—in view of Devon, of course—said nothing of consequence and strode away as Fey approached. *The Hearts on Fire banquet is Saturday, and the dance is next Monday. After that, this'll all be over.*

"What is up with that kid?" Fey asked. "Every minute he's creeping on you."

"I know," Ani said. "He's like obsessed or something."

Fey watched him walk away, then looked at Ani. Her eyes narrowed.

"No he's not. When he's on to a girl he gets a certain swagger." She let out a disgusted grunt. "Trust me, I know." She waggled her finger down the hall after him. "This.... This is something else. Something weird." She looked at Ani. "Watch your back. He likes them small and pale, and he'll kiss and tell."

"Is it bad that I find it somewhat flattering?" *Got to plant the seed, make it at least halfway believable.*

Fey rolled her eyes. "Maybe not. But don't end up on your back with that kid. He's a two-pump chump."

Ani recoiled. "Oh, Fey, that's disgusting."

She stared after him. "It's worse when you're there, trust me."

* * *

Maybe it was the stress, but the roller-skating party bugged her this time. She grabbed the razor and put her hands in her sleeves, frowning. Her stomach was off, like a mosquito's whine in her ear, unnerving and unsettling. It had been so long since she needed to cut, and she winced against the pain as she dragged her razor through the old scars. She sighed in relief as the tightness flowed out of her body, into the air and away. She leaned her head back and breathed a sigh of relief.

Her mom walked over from her perch against the wall, her eyes full of concern. "Are you alright, sweetie?" She had to yell over the Black Eyed Peas.

Ani nodded. "Just a little stressed. I'm fine."

"You're sure? You can go if you need to."

"I'm fine. I'm sure." Her mom walked away, and she turned her attention back to the music, her inner soul dancing while her body sulked.

* * *

As they walked out of the party, Jake's beat-up Ford idled at the curb, pumping bass through the neighborhood. All the kids were gone, as were the rest of the chaperones. Jake leaned against the fender, arms crossed. He lifted his chin at her in acknowledgement.

She gave him a little wave.

"Hi, Mrs. Romero. Ani, can I talk to you for a second?"

Ani looked at her mom, who hated it when kids called her "Mrs."

"Go ahead, honey. But just for a second."

Ani walked over. He reached inside and turned down the music so that it was no longer shaking the cab. "What's up?" He smelled like weed.

"Hey, um...." Jake shifted his feet. *Oh, no. Please don't ask. Please.* "Do you want to go to the banquet with me?" *FML.*

She kept her face flat, devoid of affect. "It's really nice of you to ask, but someone already asked me."

His face wrenched, he looked up at the clouds, then in her eyes. "Who?"

"Keegan Taylor."

His laugh was despair. "Keegan. Wedgies in the hallway Keegan. Kidney-punches in gym Keegan. Keegan." He turned around and put gloved hands on the hood of his truck, held the pose, then turned back, his palms to his forehead. "On what planet does Keegan fucking Taylor ask you out, and you say 'yes'?"

She opened her mouth, but didn't get the chance to reply.

He ran to the driver's side, got in, and slammed the door. Tires squealed as he pulled away, fishtailing across the slippery parking lot. Ani walked to the car, her mom already inside, the windows frosty.

She got in and closed the door, and was greeted by a raised eyebrow.

"That looked exciting."

"He asked me to the banquet."

The eyebrow dropped. "Interesting. Under other circumstances, would you have said 'yes'?"

She didn't have to think about it. "Not in a million years."

"Good. That kid's bad news."

* * *

Fey sat down next to her and the bus lurched forward. "Keegan Taylor is taking you to Hearts on Fire." There was no sign of the iPod.

"Yes," Ani said. She kept her eyes on the seat in front of her. "He is."

Fey shifted in the cramped seat so that she was wedged in backward. She looked in Ani's eyes. "Spill."

Ani glanced at her, then out the window. *I knew this wouldn't work.* "He asked me out, I said yes. That's it."

"Bullshit." Fey grabbed her by the chin and turned her head. "You look me in the eyes and tell me the goddamned truth or we're not friends." She stared at her, waiting. "I'm serious."

Oh, Fey. In another life I'd never stand for such a stupid ultimatum, but I need you. "Mike is paying for us to go together to get Devon off his back."

Fey's jaw dropped. "Shut up!" She punched Ani in the shoulder. "How much?"

"Three hundred." Ani grinned.

Fey's eyes moved up and down Ani's body. "You're screwing Keegan for three hundred—"

Ani sucked air through her teeth. "I am not screwing him. We're just going to the banquet and the dance, and that's it. No kissing, no groping, no nothing. It's just for show."

"Sure."

"It is."

"Well," Fey said, getting out the iPod. "You keep telling yourself that."

CHAPTER
18

Ani looked at herself in the full-length mirror mounted on the bathroom door. Her black dress was form-fitting from neck to ankles, with a high collar, long sleeves with lace cuffs, and lace flair at the bottom. With high-heeled leather boots, the only skin showing was her face and hands. Red lipstick and nail polish popped against her white skin, and for the evening she'd toned down the black eyeliner and mascara from 'emo freak' to 'emo lite.' Except for the eyebrow rings, lip ring, nose ring, and safety pins in her cheek—which she had reduced to six for the evening—she thought she looked downright good.

She touched up her lipstick, then called out. "Hey, Mom, are these boots too much?" She shook her head. *It's weird not having her in the house. Or the state.* She snuffed the incense, spritzed a cloud of vanilla perfume, and stepped through it.

She used the railing to totter down the stairs, opened a bottle of water, and sat at the piano. She walked her way through Grigor Iliev's *Remains from the Past*. She didn't much care for modern composers, but Iliev's work was special, and this piece in particular was haunting and beautiful. When she heard the throaty rumble of Keegan's Camaro in front of her house, she cut the piece short and grabbed her purse.

The doorbell rang. She took a shot of the water into her mouth, inhaled it, then clopped across the floor in her heels. She looked through the peephole. *Oh, great. A rose.* She opened the door. Keegan looked respectable in an olive-green suit, goldenrod shirt, and crimson tie. He'd gotten a haircut—high and tight—and wore a little too much cologne. His eyes wandered up her body to her face.

"Is that for me?" she asked, plucking the rose from his hands.

"Yeah," he said. "You look nice." *It's called not eating and a padded bra.*

She tossed the rose onto the piano without smelling it and said, "Let's get this over with."

His cocky grin collapsed a little. "Yeah, sure. Sooner in, sooner done." *That's what Fey said.* His eyes left her, then alighted on the deadbolts. "Dylan?"

She nodded. "Had them installed after the concert. Decided they were a good idea either way."

"Yeah," he said. "That was some freaky shit."

"Um, yeah."

She herded him out the door and locked it, and Keegan stepped off the stoop into the snow to let her go by. *Ladies first, I guess.* Her heels clop-scraped their way down the dry sidewalk, salt crystals crunching underfoot. Keegan tried to open the door for her, but she did it herself and got in. He held it, then shut it after making sure her dress wouldn't be caught.

His car was immaculate, without a trace of dust or dirt. It smelled clean, like Febreeze and lemon zest. *He'd better not be trying to impress me.* Keegan got in and turned up the heat. "Are you comfortable?"

"Sure."

Ani drummed her nails on her purse as they made their way toward school. Keegan watched the road, hands at ten and two, and almost obeyed the speed limit. The radio protested the awkward silence with low-volume Led Zeppelin.

Keegan laughed, short and harsh. "You know, I used to dream about taking you to the Valentine's Banquet when we were in middle school." *Oh, great.*

"Wish fulfilled," she said. *Now shut up.*

"Not exactly how I imagined it, though."

"What a shame." *A tiny part of her meant it.*

"Look," he said, raising his voice. "I know you're here because Mike asked you to be, *bribed* you to be. I get it. People suck, life sucks, high school sucks. But if we're going to pretend to like each other, you need to get the stick out of your butt."

She smirked. "Very well, consider it removed. I'm sorry I'm not the girl I was in junior high, and I'm sorry that our friendship suffered for it. We can pretend we're back in sixth grade if you want." She looked at him sidelong. "I'm warning you, though, if you try to put snails in my hair it will be the last thing you ever do."

He chuckled. "Fair enough."

* * *

They pulled into school, chatting about the time Leah slid across the turf on her face and spent the rest of the game with a green forehead. It was a good memory infected and sickened by years of rejection and mockery. She laughed anyway.

They got out of the car, and she traversed the slippery sidewalk with Keegan's help, her hand on his arm for stability. Using him as a crutch, she found she could just manage to not drag her foot. They arrived at the gym doors, and Ani had to suppress an eye roll—pink streamers, pink tablecloths on tables for two, pink napkins, white banners with red intertwined hearts surrounded by pink flame, and to top it all off she was the only girl not wearing a pink dress. *I'm all for cutesy pink, but this is disgusting.*

As they walked in, people stared. Ani was used to all kinds of looks—disgust, dislike, hate—so she was surprised to see envy. Boys looked at her with unabashed interest, and girls glared. Keegan strutted to their assigned table, pulled out her chair, and pushed it in once she'd sat. He sat across from her, his grin smug.

"Okay, this is freaking weird," Ani said.

"I told you. You look wonderful tonight."

She smiled, flattered in spite of herself. "If you start singing Clapton—"

"I know, I know. No looking, no touching, no singing on pain of death. All fun will be pretend. I won't even enjoy the food." *He does have a charming little smirk. If he weren't such an egomaniacal ass, some girl could make something of him.*

Mike and Devon were seated behind her, so that she couldn't see them while seated at the table. *Just as well.* "Is she buying it?" she asked.

Keegan nodded. "Looks like it. She's only got eyes for Mike, but keeps glancing this way whenever he's not looking."

"Good." *Maybe this won't be a complete waste of an evening.*

The appetizer was bacon-wrapped asparagus, which she skipped. Everyone "knew" she was a vegan, which gave her an excuse to avoid most food most of the time. The enzyme dealt better with vegetables than meat, and they flushed out much easier. Keegan ate both servings in under a minute.

For an entree Ani had a grilled Portobello "steak" with some kind of coconut sauce over rice. Like all food, it didn't taste like much of anything, and she picked at it, chewing mechanically. Keegan had steak, and as he cut into it, red juices leaked out onto his plate. He drew his knife through the seared flesh and revealed the rare pink inside, glistening with moist succulence that—

"I thought you were a vegetarian." Keegan said.

Her eyes snapped away from the steak. "I am." She forced herself to look in his eyes, and not at his plate.

He popped the hunk of meat into his mouth and chewed, speaking around the food. "You could have fooled me. That looked like love."

His fork moved back down to the plate, and he cut another piece. Her eyes followed the red liquid as it pooled around his mashed potatoes. She forced them to look at her mushroom, limp, brown, and lifeless.

She set her napkin on the table and stood. He half-stood as she did so, then sat back down.

She held up a finger. "Excuse me. I need to use the restroom." She tried not to hurry as the hunger clawed at her gut, her eyes dancing from plates on the tables to the heads of the people sitting at them. Her mother had given her a dose of serum before she left for the Keys, so the feeling shouldn't have been that intense. The hallway was torturous, each step a struggle not to run. She walked into the bathroom, her thoughts on red, bloody meat and brains.

She locked the door and sat on the toilet. She rummaged through her purse for the razor. *Dammit, where are you?* It wasn't there. *No. This can't be happening.* She scrambled for something, anything sharp. *Mascara case, tampon, powder brush—bloodbrainsbrainsbrains—*

SAFETY PIN! She dropped the purse and reached up to her cheek, undid a pin with shaking fingers, and stabbed herself in the wrist.

She gasped in release and her eyes rolled back. She stabbed again, and again, dragging the pin through her skin in ragged tears. Six, seven, ten times. She shuddered, relieved. She breathed out, a long, slow sigh.

"Jesus, you are a freak."

Her eyes snapped into focus. Devon stared down at her from over the stall wall, her lip curled in a disgusted sneer. *She must be standing on the toilet.*

"Devon! I... Please, don't tell Mike."

Devon's expression twisted into rage. "You mean Keegan?" She reached down and grabbed Ani's hair. "I'll kill you, you—" The wig pulled off and Devon fell backward into her own stall, her mouth open in surprise.

"Holy shit, Cutter. Not even your hair is real."

"Devon." Ani undid the latch on her door. "You give that back."

Devon bolted for the bathroom door, Ani right behind her. She lost her footing on the tile and crashed to the ground, pain exploding through her injured hip. Devon cried out in triumph as she made it to the hallway. Ani heard her footsteps retreat toward the gym as she pulled herself up with the vanity.

A dead face stared back at her. Lifeless, stringy wisps of hair on a bald, spotted dome. Wincing, she pulled her compact from her purse and held it behind her head. The scar from when Dylan had caved in her skull was an enormous pink X mottled with fleshy white. *I can't go out there like this.*

She leaned against the wall and sank down to the floor, staring straight forward, the back of her head against the wall. Two minutes passed. Then five.

Leah and Rose walked in.

"Aren't you coming out, freak?" Leah said. "Your date's looking for you."

Eyes forward, she replied. "I need my wig. Or a hat. Please."

Rose knelt down in front of her and ran her hand over Ani's head. "Wow, you really are a freak. What is it, herpes?"

Ani stared straight ahead. *Go away. Leave me alone.* "Please go get my wig."

Leah nudged her with her foot, while Rose took out her phone. "C'mon, freak," Leah said. "Smile for the camera."

Ani looked up at Rose. "If you take my picture like this, I'm going to—"

"What, cut yourself?" Devon asked as she walked in. She looked down at Ani with a cruel smile, but she spoke to her friends. "What did I tell you, a total freak show." *Self-preservation first, revenge later.* She used the wall to stand as Rose took pictures. "Smile, bitch," Devon said.

Ani snatched the camera out of Rose's hand and threw it with all of her supernatural strength. It shattered against the wall. Rose gasped in outrage, then slapped her. Ani's cheek stung, and she raised her hand to touch the raw flesh. Rose slapped her again, tearing a safety pin from her other cheek.

Then they were on her. Fists and elbows punished her, clawed hands tore at her dress. She covered her face with her arms and dropped to her knees, so they kicked her. *I can stop this. I can hurt them so badly that they can never hurt anyone ever again. I'm stronger than any of them.*

Another voice, her mother's voice, spoke to her through the abuse. *But if you do, they will know something is wrong with you, something different and special. You can't let that happen.* She was right, even when she wasn't here. Ani grunted as a foot cracked her rib, and thanked God they weren't wearing boots. It didn't hurt that much anyway, not as much as it should have.

She looked through her fingers as a male voice broke through the pummeling blows. "Hey! HEY!"

Devon yelped in astonishment as she flew sideways, rebounding off the stall and falling to her butt. Mike grabbed Leah and Rose by the hair, yanked them backward and dropped them on their backs.

"You..." Devon said to him, her voice more angry than hurt. "You hit me." She reached up and touched her bloody lip. "You fucking hit me!"

Mike shook his head. "No, I pushed you. But if you don't stay the hell on the floor, I will hit you." He looked at Leah and Rose, who glowered up at him. "You, too." Leah pouted, the sullen sulk of a girl whose Dad took away her toys. He helped Ani to her feet.

Devon crossed her arms. "We are through, Mike."

"No shit," he replied, still holding Ani's fingers.

Ani reached down and picked Rose's micro-SD card off the floor. She put it in her purse as Mike interrogated Devon. "What did you do with her wig?"

"FUCK you."

He took off his jacket, draped it over Ani's head, and took a step with her out the door. She winced in pain, almost falling, and he swooped her into his arms and carried her. People gaped as they passed the gym, but he backed out the door and went straight to Keegan's car.

Ani refused to go to the hospital, so they rode in silence as Keegan drove them home in the falling snow. Mike helped her up the walk, but she held him at the door. She pulled his coat from her head and thanked him, tried to ignore the horrified look in his eyes as he tried not to look at her gruesome skull, and went inside alone. She locked the door, fastened the dead bolts, and sat down on the couch. The house felt empty.

There's no one home. No one alive, anyway.

* * *

She got out of the bath the next morning with a different perspective. After spending a few hours in self-pity, she'd looked at the facts.

Fact One: Devon, Leah, and Rose are psychotic bitches. *I already knew that.*

Fact Two: Mike had come to her defense. *He cares about me.*

Fact Three: Devon and Mike had broken up. *After he knocked her over and bloodied her lip, something she'd never forgive.*

Fact Four: Mike had carried her, like a knight in shining armor. Like a romance-novel fantasy. If it weren't for what came before it would have been the most romantic moment of her life. *Maybe it was anyway.*

Fact Five: That's pretty pathetic.

She allowed herself a smile. *It's pathetic, but it's my pathetic.* She put on a spare wig and spent the morning painting, one canvas after the next, and every one of them Mike Brown. If she couldn't quite capture his green eyes, her muse would forgive her.

Late morning, Mike stopped by. She looked at the doorknob, then at the paintings, and back at the door. *Ah, crap. I can't let him see those.* She wiped paint on her sweater, put one foot in front of the door so that it could only open a few inches, unlocked everything, and cracked it open.

Mike looked relieved. "Hey, Ani. How are you feeling?"

She squinted into the sunlight. "I'm okay." Her ribs were sore, but no more than that.

His eyes moved up and down her body, but not in the usual way men's eyes did. He grunted. "You look a lot better than I expected." *That happens when you don't bruise, have extra-hard flesh because you bathe in a vat of chemicals, and have a mom with access to the best regenerative drugs money can buy.*

"Thanks. And thanks again, Mike." She forced the next words out. "Sorry about you and Devon."

He snorted. "I'm not. I can't believe I stayed with her this long...." He raised his eyebrows. "Can I come in?" *Why did I have to paint those stupid paintings?*

She sighed. "I don't think so. Not right now. My mom would kill me if I had a boy over when she wasn't home."

"I'm not 'a boy.' I'm Mike Brown from down the street." He winked at her. "Besides, she doesn't have to know."

"Yeah, she does. You know this block. The neighbors talk about everything."

He grimaced. *You know I'm right.* "Yeah. Okay," he said. He looked at her again, this time with more interest than concern. "See you at school."

"Sure, Mike. See you at school." She closed the door and tried not to squeal.

Her mom called at noon to ask about the banquet. She lied and said it went fine. She told the truth and said that Keegan never even tried to touch her. She told her that the entire plan "sort of backfired," and her mom didn't ask for details. *Perfect.*

The doorbell rang at lunchtime. She tried the same foot in the door trick, but Fey took immediate offense. "What, so I'm not allowed in your house now? We're not friends?" Ani moved her foot and opened the door.

"Sorry. Come on in."

Fey stormed into the living room and stopped in her tracks, staring at the paintings. "Wow." She looked at Ani, mouth still open. "Those are good. Real good. You could totally go pro."

"Thanks," Ani said. "All it takes is practice."

Fey shook her head. "I couldn't do that in a million years." She looked from canvas to canvas, then whirled around. She stepped forward and grabbed Ani's hands, her eyes wide. "So what the hell happened last night? Everyone's saying Mike beat up Devon and they split."

Ani told her what happened, even about her scar. *They saw it, so it's only a matter of time before everyone knows about it.* She explained how she got it in a bicycle accident when she was a kid.

"Then how come nobody knows about it? I mean, you told me about your hair, what with your condition and all, but that scar... Can I see it?"

"I'd rather not," Ani said.

"C'mon, just a peek." *Or I will harass you forever, or play the "we're not really friends" card....*

"Fine," Ani said. She took off her wig and turned around.

Fey didn't say anything for a moment, then, "That is so cool. Can I touch it?" Ani let out an exasperated sigh. *I don't think I could explain why my head is at room temperature.* She thought of Rose, running her hand over her head in the bathroom, and frowned.

"Why not? While you're at it want to give me a breast exam?"

"What the hell is that supposed to mean?"

Ani put on her wig and turned around. Fey's eyes blazed and her cheeks were flushed. "It didn't mean anything. Just that it's kind of personal, you know?"

Fey's face flooded with relief. "Oh. Yeah, okay. I understand. I won't talk about it either." She hurried to the door. "Look, I got to jet. See you Monday."

"Sure, Fey. See you Monday." She left in a hurry, slamming the door behind her.

Ani locked the door, trying to figure out what had just happened. She gave up by the time the deadbolts were set.

* * *

Ani called Keegan's phone and sighed in relief when voicemail picked up. "Keeg's phone, talk at the beep." The phone beeped.

"Hey, Keegan, it's Ani. Um, I'm canceling for tomorrow night. No point now, I think. See you. And thanks for driving me home." She hung up.

She bundled up against the cold—more to keep up appearances than anything else—and walked to the store. Her limp was more pronounced, and her foot really dragged now. She'd hoped it would get better in the bath, but so far it hadn't. *I'll have to make something up and have Mom look at it.* It's not like she wouldn't notice anyway.

As she walked by Mike's house, he was shoveling the walk with his mom. He waved but didn't come over to talk. She waved back, tried not to smile too big, and shambled her way to the store.

She bought a heart-shaped box of Russell Stover's chocolates from the grocery store, then crossed the street to CVS to buy a card. The pharmacy had a much better selection. It took her ten minutes to pick the right card—simple, straightforward, and not too sappy. She hid the items under her coat, returned home, and spent the evening at the piano.

CHAPTER
19

Ani skated through Valentine's Day on a cloud. Mike rode the bus to school, and it wasn't weird at all—just natural conversation—and Fey didn't even seem to mind. When Jake asked Fey to the dance before homeroom, she said "yes" without complaining about it later. Devon and Mike weren't speaking to one another, and Mike stopped to talk to Ani twice in the morning. He sat with her at lunch, and Fey was so wrapped up with Jake she didn't mind that either.

After geometry Mike gave Ani a card and a hug. He didn't ride the bus home—he had basketball practice until four thirty—so she chatted with Fey until her stop, then daydreamed out the window. She got off the bus, let herself in, and tore open the envelope.

The card was a painting of a lion standing guard over a baby lamb. *Not very Valentine-y.* She opened it and found it blank, but with a handwritten note inside.

* * *

Dear Ani,
I never told you how much you mean to me.
Saturday sucked, the worst moment of my life, but
also the best. I wish I got there sooner. I wish they'd
never hurt you, but in a way I'm glad they did

because it gave me the opportunity to hold you.
 Your dear friend forever,
 Mike

* * *

Ani ran-shuffled to her room, opened her keepsake chest, and traded Mike's card for the candy and card she had bought the day before. She signed the card, "Love, Ani" and put it in the box. Her heart couldn't bear watching him read the card, so she could give him the chocolates, ask him to the dance, and escape—he'd find the card later.

She tried to read, but found herself staring at the clock. The numbers crept forward with agonizing slowness, each tick a reminder of her mother's disapproval. *I don't care.* At five-fifteen, she couldn't take it anymore.

She stepped outside into the glorious cold, closed the door, and limped down the sidewalk, her way lit by orange halogen streetlights glistening off the snow. The salt from the night before had worn off, and the sidewalk was slick. She lost her balance, arms pinwheeling, but regained her footing with a sigh of relief. She laughed at herself, exhilarated.

A few houses down, she crossed the road, the candy still hidden under her coat. She ran her hand over the top of the mailbox marked "Brown" and felt an almost electric thrill from the freezing metal. His sidewalk was covered with a dusting of drifted snow, the pure white marred by footprints large and small.

She knocked on the door, rocking on her heels. She heard shuffling, the banging of furniture, and then the door flew open.

Mike's eyes were wide as she pushed the chocolates into his hands. "Hey, Ani! I wasn't expecting you."

"Happy Valentine's Day!" She smiled, and her eyes drew down his flushed face to land on his perfect lips. *Now or never.* "I was wondering..." He had a red smudge on his upper lip. It looked like strawberry jam, or blood, or... *lipstick.*

She took a step back, gasping, out of breath. *I can't be out of breath. I'm always... I'm...* She felt faint.

She caught movement behind him. Devon stepped into view, fastening her bra under her shirt. She gave a princess wave, her lips twisted into a cruel parody of a smile. "Hey, Ani. Nice to see you."

Ani's eyes flicked from Mike's guilty face to Devon and back. "I... I thought..." She ran.

Mike might have called after her. She stumbled through snow banks, driveways, hedgerows. Branches clawed at her clothes, her hair, her face. She didn't know where she was going. She didn't care. *Away. I have to get away.* She stumbled, more than once, but she dragged herself to her feet and kept running.

The world upended and she fell. She tumbled down a slope, her body punished by rocks, sticks, and the hard, frozen ground. Arms flailing, she pitched forward into a pile of brush. She gagged as a tree branch punched into her chest, pinning her up in the air. Legs dangling, she looked down at the branch embedded in her torso. *Missed my heart. That's good.* Her mom would notice if the pacemaker was damaged.

"Ow," she said. Her back hurt just below her shoulder blade, so she reached up and felt for the source. The branch pinning her in the air had gone right through, and she felt several inches sticking out of her back. "Wow."

Her voice sounded airy, different. She breathed in to try again, and felt air suck past the branch in her ribs. *Oh, great. Just great.* She grabbed the branch with both hands and pushed herself off the jagged wood. She was most of the way off when it snapped. The bark held firm, so as she fell to the ground, it tore out of her chest. She landed in a creek bed, the ice crackling under her rump as she hit.

She grabbed the branch and pulled herself to her feet. Chunks of something white and slimy—*lung, maybe?*—were stuck to it. "Ew!" She wiped her hand on her shirt, then looked up. The ravine wasn't very high.

She climbed out and used the moonlight to retrace her footsteps through the snow, unneeded breath wheezing in the night air.

* * *

By the time she got home, it was eight o'clock. The dance was starting. Devon was with Mike. Fey was with Jake. Mom was with her Mike. The house was empty, silent, devoid of life.

She locked the door and got in the bath, cranking *Year of the Black Rainbow.* Fey was right. It was wretched. And so was she.

* * *

When the bus pulled up to Fey's house, no one got on. Ani looked out the window. Jake's car idled in her driveway, and her mom stood in the doorway, waving the bus on. The bus lurched forward, passed Mike's house without slowing down, and continued on to school.

Greg Schulman lurked at her locker, scratching at his arms as he shifted from foot to foot. "Have you seen Jake?" *Need a fix, do you?* "I need to talk to him."

"He's at Fey's house. They're either skipping or late." Her voice was almost back to normal after a slathering of regenerative cream and a night in the bath, but it had an asthmatic quality she couldn't hide.

"Oh," Greg said. He stared at her as she got out her books for first period.

"Do you have somewhere to be," she asked?

"No," he replied, still staring. *Take a hint much?* "Can I see your head?"

"Absolutely not." Ani wasn't sure if his brain was functional enough to produce words that consisted of more than one syllable. Hopefully, he could understand them. "Go away, Greg."

He took a step back, but didn't leave. It was a relief when the bell rang.

* * *

Fey wouldn't shut up when they met in the hall after third period. "I never realized how deep Jake is. He's, like, so cool. So *deep*. We have so much in common." She flashed her eyebrows. "And not for nothing, but he ain't a bad kisser, either. And there's this thing he does—" *Don't forget to breathe, Fey.*

She let Fey ramble for a minute, then begged off to go to class. It was hard to feel happy for Fey when she was so miserable, and being so petty about it made her more miserable.

Mike always half-ignored her, but this was somehow worse. He blushed every time he saw her and turned away. *You should be ashamed.* Devon, on the other hand, wouldn't stop staring—that petty, vindictive, I-have-what-you-want look that Ani should have been above letting hurt her, but wasn't.

She turned around and bumped into Rose. She stepped back. "Sorry."

"Hey, freak, you owe me two hundred dollars for my phone."

In her peripheral vision, she saw Leah approaching from the side. *Screw this.* She looked up into Rose's eyes and shook her head. "If you try to collect it, I'll have you prosecuted for assault. Back off."

They locked eyes. Ani saw her rage and felt nothing but cold. Rose raised her hands and stepped back. *Not expecting a fight, Rose?* "Sure, freak. Whatever you say." She turned to Leah and they hurried away.

Mrs. Weller crooked a finger at her. "Ani, my room, please." *Oh just freaking great.* Ani shuffled into her room and she closed the door. Mrs. Weller's head tilted to one side, her eyes full of concern. "Do you want to tell me what that was about?"

Ani crossed her arms. "No." *I seem to be getting better at uncomfortable silence.*

"Are you sure? We take female bullying very seriously at

Ohneka Falls. There can be consequences, but you have to speak up."

"I can take care of myself."

"I didn't say you couldn't. But we can help, if you let us." Ani looked at the door, then back at Mrs. Weller. "But you have to let us." She waited. Ani let her. "Ani?"

"I heard you," Ani said. "Can I go now?"

Mrs. Weller frowned. "Yes. I'm not holding you or anything." *But you will tell my mom.*

She walked out.

* * *

Fey and Jake sat together at lunch, and Ani didn't think his hand even once left her thigh. They mooned at each other, giggling and whispering sweet nothings. They said almost nothing to Ani or to anyone else. *And this is the boy that asked me out last week.*

The day dragged to infinity, but finally the bell rang. Ani went to her locker to get her trig book. She lifted the handle, gave it a kick to pop it open, and froze. Inside was a box of Russell Stover's chocolates, unwrapped. Without taking it out of her locker, she removed the lid. Instead of candy there was a picture inside—Devon and Mike kissing on the dance floor. It was signed, "Love, Devon."

* * *

It was a relief to lock herself in her house. She was playing the first movement of Shostakovich's *Piano Concerto No. 2 in F Minor*, fast-paced and angry, when her mother got home. She kept playing as the key turned in the lock, but stopped as her mom stepped inside, scowling through her new tan.

"Shostakovich," her mom said. "Never good." She crossed the room and hugged Ani close. "What's wrong, my little baby?"

"Nothing I want to talk about." She buried her face in her mom's chest and gave her a good squeeze. "I'm glad you're home."

Her mom stroked her wig as if it were hair. "Me, too."

They held each other for a minute before Ani pulled away and tried a smile. "How was your trip?"

Her answering smile was tinged with melancholy. "It was good. We had a nice time."

"But?" Ani asked, her eyebrows raised. *Whatever's wrong, you can tell me.*

It turned into a smirk. "Nothing I want to talk about."

Ani laughed. "Fair enough. Mom...." She couldn't help but ask. "Are you and Mike still...?"

"Yes, Mike and I are still together."

"So when am I going to meet this guy?" Ani asked. *Geez, Mom, you look constipated.*

"Oh, I don't know. I want to make sure it's really serious before we start introducing kids."

"He has kids?" Ani asked.

"He has a son about your age." She kissed Ani on the forehead. "I need to pee and then get something to eat. Why don't you go back to your piano before you get in the bath?"

"Okay, Mom." *You didn't even notice my voice.* She tried for Liszt's *Feux Follets*, upbeat and happy and a strain on her technical prowess. It didn't lift her mood, but it made a good distraction. She couldn't quite play it without screwing up, but by the time the spring concert came around it would make a great show-off piece.

The idea of a concert brought her thoughts to Dylan, but she drowned them in music.

* * *

Wednesday and Thursday were more of the same—Fey and Jake in their own world, petty jibes from Devon, Leah, and Rose, and Mike too embarrassed by his own actions to even speak to her. Her life was too crowded to be lonely, but she was lonely anyway. She spent both days mired in her own thoughts and found herself composing music for the first time in weeks.

She burned through her afternoons and evenings transcribing what she had constructed in her head, semi-classical but dark and moody, not her usual upbeat dance-beat scores. *Oh, great. Much more of this and I'll actually be emo.* She couldn't wait for Friday—Monday was President's Day, and that meant nine days off if you counted both weekends. Nine days to distract herself helping Mom find a cure.

It was three in the morning on Friday when she heard the phone ring, muted and garbled through the iced formalin bath. Late-night phone calls were never good news. Never. She pushed open the lid, sat up, and the goopy chemicals sloughed off her upper body. She heard her mom on the phone. She couldn't pick out words, but her tone was clipped, agitated. She waited for her mother's footsteps on the stairs.

Her mom walked in, the phone in her hand but turned off. She looked worried, furious, murderous.

"What is it, Mom?"

"Dylan's awake. And he's talking."

CHAPTER 20

"They're taking no chances," her mom said. "He's in restraints and under guard. He's told the police—and everyone who would listen—that you're a zombie and that he was trying to save the town." Her mom sat on the edge of the tub, bundled up in her nightgown. "Fortunately for us he's also babbling about how he loves you and wants to be with you on the 'other side.' They think he's crazy and maybe brain damaged." There was an exaggerated pause.

"But..." Ani adjusted her nylon-coated bath pillow so that her face would be out of the pungent solution, and lay back. The slimy, ice-cold tingling enveloped her in a comforting embrace.

"But you need to be careful. Falsely reporting a zombie incident is a felony—not that he isn't in enough trouble—but Homeland Security always follows up. Always."

"But, Mom, no one will believe—"

Her mom held up a finger. "This means no research this week. I can still get a few things done, but we can't be going in and out of the basement. We'll have to leave the blinds open downstairs—too suspicious otherwise—and you'll need to be out and about. Walk around town, hang out with Tiffany, apply for jobs or something." Ani looked at the raised finger. She almost interrupted anyway, but thought better of it. "And... I'll get us a kitten." She dropped her hand.

"Mom, we can't get a kitten. It'll freak the hell out."

"Not if it's heavily sedated whenever you're home. You can sit on the couch and pet it. That should allay any suspicion that anyone watching you might have."

"But... I... They can't possibly believe him. There are no zombies like me. None anywhere. It's not possible."

Her mom looked out her bedroom door at the repaired banister.

"Mom?"

"Dammit, Ani," her mom snapped. "Use your head. Do you think I came up with all those serums entirely on my own? The bath? The treatment?"

"You mean people know—"

The finger shot up. "There are other researchers, yes. Other rehabilitation labs. Government labs. Nobody knows about you in particular, no. As far as I know you are the only human who has ever been infected and yet remained alive for years. You are the only one who can think and speak about other things most of the time. The only one I know of."

She put her fingertips to her forehead, her elbows on the edge of the bath. "But you're not the only zombie who has had their cravings at least partially controlled, though you might be the most successful. You're certainly the only one allowed free. You'd be special, unique, even if you weren't my baby girl." Her hand dropped.

"Holy shit, Mom." She ignored the disapproving glare. "That can't be legal."

"Watch your language." She nodded. "And you're right. It's not legal. What those other labs are doing is every bit as illegal as what we're doing here. But if we're going to cure you, something has to be done, right? I can't do it all on my own, can I?"

Ani didn't bother to answer the rhetorical question. "So you work with these people? Who are they?"

She shook her head. "It's top-secret military research. I used to work for them officially—I was never really a cardiologist—which is why I was on-hand when the first ZV outbreak hit."

"The zombie virus was man-made?"

Her mom nodded.

"Mom, did you make—"

She scowled. "Don't be ridiculous. It was the Chinese. We got a hold of their research and reverse-engineered it, tried to find a counter to it before it could be used on us. The program was canceled of course, after the first outbreak, but it re-opened under other names, other departments." She leaned in close and kissed Ani on the forehead. "We all have our reasons for doing it. Mine are just more personal than theirs." She pulled back. "Anyway, those connections allow me access to drugs and research I wouldn't otherwise have. They're critical if I'm to find a cure before I—" She choked back a sob. *What the hell was that?* "Before you graduate." She stood up and put her hands to her mouth, gasping through tears. "I need to go back to bed. I'll see you in the morning, sweetie."

"Okay, Mom."

Her mom rested her fingers on the bath lid.

"Hey." They locked eyes. "I love you."

"And I love you, Ani."

Her mom closed the lid and hurried out of the room, leaving Ani to her worries.

* * *

She spent the rest of vacation pretending to be a semi-normal girl. She practiced piano, painted, ate two small meals a day that she had to wait until late at night to flush out, and petted the drugged-up orange tabby mom had adopted from the pound. She filled out and dropped off job applications, hung out with Fey and Jake, and tried not to notice the black Lexus sedan that seemed to follow her everywhere.

By the end of break, it was gone, her mom gave her the 'all clear' and gave the cat away to one of the bus drivers. They got in one day of tests before it was time to go back to school. Sunday night she slept in the bath. She needed it—after a week without it, she was starting to smell, and her voice was getting worse.

* * *

The next week was uneventful. Fey and Jake broke up over something stupid, got back together, and broke up again. By Friday they were back to talking, and the emo crowd had settled into a sense of relative normalcy.

People whispered about Dylan, but it was just talk—nobody seemed to lend the rumors any credence. Ani talked and went to school and hung out, so she couldn't possibly be what Dylan said she was—he had to be crazy. It did have the unfortunate side effect of earning her a new nickname from the evil three.

After the initial shock, she got used to "Dead Girl" in minutes and began to appreciate the irony of it. She started responding to it as if it were her name, and they stopped. It was probably for the best that she went back to being "Cutter" and "freak."

Saturday morning she went to an interview with Luz's Soaps and Scents, a boutique that suited her needs as well as the Lair ever did. The shop was cloying, an allergist's worst nightmare of floral scents; and in addition to soap, lotion, incense, and bath salts, it also displayed work from local artists—it was perfect, and she looked forward to an excuse to get out of the house more.

She wore a nice, modest dress and toned down her makeup to the minimum possible that would still maintain her image. She took the safety pins out of her cheek—the scar was almost invisible—and carried another copy of her resume in a portfolio. She put on her best smile and walked into the shop, the jingling bell atop the door announcing her arrival.

The curly-haired Latina behind the counter smiled at her as she approached. "May I help you?" Her accent was charming, but Spanish rather than Mexican or Puerto Rican. "Bath salts are on sale, twenty percent off."

"Are you Luz?" she asked. The woman nodded. "Hi, I'm Ani Romero. I have a ten o'clock interview."

Luz gave her a flat smile, folded her hands one atop the other, and her eyes walked over Ani's pierced eyebrow, nose, and lip. "I'm sorry, but the position has been filled. We'll let you know if it opens up again."

Ani glanced at the 'Help Wanted' plaque on the counter and snorted. "Sure. Thanks for your time."

She walked home grumpy, slowing as she turned the corner to her street. An unmarked delivery truck sat in her driveway, the ramp down. She stepped behind a tree, watching. Her mom directed two men in dark blue coveralls as they maneuvered a large wooden crate on a hand dolly up the sidewalk, over the stoop, and into the house. About five minutes later, they returned with the empty crate, loaded it onto the truck, and drove off.

She let herself in—the doors were locked, as usual—and called out. "Mom?" There was no answer. She took a quick look around, and no one seemed to be home, which meant that Mom was in the basement.

She heard scrambling as she slid back the bookcase, and ran down the stairs as fast as her dysfunctional legs would let her. Her mom sat at the lab table, writing, but her face was flushed and she breathed harder than a person writing should. She looked up as Ani hit the landing.

"Slow down, sweetie, you might hurt yourself." She turned back to the legal pad.

"What was in the crate?" she asked.

"Hmm?" Her mom shook her head without looking up. "Nothing to worry about. Just something I'm working on."

Ani looked around the room. Everything seemed to be in its place. No new glassware or equipment, no boxes, no package peanuts, no nothing. Her eyes lit on the 'just in case' room door, and the padlock dangling from the handle. *Why would that be locked if I'm not inside?*

Ani didn't bother trying to be subtle; she shuffled straight toward it.

Her mom spoke up without lifting her eyes from the page. "You don't want to look in there." *Oh, yes I do.* She kept walking.

"I said stop."

Ani stopped but didn't turn around. "Why? What is it?"

"Something I need to continue my research, to push it to the next level. Nothing that will make you happy."

"I have to know—" She took another step.

"Do not look in that room. I forbid it."

Her mom frowned as Ani glanced back. "Sorry, Mom." She walked up to the door's tiny window. She put her hands around her eyes and pressed up against the glass. In the gloom she saw a figure strapped to the chair, head lolled a little to one side, gag in his mouth.

Dylan.

She whirled around, catching herself on the door lest she fall. Her mother was right behind her, wearing her doctor face.

"Mom, you can't do this."

"Too late, it's already done." She raised a finger.

"No. We can let him go before he wakes up. He'll never know, and if he remembers something, they'll think he's crazy." Ani braced for the explosion.

Her mom opened her hand, put it to Ani's cheek and brushed her hair back with her knuckles. "Ani, sweetie, we can't let him go. He's too dangerous."

"No he's not, Mom. He's crazy, so they'll keep him locked up. No one will ever believe him. We can let him—"

Her mom grabbed her face with both hands and pulled her close. "You don't understand. I infected him with ZV just before you got here."

Ani blinked in disbelief. "What?"

"You heard me."

Ani stepped back against the door and slid to the floor. "You..." She wrapped her knees with her arms. "You killed him."

"No," her mother said. "It's just until I can cure him. It gives me a specimen that I'm not so concerned with losing, so I can be more aggressive with the testing regimen."

Aggressive. "And then what? If that fails, you just find another *specimen*?"

Her mother nodded. "If I have to. I told you I would do anything to protect you, and I meant it."

"Jesus, Mom. I... *Jesus*. Have you done this before?"

She hesitated, then shook her head. "Not personally."

Ani scowled. "I have a right to know."

Her mother returned her scowl. "I suppose you do." She licked her lips. "My colleagues have done it before, and it's the reason I left their employ. They infected a pregnant woman to see if ZV transmits through pregnancy."

"Oh, my God," Ani said, horrified. "What happened to her?"

"She died."

Ani bit her lip. "And the baby?"

Her mom hesitated. "Also dead."

Ani shook her head. "You can't do this," Ani said. "It's wrong."

"We don't have a choice. It's time to grow up, Ani. Sometimes you do what you have to."

* * *

Ani got out of the bath at two-thirty and crept through the darkness. Her mother's breathing didn't change as the stairs creaked, but she froze anyway, waiting for a trap. A minute later she tiptoed to the bookcase, eased up the latch, and opened the basement door. Well-oiled, it made no noise. She stepped through and eased it shut. The concrete floor was cold on her bare feet.

Her mother took meticulous notes, years and years of spiral notebooks filled with drawings, ideas, arguments, chemical formulae, and experimental results organized by date in a mountain of filing cabinets. Ani found the earliest set of files in the back of the basement. A moan escaped the coal furnace, and Ani closed her eyes. *I'm so sorry.*

After a moment she opened them and gripped the handle. The drawer squeaked as she inched it open, and with gritted teeth she forced herself to patience. Millimeter by millimeter the drawer came open, revealing stacks of notebooks sprinkled with ancient dust. She wiped the dust off the top notebook, and found dates printed on the front in her mother's meticulous hand. She skipped forward six notebooks and found the entry for July 9th, seventeen years previous. She caught herself humming *Happy Birthday* under her breath, and stopped.

She scanned the entry, picking out important phrases. *Jane Doe stable under serum 2... C-Section scheduled... live birth, female, four pounds, eleven ounces... child is symptomatic, fever 103... time of death 9:32 p.m., remains incinerated... biopsy ZV positive...*

She looked up. Her mom frowned at her from halfway down the stairs. Her voice was soft, husky. "What are you doing?"

"Reading," Ani said. "About me?"

Her mom froze, then nodded. "Lies about you, yes." She leaned against the wall and closed her eyes. "I couldn't write the truth, not about that. If they found it..."

Ani swallowed, a useless reflex. "What is the truth, Mom? About me? My real mother?"

"I'm your *real* mother," she growled, then schooled herself. "Your birth mother, you mean."

Ani nodded, and waited. *Please, no more lies.*

Her mom looked through her as she talked. "Jane Doe. I never knew her name, where they got her. She was maybe seven months pregnant when they brought her into the lab and infected her. They kept her in an induced coma until she came to term, and the child was removed via C-section. Healthy, pink and precious, a baby girl. It was my job to test it for ZV and then destroy it. I took it—her—to my lab and administered the tests. ZV positive. And yet alive. No symptoms, no fever. Healthy. Beautiful."

Her sad smile never touched her eyes. "If they ever realized what they had, what a miracle this baby girl was, she'd grow up in a lab, forever strapped to a table, a test subject from violent birth until they found no more use for her and incinerated her. I couldn't let them do that. I couldn't. It was too far. Even for me." Her gaze drifted to the floor. "Even for me...."

Ani waited. Her mom looked up but didn't appear to see.

"So I faked the documents that she was destroyed and took her home." Her eyes snapped back to the present. "I named her Ani, and I raised her as my own, and I never told them."

Ani stood there, her mouth open in dumb shock.

Her mom walked down the stairs, put her hand on Ani's head and rubbed it affectionately. "I love you, my baby girl. I have since the moment I saw you. I had to protect you."

"You lied to me," Ani said. "Lied."

She nodded. "I did. I was going to tell you when... when all this was over. When you got better." She plucked the notebook from Ani's fingers and closed it. "There are a lot of things I wish I'd never done. Working for those men can't be one of them, because they brought me you."

She reached out her arms, and Ani buried herself in the warmth of her embrace. *Oh, my God.*

CHAPTER
21

Ani trudged through the next few days. *Dylan is dying in my basement. My mom is a murderer. Maybe a mass-murderer. My mom isn't even my mom.* She vaguely recalled blowing off Fey when she wanted to talk about Jake, and being sat down by a concerned Mrs. Weller worried about her shell-shocked demeanor. Called into the nurse's office, she had to listen as her mother snapped at her to stop being childish. *She infected him and now she's waiting for him to die so she can run her tests.*

Wednesday was Dr. Seuss's birthday, and she played piano at the assembly in the Elementary School. She just walked her way through the sheet music and hoped she didn't screw it up. The kids clapped along and seemed to like it.

She got back to the upper school too late for the bus. Rather than call her mom, she decided to walk home. A car pulled up next to her, a voice called out. Fey, from the passenger's seat of Jake's car. *No, I don't want a ride.* She waved them off and kept walking. It was almost forty degrees, warmer than her nightly bath, and the air felt good against her skin.

When she got home she could hear her mom in the basement. She didn't want to look, didn't want to know. She slipped behind the bookcase and went downstairs. Dylan was dead in the recliner, straining against the chains, drool leaking out past the gag, soaking his T-shirt.

"Oh, good, sweetie, you're home," her mother said, not looking up from her notebook. "Grab the syringes for me, would you?"

Ani looked at the lab, clean and clinical. *Is this what it looked like then? When they cut my mother open and pulled me out and burned her? Did it happen here, or somewhere else?*

"Ani!" her mother barked from above a bank of test tubes.

Ani looked at her. "I don't think I can do this. This isn't right." Dylan moaned.

"It's as right as it can be. Now get me the syringes."

She looked at the syringes, then at her mom. "No."

Her mother raised a finger and opened her mouth.

Ani cut her off.

"Don't you dare raise that finger at me. You're not my mother."

Her mother stormed around the table and grabbed her by the shoulders. She slapped Ani across the face. "Don't you ever say that again." Her voice was hoarse. "I gave up everything to be your mother. Everything. I raised you as my own, and I'm the only thing that's standing between you and the furnace. And now... And now I..." She started hyperventilating, then burst into tears.

Sobbing gasps overwhelmed her. She dropped to her knees. Ani didn't know what to do, didn't know what to feel. *You've always been the strong one.* She stepped forward and put a hand on her shoulder, patted it. Her mom grabbed her leg and cried. And cried and cried.

When she finally stopped, her eyes were red and her nose leaked snot. She wiped her face on the sleeve of her lab coat, then hugged Ani's leg again. "I'm so sorry, baby. I just don't know what to do." *Mom always knew what to do, always had a plan, and a backup plan.*

"What's going on?" Ani asked. Dylan groaned around the gag and jangled his chains behind her. *Besides the obvious.* She helped her mom to her feet and walked her to the lab table. They sat. Her mom blew her nose, threw away the tissue, then looked at Ani.

"I went to see a specialist this fall. An oncologist."

"I don't—"

"A cancer specialist. I was diagnosed with AML, acute myeloid leukemia. I've been on chemotherapy while they ran more tests. That's why I've been so tired." Ani bit her lip. "While we were in Key West, Doctor Ehrmentraut called and gave me some news. There are some cytogenetic abnormalities in the del-five-Q—"

"What does that mean?"

"It means that it's bad. Very bad."

"How bad?"

Her mom put her palms flat on the table. "Typical cases have a five-year mortality of eighty-five percent." *No no no no no not my mom not my mommy.* "Sometimes it can be cured. The first chemo didn't go so well. We're going to run a more aggressive battery soon. I'm going to feel sick—sicker—and I'm going to lose my hair, and my energy.

"But I'm already tired, and I don't feel good. And if I'm going to cure you, I need to do it before I... soon. And I can't do it without your help. I need my baby beside me. Please, sweetie." She reached across the table and grabbed Ani's hand.

Ani squeezed. "Okay, Mom. Okay. I'll help. On one condition."

"What?"

"If things don't work out with Dylan, we stop. No more people die so I can live."

"Okay, sweetie," her mom said. She gave Ani a tight smile. "Let's get to work."

* * *

Friday good. End of twenty-five weeks bad. Ani got her unofficial grades from her teachers. *D in AP History, D in English.* Parent-teacher conference requests had been sent home that morning. *I'm dead. Extra dead.*

"Come on," Fey said. "What's the worst that could happen?" *Home school.*

"Summary execution," Ani said. Jake laughed, and she punched him in the arm. "It's not funny, Jake. My mom is going to kill me."

Jake rubbed his arm. "Your mom has a stick up her butt."

"Doesn't she know already?" Fey asked. "I mean, she works here and all."

Ani shook her head. "Apparently she has to contact the teacher the same way any other parent does. Union rules or something."

"That's stupid," Jake said. Ani shrugged.

"So," Fey said, "that means she's getting a letter in the mail just like anyone else would?"

Ani nodded. "It'll be in the mailbox when she gets home."

Fey grinned. "It doesn't have to be."

"Mom beats me home every day, if she doesn't give me a ride. There's no way to hide it from her."

Fey coughed, then smirked. "Wow. I don't feel so good."

Jake ran his tongue over his front teeth. "You look pale. Maybe you should go home early."

Ani's eyes widened. "If someone sees you—"

"Then I did it myself," Fey said, "trying to do you a favor. You didn't put me up to nothing."

Ani sighed. "Why bother? It's just delaying the inevitable. She'll find out when five week reports go out anyway."

"True," Fey said. "But what's wrong with delaying the inevitable?"

Ani bit her lip. She looked at Fey, then down the hall toward the nurse's office. "Yeah, okay. I owe you one."

* * *

Her mom ate dinner while Ani painted, ungrounded and un-yelled at. *For now.* Another brush stroke completed the hull of a sailboat, and she started on the sail. The doorbell rang. Ani got up, but her mom beat her to it. She checked the peephole, unlatched the dead-bolts, and opened the door. Fey stepped inside, chomping gum.

"Miss Daniels," her mother said. "What can I do for you this evening?"

Fey held out an envelope. "Hi, Mrs. Romero. This was in our mailbox by mistake. Thought you might want it." Her mom plucked the envelope from Fey's hand. Ani recognized the school's logo, and tried to come up with an insult deadly enough for the occasion.

"Thank you, Tiffany." Her mom stepped out of the way as Ani pushed past her.

"Fey, can I talk to you for a minute?"

"Sure," Fey said. Her upper lip was curled in a tiny sneer. Ani stepped outside and closed the door, her wide eyes asking the question for her. "Not for nothing, Ani, but next time I want to talk to you about something, try not blowing me off. Consider this a lesson in friendship." She turned and tromped through the snow toward her yard.

Ani watched her go, then walked inside to face her mother, who was already frowning at the letter.

"Why am I being asked to parent-teacher conferences, Ani?"

"I've been under a lot of stress, Mom. Maybe they want to talk to you about that. Mrs. Weller's been concerned about me, referred me to the psychologist and everything."

"Well," she said, "I guess I need to keep Thursday night free."

* * *

When Fey got on the bus, Ani scowled at her.

"What?" Fey smirked. "Tell me you didn't deserve that."

"I..." Ani sighed. "I'm sorry I blew you off, Fey. But—"

"But nothing." Fey shook her head. "I'm not your part-time friend, there only when it's convenient for you. We're either friends or we're not."

Ani held up her hands. "Yeah, okay, I get it. I didn't realize I was being such an asshole." *Sometimes I forget and expect you to make sense.*

"Apology accepted, asshole." Fey sat, shoved Ani toward the window with her hip, and held out an ear bud. "Happens to all of us."

They chatted about Jake over Death Cab for Cutie—he was still interested, Fey wasn't—and Ani gave her some lame advice founded on nothing even vaguely approaching experience with that sort of situation. The one time something like it had happened to her, she'd died and gone emo. That had taken care of Keegan's interest without further effort on her part.

They cut eighth period to smoke cigarettes behind the gas station across the street and talk about nothing. A certain amount of calculated trouble was expected of her, and Fey was always a willing participant.

Fey was complaining about the lack of good jobs in Ohneka Falls when she took a silver box out of her purse. Ani stared in amazement as she popped it open, scooped out a hunk of white powder with her pinky fingernail, and snorted it. She snapped it closed, sighed, and shook herself out. "Wow."

Ani's mouth opened, closed. She tried again. "Fey, what the hell was that?"

Fey quirked a smile. "Fuzz. You want some?"

"What the hell is fuzz?" *Because it looked like freaking cocaine.*

"It makes you fuzzy. Warm. Happy. Want some?" She hesitated with the case halfway into her purse.

Ani shook her head. "No, Fey. I—You shouldn't have any either." *Holy crap.*

Fey rolled her eyes. "Don't start. I get enough of that shit at home. If you're going to go all prude, I'll go back to study hall." *Stealing alcohol and cigarettes for my friends, and I'm prude?*

"I was just saying that—" Fey put her index finger to Ani's lips.

"Yeah, I know. I got this. It's fine."

Ani grabbed her wrist and lowered it. *What does, "I got this" even mean?* "Yeah, um, I'm going to have to ask you to not do that in front of me."

Fey rolled her eyes again. "Whatever. Give it a month you'll be doing it with me. Just watch."

At a loss for words, Ani lit another cigarette. Fey gave her a lazy smile.

"Got another?"

Ani sighed. "Sure, Fey."

Shit.

* * *

It was the second Tuesday of the month, so that evening Ani found herself at the elementary skating party, selling candy. The moment she walked in, she felt the familiar, disconcerting feeling simmer in her gut. As the evening passed, she tried to enjoy the music and the atmosphere, but more and more her eyes were drawn to the delicate shapes moving under the flashing lights, and her gorge rose in her throat. She forced down the feeling and fumbled through her coat for her razor. It took the edge off, but didn't kill it.

The DJ put on Abysmal Dawn, but nobody wanted to skate to death metal, so she got mobbed. Ravenous children looking for a sugar buzz surrounded her, a press of delicious flesh with an undertone of young, delicious brains. She dragged the razor lengthwise down her wrist once, twice, and it didn't help. She put her hand to her mouth and wiped away a string of drool—and that was too much.

She pushed out of her chair and it clattered to the floor as she stumbled away. She looked at her mom, tan and lean and full of hot blood, gasped out "Mom" in desperation, and stumbled into the bathroom. Once past the door she dropped to her knees and dug her fingernails into her thighs, her eyes squeezed tight in concentration. Behind her eyelids the world got darker, and darker.

An arm went around her neck, putting her in a choke-hold. Her eyes snapped open and she saw her mother in the mirror, one arm around her neck, the other raised above her head with an auto-injector. The hand came down onto her wig. She wanted to bite it, chew it, taste it, but she kept herself still. It was the hardest thing she had ever done.

There was a hiss as the CO_2 cartridge injected serum into her brain. Warmth flooded her head, dissolving the hunger as her mother pulled her up against the door and produced a revolver from her purse. Ani stared at it through the mirror as her mom cocked the hammer and shoved her across the room.

"Sweetie?" she asked, half-raising the pistol.

Brains! It was a pathetic thing now, weak and starving. Ani nodded, a near-imperceptible jiggle of her head. "Better every second, Mom."

They waited like that, her mom against the door so that no one could barge in, one finger on the trigger. One minute, then two. The last vestiges of the hunger faded into a familiar low burn—it would be gone in hours.

Finally, she flexed her hands and shook it off. "All good." Ani looked at her mom and smiled. "Thanks, Mom." *That was close.*

Her mom un-cocked the revolver and put it back in her purse. "Go home. I'll see you when we're done here."

"Good idea," Ani said, though it was clear it wasn't a suggestion. She walked home, sick to her stomach—but this time it was only emotion. *She has to protect herself. Has to protect those kids. From me.*

* * *

By the time her mom got home, Ani felt a thousand times better. The cravings had all but disappeared. Still, her mom was worried, and a worried Mom always led to more restrictions.

Ani opened the door and started right in. "Mom, it was the crowd. I felt fine all day. I had no problems, no issues. Everything was fine when I got there, too."

"But everything was not fine when the kids rushed the table." Her mom stepped past her and hung her keys next to the door.

"No. That was a big problem." Ani closed the door and locked it.

Her mom walked into the kitchen, poured herself a cup of coffee, took a sip, and added a splash of milk. She took another sip, nodded, then set the cup on the counter. "I'm sorry, honey, but I don't think you're going to be able to go to any more skating parties." Ani didn't even bother trying to object. "I can forge you a prescription for an epi-pen, and you can carry an auto-injector in your purse, just in case. People will look at you funny if you inject yourself in the skull, but it beats the alternative." She took another sip, her eyes on Ani over the mug. "So what are we going to do about school?"

"What do you mean?"

"There will be situations where you're forced into contact with large numbers of people at once. Assemblies, fire drills..." *Locker rooms, band pits, group projects. I'm screwed.*

"Claustrophobia," Ani said. "There's another girl who graduated a few years ago. She was diagnosed with claustrophobia and got to skip out on all that stuff. The school was really good about it."

"Okay," her mom said. "Claustrophobia it is. Just don't get caught in any confined spaces."

CHAPTER 22

Thursday night her mom left her at home to go to parent-teacher conferences. Mrs. Weller and Mr. Gursslin both wanted to talk to her about Ani's grades, while Mr. Bariteau wanted to talk to her about a summer symphony program up in Rochester. *Not very likely the way things are going, Mr. B.* Trapped at home with impending doom hanging over her head, Ani waited without an iota of grace or patience.

She tried to paint, but her muse had abandoned her. She tried to read a book, but was too distracted. Her fingers were clumsy on the piano keys. *Mom's going to get home and say I'm never going to school again. Between the skating party and my grades, it's too big of a risk for not enough reward... but I have to interact with other people, so she can't do that. Can she?*

When her mom walked in the door, Ani gave her a fresh cup of coffee, one cream. Her mom hung up her coat, took the coffee, and set it on the table without tasting it. She produced several crumpled papers from her pocket and smoothed them out on the table. Only then did she look at Ani.

"Two D's, two C's, and two A's. Completely unacceptable."

"I know, Mom. I've had a lot on my mind."

Her mom clucked her tongue. "Most of what you have on your mind, you only learned in the past week. You have missing assignments in English and poor test grades in Trigonometry this entire quarter. You only did half of your daily math homework. There's no point in ensuring you have a future if you're not going to do your part to ensure it's worthwhile." *Ouch.*

"There's still five weeks left, Mom. I'll pull my grades up. I promise." *I will, I will, I will!*

"You associate with Tiffany and Jacob because they provide you necessary cover and social stimulation. You aren't supposed to become one of them."

Part of Ani was offended on their behalf. *I like Fey. And Jake. Sort of.* "I know, Mom. They don't really have anything to do with this. It's all me. I accept full responsibility." As soon as she'd said it, she knew it'd never fly.

"Well, in that case, I will have to see a significant improvement by the end of ten-week period—that's less than a month away—or I will pull you out of school and deal with your education myself. With everything that's been going on, I've been considering it anyway, but I know you don't want it."

"Just tell me what I have to do." *Please, please make it something I can.*

"I want to see your lowest grade as a B in four weeks, or you will not be returning to Ohneka Upper School for your senior year."

Ani stifled a sigh of relief. *B's. I can do B's.* "Okay, Mom."

*   *   *

Ani went to school and begged for mercy.

Mr. G. was awesome. He told her that if she made up all of her back work he would give her half credit for it, and allow her to do corrections on her exams. He'd always been a pushover for anyone willing to try, even if they hadn't yet lived up to their end of the bargain.

Mrs. Weller was another story.

She stayed after school and waited outside the door for the other kids to leave. When they were gone she stepped into the doorway and tapped her knuckle against the metal frame. She caught herself chewing her bottom lip and forced her mouth closed. Mrs. Weller looked up from her desk and smiled. *A smile! Good start!*

"What's up?" Mrs. Weller asked. *The ceiling, ha ha.* Ani squelched her nerves and forced her voice to neutrality.

"My mom told me about your conversation last night. She's not very happy with me at the moment."

Mrs. Weller stood from her desk, her brow furrowed. "Neither am I. You shouldn't be, either. I'm worried about you."

Ani looked down, realized there was no way to pull attention away from herself and still have the conversation, so she looked back up. "I know. I know I screwed up, and it's all my fault, and I can do better. I will do better. I was just wondering what I can do to pull my grade up."

Mrs. Weller sucked air through her teeth. "Boy, Ani, the marking period is six weeks through." She opened her grade book and scanned Ani's entries. "You turned in a lousy research paper, and didn't even bother to hand in two critical-lens essays. That doesn't even count all the regular homework you've missed."

Ani cringed. "Is there any way I can make any of that up?"

Mrs. Weller shook her head. "No. I don't accept late work, and I don't accept incomplete work." *Damn. Humility didn't work. Time to beg.*

"My mom's going to home school me if I don't pull up my grades. Seriously. Can you make an exception? Please?"

"You want me to compromise my academic standards to help you fix your screw-up? What kind of lesson would that be teaching you?" *You won't be teaching me any lessons if I don't get a B!*

"I'm begging. Can I do something? Anything? Extra credit?"

"Extra credit is for people who have done all of their regular credit, which you have not. You have four weeks left. If you get A's on the assignments you have left you should be able to pull a C."

"Is there anything I can do to get a B?" *Please.*

Mrs. Weller fiddled at her computer for a minute. "According to my math, no. It's too little, too late." *Oh, no.*

"Thanks, Mrs. Weller," Ani said. *So this is what impending doom feels like.*

"Any time you need extra help, you come see me. I'll make sure you get that C." *Great. Just enough to be not enough.*

"Okay."

* * *

Ani was in her room, talking to Fey on her house phone, alert to any clicks that would indicate an eavesdropping mother.

"Mrs. Weller's a bitch," Fey said. "Her and life."

"No kidding," Ani said. "She was completely unreasonable. She wouldn't do anything for me, and now I'm screwed."

"Look on the bright side," Fey said. "Now you don't have to do nothing for any of your classes. You're screwed either way, why bother?" *Exactly the lesson Mrs. Weller's trying to teach me, I'm sure.*

"I have to do something. I can't get pulled out of school." *You don't understand. I spend eight hours a day staring at the inside of a fridge, and most of the rest of it at home doing the same thing over and over again. School is my only break.* "I'll go crazy."

"Too late," Fey said.

"You're hilarious," Ani said. "Look, I've got to finish this book by Monday. I'll catch you later."

"Sure." Fey hung up.

* * *

Ani planned to spend the weekend reading and studying while her mom worked in the basement. Schoolwork was the perfect excuse to avoid going down there, and it helped that her mom didn't talk to her about Dylan's "progress." She tried not to think about it, but it made studying difficult.

Saturday afternoon the phone rang. The caller ID said "Daniels." Ani turned her book over on the table and snatched up the phone before her mom could get it in the basement.

"Hello?" *You know I'm trying to study, Fey.*

"There's a band playing down at Dusty's tonight. I kind of dated the bouncer for a while and he'll let us in no charge." *I don't want to know what 'kind of dated' means.*

"Yeah, I can't do it. I've got too much to do."

"Shut up. You can't study all the time."

Let's see... A large crowd in a small space, darkness and flashing lights, drunks riding each other on the dance floor, blood in the mosh pit. And I'm sure the music sucks. "There's no way, Fey. I have two assignments to finish by Monday, and they're not going to do themselves."

"Yeah, whatever. We'll pick you up at ten." She hung up the phone before Ani could object.

She was still reading when ten o'clock rolled around. She heard a car idle outside her house, beep the horn twice, idle some more, and then peel out, running the stop sign at the end of the block.

* * *

Early Tuesday morning the phone rang. Ani looked at the clock before picking up. *Five fifteen.* She'd been out of the bath for an hour studying for an AP History quiz, and her mom wasn't up yet. The Caller ID read "OFCSD."

She picked up on the second ring. "Romero residence."

"Hello," said a recorded man's voice. "This is Superintendent Jim MacIlwaine. Due to the overnight snowfall, all Ohneka Falls schools are closed today—"

She hung up the phone and limped to the window. Tree limbs bowed under the weight, and the top of the mailbox was a small lump in a sea of white. *There must be three feet of snow out there!* She walked past the kitchen to the master bedroom and knocked.

"Snow day?" her mom asked through the door.

"Yep." *At least something goes my way now and then.*

"I looked outside when the snow rang. I'm going back to sleep for a few hours." *'Snow rang?' More sleep sounds like a good idea.* Ani missed sleep. It wasn't what she missed most about living, but it was something that all mankind had in common. Everyone but her.

She stopped studying for a quiz she wouldn't be taking, and with nothing better to do, started on another back Trig assignment. By dawn the snow had stopped, and the sun rose in a blue sky devoid of clouds. She checked the forecast online—low 50's and sunny. *You have to love mid-March.*

Her mom slept until ten-thirty, well later than any time in Ani's memory, and when she emerged she looked exhausted. She made a tuna sandwich and sat at the table, chewing mechanically.

"You look tired, Mom."

She nodded and kept chewing.

"Chemo?"

She took another bite.

"Do you want to go back to bed? I can get you in another hour."

She shook her head and set down the sandwich. "This research won't do itself. There's nothing for it. I'll be okay—some days are just harder than others."

She went into the basement having only eaten half of her sandwich. Ten minutes later she rushed into the bathroom and threw it up, but she didn't complain.

* * *

By noon the work crew had cleared the roads, and the town's giant snow blowers had cleared the sidewalks.

Feeling a little caged in, Ani bundled up against the cold, put on a wide-brimmed hat to block out the sun, and called down the basement stairs. "I'm going for a walk!" *Not quite asking for permission, but good enough.*

She heard nothing for a moment, then, "Okay, sweetie! Don't be gone too long!"

She opened the door and was blinded by the glare off the snow, so she ducked back inside and grabbed a pair of sunglasses. Fortified against the elements—the elements she cared about anyway—she set out. She turned right as she always did, passed Fey's house and took another right at the corner. *Once around the block should about do it.*

Mike jogged past her, twice, and while he replied when she said hello, he didn't stop to talk. Ever since Valentine's they were less than friendly—not mean, exactly—just... uncomfortably uncommunicative. *Which means he ignores and avoids me while I spend half my time trying not to think about how much I miss him.*

She was saved from her thoughts when Jake's car veered onto the curb in front of her. A boy she didn't recognize sat shotgun, Fey in the back.

"Snow day, bitches!" Jake hollered, pounding the steering wheel with the palm of his hand. *Classy.*

"What's up, guys?" Ani asked.

"Just cruising," Fey said. "Want to join us?"

Ani bobbed her head back and forth. "Um... I do, but I'm grounded. I told my mom I'd just be around the block and back home."

Fey rolled her eyes. "What she doesn't know—"

"She'll know, Fey. Mom knows everything."

Fey threw up her hands. "Whatever."

Jake hit the gas, and they were gone.

* * *

She got home, kicked the slush off her boots on the stoop, and left them by the door. "I'm home!" she yelled. There was no reply.

"Mom?" She looked out the window—the Audi sat in the driveway, covered in half-melted slush. The house was silent.

She shambled over to the couch, reached over the back and behind it. Her hands touched metal brackets, but no gun. She froze, listening. She didn't hear any movement, upstairs or down.

She shuffled to the piano, floorboards creaking under her step-drag limp. She grabbed a brass candlestick, pulled out the candle and set it on the windowsill. She hefted the candlestick. With her unnatural strength, she could brain someone with it, no problem.

She moved to the bookcase and pushed it back. The basement door was ajar. She stopped breathing to be as quiet as possible, pushed open the door with her left hand, and listened. *Nothing.*

Her first step was quiet. Despite her efforts her second step was a lurching half-fall onto the second step down. *Damn hip.* She gave up on stealth and hurried down the stairs.

The door to the 'just in case' room was ajar, and there was no sign of her mom. She ran to the lab table, yanked the phone off the cradle, and dialed her mother's cell. A mechanical woman's voice from inside the furnace said, "call from home... call from home...."

She hit 'end,' dropped the phone, and hefted the candlestick two-handed. "Mom?" No reply. She crept closer, wedged the door with her foot, and looked inside.

Her mother lay on her back in a puddle of expanding blood. The chair sat empty. Ani tore open the door and fell to her hands and knees at her mom's side. She put her hand to her neck. *Strong pulse.* She tore her eyes from the pool of blood and ran her hands over her mom's scalp, trying to find the source of the blood.

Her mom had a cut on the side of her head, and her hair was matted with blood. Ani pulled a jagged piece of glass from her scalp, and blood gushed from the wound. She rushed into the lab, grabbed a bandage and styptic powder, sprinted back, dumped the powder onto the cut and wrapped her mom's head. The bleeding stopped, and Ani sighed in relief.

The furnace door slammed closed behind her. The bar dropped down.

She lurched to her feet and looked out the window. Dylan's face was inches from hers, separated only by a pane of bullet-proof glass. His eyes were bloodshot, crazy, but he looked alive, or nearly so. *As alive as me.*

"We've been here before, Ani," he said, his voice calm. "You in this room, me out here with the button."

She swallowed. "I tried to help you—"

"I know. I heard you argue for me when I was first brought here. It's the only reason you're still alive." His eyes moved to her mother. "That woman is a monster. Evil. She deserves to die." *I can't argue with that, but I can't agree either. She's my mom.*

"What about me, Dylan? Are you going to kill me, too?"

He frowned. "I didn't know it would be so cold."

Her mother shrieked, and she whirled around. A keening wail erupted from her mom's throat as she scrambled backward to the wall, her back slamming into a propane intake pipe. As Ani reached her she grabbed her purse and yanked out the revolver.

Ani stepped in front of the door. "Mom, don't!"

Still screaming, her mom put the pistol under her own chin.

Ani dove forward and slapped. Something crunched.

The gunshot was deafening in the tiny room. The pistol clattered across the floor to the other side of the recliner. Her mom still screamed, clutching her hand to her chest. Ani grabbed her wrists and yanked them apart, surprised at how effortless it was.

"*NO!*" her mom screamed. "*I WON'T BECOME ONE OF THEM! I WON'T!*"

Ani shook her. "Mom! You're okay! You just cut your head!" She was hyperventilating, and the high-pitched wail returned. Ani held her, waiting. "It's okay," she said, calming her voice. "Mom. You're going to be fine. It's okay." *If Dylan doesn't incinerate us both.*

After a minute the panic in her eyes faded. "He didn't bite me?" The naked hope in her voice hurt.

Ani shook her head. "No, Mom, he didn't bite you. You cut your head on some glass."

Sobbing, she grabbed Ani around the neck and squeezed. After a minute she pulled away. "Where's Dylan?"

Ani turned around, then looked out the window. "Gone. Dylan's gone."

They found two of Dylan's fingers on the other side of the recliner—he'd bitten them off to escape. Ani's slap had saved her mom's life but broken one of her fingers. They made a crude splint and then assessed their options for getting out.

The room was designed to hold back a mindless zombie, not a thinking human. They used surgical scissors to pry the pins out of the hinges, removed the door, and were free.

The house was quiet. A cautious look around found nothing. The cops didn't come. The world didn't end. No phone calls, no black helicopters, no incineration squads. They never found the shotgun.

* * *

Two days later Ani sat in Mr. Gursslin's room after school. *This is insane.* She finished her makeup test and set down her pencil. Part of her brain screamed in panic as she went through the motions of high school life. Dylan was out there somewhere. He was dead, like her, and contagious. She stood. He had no one to turn to, nowhere to run. No one to give him serum when the craving overcame him. He was doomed, and damned, and would bring fire and death. That her mom was "handling it" was no comfort.

"Ani?" Mr. Gursslin asked. "Are you just going to stand there, or are you going to hand that in?"

"Sorry," she said. She handed him the test. "I think I did okay." *We're all going to die.*

"Good," he said. "Just one more to go and you should be all set."

"That's great, Mr. G. How's next Tuesday?" *Dylan's going to bite somebody, and they'll quarantine the town and burn everything and everyone.*

"Next Tuesday is fine."

"Okay." *Nothing is okay. We're going to burn and it's all my fault.*

"Are you alright?" he asked.

"Sure," she said. *My mom tried to kill herself so I broke her finger.* "Bye Mr. G." *So she wouldn't be like me.* She walked out of the room. *She'd rather die than be like me.*

She remembered something about Fey trying to talk to her about something as she passed her locker. She couldn't figure out how she got home. She helped make her mom some dinner, did her homework, and got in the bath.

She'd rather die than be like me. It didn't matter. She closed her eyes, sank into the cold, chemical syrup and thought of fire.

CHAPTER
23

The weekend came and went without a ZV outbreak, without kidnapping or murder charges, without any talk of Dylan at all. Minus the omnipresent feeling of impending doom, it was almost boring. It was as if the world-changing events of the previous Tuesday had never happened, as if Dylan had never been killed in their basement, never reanimated, never escaped. Aside from her mother's broken finger, life was... *normal*.

* * *

Late Thursday afternoon, Ani was halfway through a book report on *The Jungle* when her mom came in the door and plopped down the groceries.

"How was your appointment, Mom?"

She pursed her lips. "Not bad, all said. Nothing new, and what's there is a bit better. The chemo and radiation seem to be doing the trick."

Ani grinned. "That's great!" She started sorting the groceries into fridge and not-fridge. *Since when does mom eat Nutella?* "Isn't it?"

"Yeah, sweetie, it is. Better than we'd hoped, anyway. They're going to knock it into remission and then do a more aggressive treatment—it's called consolidation—to keep it from coming back." She grabbed the milk, eggs, and butter and put them in the fridge. "Hopefully."

"So that's, like, a cure?"

Her mom shrugged. "A month ago I would have given me eight-to-one odds. Now I'd say it's more like three-to-one."

Ani hugged her around a box of Mac 'n' Cheese. "Better is better, right?"

"Better is better."

* * *

Monday the twenty-eighth was a "Superintendent's Conference Day," which meant another day off for students, but staff had to work. Her mom stood at the door, taking an inventory of her possessions before leaving for the day. Ani sat on the piano bench facing the living room, an easel in front of her. The thought of Dylan sneaking up behind her made playing the piano unacceptable. The way was cleared for her to bolt into the basement should the need arise.

Her mom's eyes lit on the bookshelf, then locked on Ani. "One more time."

Ani returned the stare and repeated the instructions. "If Dylan shows up, get to the basement. The new shotgun is at the bottom of the stairs, loaded and chambered. Hold him there or shoot him if he runs. Under no circumstances shoot in the house proper or outside. Call that number you gave me. No cops, no neighbors." Ani also had the pepper spray in her pocket—they'd tested it out on her and it hurt like hell, so it should work on Dylan.

The morning passed without incident, and by noon her canvas was an abstract nightmare of red, black, and gray, more a feeling than a picture. The mailman walked by, so Ani went to the window and looked outside, careful not to touch the curtains with her paint-smeared hands and forearms. Mr. Washington was taking advantage of the thaw to clean sticks out of his yard, the mailman was still on the block, and down the street a Frontier Communications crew fiddled with something on a telephone pole. *Plenty of witnesses.*

She didn't bother to put on a jacket as she got the mail,

waving to Mr. Washington on her way back inside. He waved, and she tried not to think of poor Mac, dead in the street. She closed the door, latched the dead bolts, and looked at the pile—three bills, four pieces of junk mail, and a padded envelope.

The manila envelope was sealed but had no postage and no writing. She frowned, turning it over in her hands. *Nothing on the back, either.* From inside the envelope a phone rang.

She sat on the piano bench and tore the envelope open. Inside was a cheap Nokia pre-paid. It rang again. The caller ID gave a phone number but no other information. She pressed 'Send' and put the phone to her ear.

"Hello?"

Silence. Then, "I need your help." Dylan's voice was husky, coarse.

Ani looked out the window. If he was hiding in view, she couldn't see him. *But he knew the moment I got the mail.* She picked up the house phone and dialed her mom, holding the receiver to her head so they could both hear Ani's side of the conversation.

"I don't see any reason why I should ever help you, Dylan. You tried to kill me."

"This isn't about you," he said. "I need an injection, or... or..." His voice faded into a pathetic whimper. "I'm so hungry." Her mom picked up as she replied.

"Dylan, you need to come back to the lab—"

"I can't do that. I won't be chained to a chair again. I'd rather die than be under the control of that woman." Ani tried to listen for anything on his end of the phone that would betray his location. She heard only silence. "I need the serum. Soon."

"I have extra serum," Ani said. Dylan was crazy, but he didn't deserve this. No one deserved this. "I can give it to you."

"Stall him," her mom whispered. Then she hung up. *So you can kidnap him again? Chain him to the chair? Kill him again? Burn him?*

"I'm not going in there," Dylan said. "Put it in the mailbox and I'll get it."

"Okay," Ani said. "I'm sorry for what happened to you, and I'll help you, but you have to stay the hell away from me. If you come into my house again, I'll kill you for real." She peeked outside—Mr. Washington was still there, and so was the Frontier crew—then walked to the mailbox. She pulled the auto-injector from her purse, put it in the box, and hurried back toward the house.

"Thank you," Dylan said. She shivered in revulsion at the thought of him creeping on her. The phone clicked.

"Hello?" she said. The dial tone rang in her ear.

She was halfway up the sidewalk when Mr. Washington called to her in his deep baritone. "Hey, Ani!" *No, no, not now.*

She lurched to a stop and turned to face him. "Yeah?"

"You forgot to put the flag up."

She looked back at the mailbox, rolled her eyes for effect, and shambled toward the road. A pickup truck drove past, and she eyed the bed. *Are you in there, Dylan?* She walked back up the sidewalk, thanked Mr. Washington, and went inside.

She felt safer behind the locked door, and safer still near the shotgun. Ani wondered if her mom would get home before Dylan got to the mailbox. She waited on tenterhooks for something, anything to happen.

A man in dark blue sweat pants and a brown RIT hoodie jogged up to the mailbox and put his hand on it, as if resting. Ani could only see his mouth, but she was sure it was him. As Dylan opened the mailbox and grabbed the injector, Mr. Washington cried out. "Hey, you! Stop!" Dylan took off, Mr. Washington in pursuit.

Ani bolted out the door. "Mr. Washington! It's okay!" In his early eighties, he didn't have a chance in a footrace anyway.

Confused, he turned around. "That man stole your package!"

She threw up her hands. "I saw from the window. Don't worry about it. It's not worth getting hurt over. I'll just send another one."

He started back toward her. Dylan ducked behind the Miller's house and disappeared from view. Mr. Washington scowled at her. "You playing straight with me, girl?"

"Yes," Ani said. "It's no big deal."

His scowl deepened as her mother's Audi screeched around the corner. She slowed as she approached the house and angled into the driveway. She killed the engine and made a show of taking her time getting out.

Mr. Washington frowned at her the entire way. "Sarah," he said as she shut the door. "A man just took something from your mailbox. Something left there by your daughter just a minute ago."

"Thank you," her mom said, grabbing Ani by the arm. "We'll discuss this inside." She marched her up the walk and into the house, then slammed the door. With a glance to the window she said, "I'll think of something." She turned her attention to Ani. "You gave him your auto-injector."

"Yeah," she said. "I figure he'll be back for another one and you can try again. I couldn't stall him any longer."

"That's okay," her mom said. "We'll get him next time." Her eyes scanned the neighborhood from behind the blinds. "We have to."

"I know, Mom." Ani looked at the Audi. "What did you tell work?"

"Nothing. I answered my phone and then left."

"Are you going to get in trouble?"

She thought about it. "Mr. Washington witnessing makes an excuse more difficult. Not medical, not psychological... I'll come up with something." She looked at Ani. "Now, tell me what happened."

* * *

The weekend passed without further incident. Ani had almost gotten used to the vague feeling skittering in the back of her head—the feeling that at any moment the entire town would become a charnel house of blood and fire. Sunday night she reminded her mom to write out a check for SAT registration.

* * *

Ani sat next to Fey in the cafeteria. She set her SAT registration form on the table and scanned the directions. "Did you remember your check?" she asked.

Without looking at her, Fey used the dull half-pencil they'd each been given to fill in the bubbles. Ani tried again. "Do anything fun over the weekend?" Fey picked up her form and slid down to the end of the table. *Oh, great. What now?*

By the time Ani had finished her form, Fey was gone. She went to her locker, gathered up her books, and headed to the bus. The late run was less crowded than the two-thirty, and the bus was half empty. Fey sat in the second seat back, well forward of their normal spot. Ani walked up to her, but she didn't move to let her past, so Ani sat in the seat across the aisle.

Fey stared straight forward, her music so loud Ani could hear the lyrics. Ani tapped her on the shoulder. Fey tore the headphones off her head and glared at Ani. "What?"

Ani cringed back. "What did I do?"

"Nothing," Fey said. When she moved to put the headphones back in, Ani grabbed her wrist.

"No, seriously?" The bus jolted forward and rolled out of the bus loop.

"Yeah, seriously. You've barely said shit to me in two weeks. It's like I'm a fucking ghost."

"Tiffany, language!" the bus driver snapped.

She changed her tone without letting up her glare. "Sorry, Mrs. Sidlauskas." Ani thought about it. *Yeah, maybe this one's on me.*

"Sorry, Fey. I didn't realize—"

"No, of course you didn't. Again. You've been a fu—" Her glare flashed to the rear-view mirror. "A freaking zombie lately."

Ani bit her lip. "I know. I've had a lot going on." *You don't have the slightest idea.*

"Not for nothing, but the world don't disappear when your life gets all emotional. You can talk to me." *No, I can't.* "Tell me anything."

Ani's mind raced for a reasonable topic. She lowered her

voice. "My mom has cancer."

Fey's mouth opened. "You're shitting me." Mrs. Sidlauskas glared at them through the mirror. Fey stood up. "Yeah, give me a fucking detention, see if I care."

The bus lurched to a stop. They didn't get the chance to finish the conversation.

* * *

Ani played the piano until ten o'clock, waiting for Fey's inevitable call. Her mom had gone to bed early—she'd been doing that a lot—so she kept the phone next to her. She took it with her as she stripped for the bath, then gave up. She looked down at the icy, chemical goop and a thought occurred to her.

She shuffled to the computer and opened up a web browser. In the search field she typed "formalin carcinogen." The first link was the Wikipedia page for Formaldehyde. She clicked it, scrolled down to "safety," and read. A phrase jumped out at her.

* * *

Formaldehyde is a known human carcinogen associated with nasal sinus cancer, nasopharyngeal cancer, and acute myeloid leukemia.

* * *

Her mother's words came back to her as she closed the browser and shut down the computer. *I gave up everything to be your mother. Everything.* She couldn't cry, so she did what her mom would want her to do. She got in the bath.

* * *

That Friday they got their third marking-period grades. She

had an A in band and art, of course, and everything else was a B...
Except for English. The C crawled up from the page and infected
her brain, where it pulsed and throbbed in time with her clockwork
heart. *HOME-school. HOME-school. HOME-school.*

Ani didn't bother begging Mrs. Weller for clemency—that
road was a dead end with road-kill on it. *No point in waiting.* As
soon as the eighth-period bell rang, she skipped her locker and
went straight to the nurse's office.

Her mom sat at her desk, scribbling on a form, her brow
furrowed in concentration. She glanced up and then back down.
Ani waited until she finished, then stepped farther into the room.
Her mom set down the pen and met her eyes. "Well?" She held out
her hand. *I'm screwed.*

"I'm screwed," Ani said. She handed her the report and tried
not to gnaw on her bottom lip. "English is a 'C.'"

Her mom's lips formed a tight line. "Almost an impressive
recovery."

"Thank you," Ani said. *Oh, God, please don't take that as
sarcastic.* "Mrs. Weller wouldn't budge."

Her mom exhaled. "Well, I can hardly punish you for not
doing the impossible." She looked up from the desk and steepled
her fingers, and Ani dared to hope. "Straight A's fourth quarter, no
exceptions except PE. Last chance."

Ani bounced on her feet. "Thank you, thank you, thank
you!" She shuffled out of the room with a giant smile.

"Cutter looks happy," Devon said from behind her.
"Mommy must have given her a new razor."

Ani rolled her eyes without turning around.

"Miss Holcomb," her mother's voice rang down the hall. "In
my office, please."

Ani hazarded a glance back. Leah's eyes were wide, while
Devon glared at Ani. *Yeah, that was totally my fault, you psycho.* She
headed for the bus.

She sat down next to Fey in their usual seat, well out of
earshot of Mrs. Sidlauskas. Fey handed her the headphones—today
it was *God or Julie*—and the bus started to roll. Ani let the

depressing music carry her thoughts aloft. *Mom's looking better. I'm not getting homeschooled. Fey's given up on hating me for now.*

Her eyes lit on Fey's hair, the black now streaked with white and pink. They followed a pink strand from the part to her delicate ear, then downward to her neck. Fey's neck was creamy white, like porcelain. A vein pulsed in the side of her throat, the hot blood just beneath the surface—

"Hey," Fey's voice snapped her out of her reverie. "If you try to kiss me I'm elbowing you in the face."

Ani recoiled and put her hand to her mouth. She drew it across her drool-soaked lips and laughed. "Wow, Fey, I was in my own little world there." She tried not to think about the blood, the flesh, the brains next to her. *That's Fey. Not meat. Fey.*

"Well, keep your own little world to yourself," Fey said, eyeing her askance.

Ani turned away from her, palmed the razor from her purse, and put her hands in her sleeves. As the blade split her skin she closed her eyes, anticipating release. It didn't come. She cut harder—nothing. Nothing but the rising queasy desire in her stomach.

She counted the houses until Fey got off the bus, and two houses later stumbled onto the sidewalk. *Brains.* She limped to the door and pulled her keys from her purse with shaking hands. *Blood. Fey. Brains.* She dropped them and swore as she scrambled to find them in the grass.

She felt cold metal against her fingers and closed her fist. *Got it!* She picked them up, tried to put the key in the lock, and missed. *Fey, blood, meat, brains–brains—brains.* She tried again, got it, then moved to the next as drool pattered on her shoes. It took her three tries. Her eyes wandered to the Washington's house. Mrs. Washington was a local civil-rights hero who'd marched with Dr. King. She was in her early seventies, an invalid. *Helpless, defenseless...*

She brought the razor down to her thigh and raked upward, slicing through her black jeans, splitting skin and muscle. She gasped in relief as the craving subsided. She leaned against the doorframe, savoring the pain and the peace that came with it. With a sigh, she inserted the key in the final lock, and went inside.

Out of sight of the neighborhood, she jammed the auto injector into the base of her skull, just in case. That done, she wrapped the ruined jeans in a plastic grocery bag and threw them away, grabbed pajama pants from her room in case her mom got home early, and went into the bathroom. She used the full-length mirror on the door to get a better look at the cut marring her thigh.

Maybe six inches long, at its deepest she could see the gray-brown of bone. The muscle had been severed clean, right down the middle. She winced as she touched the raw flesh underneath.

She stood, grabbed the first-aid kit from the cabinet, and popped it open. She squirted "Liquid Bandage" into the wound and squeezed it shut. The bottle was labeled "For topical use only. For deep cuts, consult a doctor." *For zombie flesh cuts, consult a witchdoctor.*

Once it had bonded, she limped her way to the basement to stitch up the outside. She grabbed the suture thread and a needle, threaded it, tied the loop, and stitched the wound closed. She stood and put weight on it, then bounced a little. It hurt, but the stitches held. *Perfect.*

She bent down, put one leg in her pajama bottoms, and froze. *Did I just see...* She looked up. The 'just in case' room door stood barred and padlocked. She shuffled forward, eyes wide. *No, please. Not this. Anything but this.* She peered inside.

A corpse writhed in the recliner. It was an old man, bald with tufts of white hair, blotchy and fat. It moaned through the gag, all but inaudible through the door. It wore a hospital gown and steel manacles like you'd see in movies with old dungeons. Its dead eyes were wide and murderous, as Dylan's had been.

Ani sat on the floor, stunned. She was still sitting, staring at the door, when her mother got home. She wasn't sure what time it was, but through the safety glass she could see that the sun had gone down. Ani heard her call out, then heard her come down the stairs.

"You promised," Ani said, still sitting, facing the door.

"I promised that I would do anything to protect you. Even if that means lying to you." Ani closed her eyes and saw her mother, pistol pressed up against her chin. *Not anything. Not what you did to this man. You'd die before you became what he is. What we are.*

She clambered to her feet and turned to face her mother. *Dylan's monster.* "We made a deal." Her mom's gaze drifted downward. Ani looked down, realized she had one pant leg around her ankle, the stitches exposed for her mother to see.

"What happened to your leg?"

"You're not changing the subject, Mom. We made a deal. Nobody else dies. You agreed."

Her mom scowled. "This man was terminal. He had hours to live. Less." Ani had felt a lot of things about her mom recently: confusion, love, shock, pain. Hate was new, powerful and consuming, as dangerous as hunger. *If this is what it's like to grow up....* Ani felt sick to her stomach as she made up her mind.

She slammed her hand back, heard a gentle whoosh of air, felt the heat even through the door. Black-orange shadows danced on her mother's face, her mouth creased in disapproval.

"Next time it will be me in there, Mom." Her mom opened her mouth and Ani held up a finger. "No deals, no promises, no lies. I won't let you do this again. I'll die first. Forever. Do you understand me?" Her mom nodded. She dropped her finger.

"That was rash," her mom said.

"We're not discussing it," Ani snapped.

Her mom nodded. "Alright, then, can we discuss your leg?"

Ani stepped in to the other pant leg, pulled up the pink Hello Kitty pj's, and tied the drawstring. "I need another dose. Or a stronger dose. Or something new."

"You just incinerated 'something new.'"

"Then get me something old."

* * *

The older serum didn't work quite as well, so Ani skipped school with the "flu" on Monday and Tuesday. Tuesday night was the monthly skating party, and while her mom sold candy, Ani stayed home, never too far from the shotgun. If she drew patterns in her thighs with a razor blade just from thinking about the crowd of kids, that was the price for her refusal to compromise.

* * *

The rest of the week was almost nice. Fey acted normal again, her mom seemed to feel a little better since they'd altered her chemo, and the school was abuzz with spring break plans. Jake was being dragged to the Bahamas where his mom would almost definitely force him to get a tan and lounge around by the pool, and he wouldn't shut up about what a drag it was. The rest of the world pretty much ignored her—that included Mike, but there were worse things. If her mom had any news about Dylan, she kept it to herself. Ani tried not to think about the ashy remains in her basement.

CHAPTER
24

Ani stopped pretending to search for a job. She didn't want to work in a tattoo parlor, and nobody else would even interview her once they got a look at her facial piercings. Travis was going to re-open the Dragon's Lair, though it wouldn't be until June, but Ani had enough money saved to get by until then. *You need a life to have bills.* Ani found herself spending most of her spring break in the basement with her mom.

Wednesday afternoon the phone rang. The caller ID said "The UPS Store," so Ani picked it up and hit 'Send.' "Hello?"

"Hello, may I speak to Ani Romero please?" said a pleasant female voice.

"This is she," Ani said.

"Hi, Ani, this is Greta Haberstro from the UPS Store. I understand that you stopped in for an interview but were turned away?"

"Yeah," Ani said. "I was. They didn't like my taste in jewelry."

"I'm so sorry that happened." Greta laid on the fake sympathy pretty thick. "Would you be willing to come in tomorrow at ten?" *Desperate, are we?*

"Just a second." She put her hand over the receiver and asked her mom.

"I have a doctor's appointment," her mom said. "You'll have to find a ride."

"I'll be there," Ani said. *If I have to walk.*

"Wonderful," Greta said. "I'll see you tomorrow at ten."

Ani pressed 'End,' set the phone on the table and looked at her mom. "Oncologist?"

"At ten-fifteen. He's doing a round of tests after this latest bout of chemo. It's a little early yet, but insurance is covering it and he thought it'd be a good idea."

"Okay," Ani said. "I'll ask Fey."

* * *

Jake picked her up in his mom's tiny four-banger Hyundai Excel the next morning at nine forty-five. She got into the car, cradling the faux-leather portfolio that held her sparse resume. "You're late." He hit the gas before she'd shut the door, and she had to scramble to get her seatbelt on. "Shouldn't you be wearing your seatbelt?"

"What are you, my mom?" Jake asked. He made a rolling stop at the sign and turned right. *It's exactly this level of conversation that makes you such a hit with the ladies, Jake.* Even so, he grabbed the belt and fastened it a split-second before the oncoming truck swerved.

Straight for them.

The sound was so fast her brain had a hard time processing it, a violent crunch that consumed her every thought. Ani had never heard anything so loud, but it was nothing like in the movies. Her head rebounded off the dashboard and the world hazed red.

Mouth open, she turned to Jake as life shifted to slow motion. He held his face with both hands, bright red blood gushing around his fingers. Hunger consumed her. She reached for the bloody flesh, grabbed its arm, tried to pull it closer. Her hands slipped on the blood, and she cried out in anguish as the meal was denied. She licked the blood from her hands as something pulled her out of the car.

She twisted free and turned, furious. Dylan's fist caught her in the temple, and pain exploded as she heard bone crack. *Mine or his?* It shocked her back to herself even as she fell. She flopped to the ground as he grabbed her purse and tore it in half. The contents rained down on her: keys, Tic Tacs, cigarettes, makeup, tampons. Dylan caught her auto injector before it hit the ground and jammed it into his temple.

She tried to stand and he stomped her to the ground. She gasped as her ribs cracked. He stomped again and again. With each blow, the hunger faded in the blissful release of agony. Her vision clouded.

He fell on top of her, straddling her, and beat her. His fists rained down on her shoulders, chest, and ribs, each blow a stinging rebuke. *I'm dead because of you. You let your mother do this. This is your fault. Yours and yours alone.*

As the world went black, a righteous angel appeared. Shirtless and covered in rippling muscle, the seraphim's green eyes burned with the fury of God unleashed on an immoral world. *So beautiful.* After such an incredible sight, Ani knew she could die happy. Something didn't fit. *Why does the Angel of Death have a shovel?*

Mike swung, taught muscles straining, and the flat of the metal blade caught Dylan in the side of the head. Knocked sideways, Dylan scrambled to his feet, snarling. Mike filled her vision as he stepped over her and swung again. She heard metal contact flesh-covered bone, and then he looked down at her. She fell into his eyes, and was lost.

She sobbed as his eyes left her, unable to think except to gasp for more. She felt strong arms lift her like a baby, carry her to safety. A cloud enveloped her, and she slept.

* * *

Ani opened her eyes. It was such a strange feeling, to have been unconscious, unmoving, helpless, that she snapped to a sitting position. "Jake!" she cried.

"He's okay," her mom said. "He didn't even break anything." A blinding light hit her eyes. *Penlight.* Her mom moved it to the other eye, then switched it off.

"Where's Mike?" Ani asked.

"I'm here," he said. As her eyes adjusted to the brightly lit, stark-white room she saw his face. *My angel...* Her mother's voice murdered her daydream.

"Because of your condition I had you transferred to the care of Doctor Banerjee. He's an old friend of mine who specializes in these kinds of things." Her mother's eyes were a warning.

Ani closed her eyes and leaned back into the pillow. "Are you sure Jake's okay?"

Mike responded. "He'll be fine. A little banged up, and his car is totaled, but he's supposed to be released in a few hours."

"My daughter needs to rest," her mother said. "You should go."

"No, wait!" Ani said, opening her eyes. She looked at her mom. "I want him here." She grabbed Mike's hand. "I want you here. Please stay."

He leaned over her and gave her a hug, wrapping her in his arms, strong but gentle. "Of course."

She ignored her mom's glare. She closed her eyes and her consciousness drifted, neither awake nor asleep, his hand warming hers.

* * *

The State Police intensified the manhunt for Dylan, not only for the previous charges and his "escape" from the mental institution, but this time for attempted vehicular homicide. Dogs, helicopters, and volunteers scoured Ohneka Falls and the surrounding area. The police dogs refused to follow his scent, but a man from Corning reportedly had given him a ride as far as Binghamton in the back of his truck, and the trail from there was cold.

Sunday morning—Easter—Ani and her mom went to church. With heavy makeup on her face and most of the damage contained to her torso, she looked almost uninjured. The pastor greeted them as strangers, which was no surprise. The two to three times a year that they went weren't enough for Ani to remember his name, either. She fidgeted through the ceremony and bounced her way to the car.

The day held an air of excitement. They were going to the city for dinner so that Ani could meet her mom's mystery boyfriend and his son. Ani was thrilled, even though it would mean a mechanical flushing when she got home.

"What if I don't like him?" Ani had asked her mom.

"You will," she'd replied, but she looked nervous.

Jake was out of the hospital. Ani's mom gave her a ride to his house so she could personally deliver a card. *No flowers. The last thing I need is that kind of misunderstanding.* There were half a dozen cars in front of his house, and he answered the door himself, nose bruised and swollen.

"Ani! Hey! How are you feeling?" He gave her a gentle hug. Startled, she returned it, her head brushing against the bandage on his scalp.

"Good, Jake. How are you?" She pulled away. His eyes were bright and alert, and all things considered, he looked pretty good.

"I'm okay. I'm glad you're all right. Come on in." He stood aside so she could go past him.

"I can't stay. I'm leaving for Rochester in a little while. I'm sorry I didn't see you more in the hospital—"

"It's okay. You had your own recovering to do. I'm sorry I didn't see the truck. I should have seen, well..."

"There's nothing you could have done," Ani said. She held out the card. "This is for you."

"Thanks," he said, and shoved it unopened into his pocket.

"Look, I need to get going. It's good to see you."

"You, too," he said. "I'm glad you're okay." He hugged her again. This time he held it and squeezed.

"Careful," she said, and he let up the pressure without letting go. She patted his back, pried herself loose, and turned back down the sidewalk toward her mom's idling car. "Happy Easter, Jake."

"You, too, Ani."

* * *

The Crystal Barn was more "crystal" than "barn," with high ceilings and chandeliers of gold and crystal. *Whoops.* She felt underdressed in her black turtleneck and slacks. Her mom looked somehow radiant and exhausted in a black dress a little too low on top and high on the bottom, her diamond earrings sparkling in the diffused light. *At least we match.*

They approached the tuxedoed maître d' and her mother said, "Brown, party of four." *There's no freaking way your boyfriend's name is Mike Brown.* And either it was Ani's imagination, or her mother was looking anywhere but at her.

"The rest of your party has not arrived," the host said. "Would you like to be seated, or would you care to wait?"

"We'll sit," her mother said. The host led them to their table—they pulled their own chairs out, thank you—and left them alone. It wasn't her imagination. Her mom looked at the chandelier, the wallpaper, the ceiling... everywhere but at Ani.

"Your boyfriend's name is Mike Brown," Ani said. *This is so not funny.* "Mike. Brown."

"I'd have told you earlier, sweetie, but I wasn't sure how you'd take it." The server interrupted, dropped off four menus, and left without taking their drink orders.

"That's a heck of a coincidence," Ani said.

Her mom licked her lips. "It's not a coincidence." *This absolutely can't be happening.*

"You're dating Mike's *dad*?" Ani wanted to scream. "*My* Mike?"

"He's not your Mike." Her mom smiled over Ani's shoulder. "And here they are now."

Ani turned to look. Mr. Brown had put on weight since she'd last seen him, but otherwise looked like an older, graying version of his son. Mike belonged on the cover of *GQ*, ruggedly handsome in a blue three-piece suit. When he noticed them, his face darkened to a thundercloud. *Surprise.*

They approached the table and her mom stood for a quick kiss, then they all sat. Mr. Brown and her mom made small talk while Mike glared at Ani from across the table. Ani shrugged at him, but he didn't let up. When she tapped his leg with her foot, he shifted out of the way.

Mr. Brown ordered appetizers for all of them—escargot, bacon-wrapped lobster, and a duck quesadilla. Being a "vegan" meant she didn't have to touch any of it. She looked at the menu to avoid looking at Mike. It gave her another reason to scowl.

"There's nothing vegan on this menu," Ani blurted, interrupting their small talk. *Just because I'm a fake vegan doesn't mean I can't get offended on their behalf.*

"I thought of that when I picked this place," Mr. Brown said. "There's a vegetable grill pasta on the back page."

"It comes with feta cheese. And pasta has eggs in it anyway."

"Oh." He had the decency to look chagrined. "How about the

garden salad?"

She read the entry. It looked safe. *Damn.* "Okay, I guess I'll have that."

Their appetizers came. Mike ate in sullen near-silence as their parents pestered them about school. They both gave as close to monosyllabic answers as they were able. Her mom glared at her, and Mike's dad glared at him, and both tried too hard to have a good time.

When the server took their orders, ladies first, Ani asked for the salad.

"What kind of dressing would you like?"

"What are my options?"

The server's eyes rolled up as she recited the list from memory. "Um, buttermilk ranch, peppercorn ranch, parmesan vinaigrette, French, Russian, and Italian."

"Do you have anything vegan?"

"Italian—"

"Has cheese in it," Ani said.

"Russian—"

"Made with mayonnaise."

"French—"

Ani rolled her eyes to her mom, who glared without sympathy at the act. "Worcestershire sauce, which is made with anchovies." She rolled them back to the server. "Just bring it dry."

"One dry salad." She moved on to Mr. Brown, who seemed uncomfortable ordering veal in front of a vegan, but he did it anyway.

When the server left, her mom pestered Mike about Devon. "Where's she going to school? What is she going to study? What do you guys do for fun?" Mike responded to each question with no enthusiasm or detail. Images of Devon fastening her bra in his living room throttled Ani's mood. *You don't want to know what they do for fun.* By question six or seven, she was ready to scream. *Maybe if I fake a seizure they'll let me leave.*

"So, Ani," Mr. Brown said. "Do you have a special man in your life?"

Ani closed her eyes so she wouldn't look at Mike. With her eyes closed, he was all she could see. *I can't do this.*

"I'm a lesbian," Ani said.

"Ani!" her mom scolded. "Be polite!"

"Him first. It wasn't a polite question."

"You apologize right this—"

"Him first!"

"Ani, this is not—"

Mike interrupted her, his voice quaking. "So the two of you have been dating since mid-January?"

"Yes," Mr. Brown said, a fake half-smile on his lips. "A few weeks after Christmas."

Ani saw where this was going and shrank down in her seat. *Don't be too grateful about the change of topic, Mr. Brown.*

"So during February break, when we were supposed to go ice fishing and you canceled, you were with Mrs. Romero?" Mr. Brown scowled at his son. Ani tried to make herself even smaller. "And our weekend in March when you were supposed to give me a tour around the U of R? Or last weekend, when—"

"That is enough," Mr. Brown said.

"Yeah," Mike said. He pulled his napkin from his lap and dropped it on the empty plate, then shoved back from the table. "It is." He stood and stormed out.

Her mom glared after him. "Now that's childish. How is he going to get home?"

"He's got the keys," Mr. Brown said. "He'll probably just leave."

Ani stood. "I'll go talk to him."

"As long as you don't leave with him," her mom said. "He needs to come back in here and eat like a civilized person." *Yeah. Civilized. Awesome.*

Ani got to the door as Mike started the engine. Mike pulled out of the parking space and she stepped in front of the car. She'd never seen him so angry, not even clubbing Dylan with a shovel.

"I can't believe you didn't tell me, Ani."

She opened her mouth to reply and he gunned the gas. She stepped out of the way as he squealed out of the parking lot. *I didn't know* died on her lips.

When she got back to the table her salad had arrived, dusted with grated cheese.

CHAPTER 25

It was a relief to get back to school. Mike's embarrassed avoidance had been replaced with rage-filled shunning, and he wouldn't let her explain. He doted on Devon whenever she was around, much more than he had before, but it was petty and mean-spirited, and from the looks Devon gave him, she'd caught on.

Careful, Mike. Thinking about me at all—even if it's hate—brings out her inner psycho. Getting dumped would serve him right for jumping to conclusions.

"You," Fey said, interrupting her thoughts, "need a freaking hobby." She opened Ani's purse, plucked out a cigarette, and tucked it in her cleavage.

"Excuse me?" Ani asked. *I have lots of hobbies. I paint, play the piano, write music—*

"Every time I think you're done with that jerk, you go all dreamy-eyed-stare-y." Fey grabbed her by the shoulders and shook her. "Earth to Romero. He's not interested. Give it up."

"I gave it up a long time ago," Ani said. *Until I'm cured.*

Fey tapped her on the forehead. "In there, maybe," she said. She poked her in the sternum. "Not in there."

"What the hell do you know about it?" Ani said. She slammed her locker and walked away.

* * *

That night Ani was reading in her bedroom when she heard a

tap against the window. She looked over and saw another pebble bounce off the glass. Frowning, she walked to the window and looked down. Fey stood in her yard, wrapped in a parka too big by half.

Ani opened the window and kept her voice low. *Not that it matters.* These days her mother slept like the dead. "What do you want, Fey?" The air was warm for an April night. She held up the book. "I'm busy."

"Just get the hell down here so I can apologize," Fey said. She dropped the pebbles she'd been holding right in the grass. Ani imagined Dylan lurking in the shadows, waiting to pounce.

"I'll let you in," Ani said. She closed the window, hobbled down the stairs, and opened the door. Fey walked in, and Ani closed and re-locked the door.

"Paranoid much?" Fey asked.

"No," Ani said. "Just careful." *The only place he can get serum is here.*

"They still haven't found him, have they?" Fey sat on the couch, bounced up and down a few times, then settled in. "Nice couch."

Ani sat on the piano bench and folded her hands on her knee. "Look, I'm sorry for freaking out at you today..."

"My fault," Fey said. "I know there are some topics I just shouldn't bring up, but my mouth goes faster than my brain."

While my brain always wanders to the same place.

"Don't sweat it."

"Still friends?" Fey asked.

"Of course," Ani said. "But we won't be allowed to be if Mom catches you in here."

Fey rolled her eyes. "Oooh, Mommy."

* * *

The next day Fey grabbed her arm as they passed in the hall, spinning her around. "Ani, did you find an earring after I left last night?"

Ani shook her head. "No, but I didn't look either. What's it look like?"

"Let me know if you do. It's a real diamond."

"Sure," Ani said. "Maybe it's in the couch cushions."

It wasn't.

* * *

That night her mom swept the floor while Ani practiced Rachmaninoff. *I'd rather be painting, but these days all I ever paint is Mike.* She had several paintings of Mike-as-Seraph that she was too embarrassed to show anyone she knew, even her mom. *Maybe especially Mom.* She knew they were excellent in terms of technique, her best work ever, so she'd put them in her college portfolio—only Mr. Frazer and the admissions officers would ever see them.

Her mom bent down and interrupted her music. "What's this?" She held up a small, sparkling earring.

"Oh, wow, I think that's Fey's," Ani said.

Her mom frowned. "How did it end up behind the loveseat?"

"It must have stuck to my clothes or something. She lost it yesterday at lunch. She was really freaking out about it." Ani walked over and took it from her mom.

"Yeah, this is hers. So weird that you found it. I'm going to run it over to her."

Her mom's frown deepened. "It's getting dark."

"It's two houses away. You can watch me from the window."

Her mom *tsk*-ed. "Hurry up."

Ani threw on her boots without lacing them up and trudged across the Washington's back yard to the Daniels's house. The lights were on both upstairs and down, and System of a Down blared from Fey's window. Ani looked in the side door and didn't see anyone in the kitchen or dining room, so she knocked. She waited, tried again. Nothing.

The darkness at her back creeped her out. She tried the doorknob, and the door opened. "Hello?" she yelled. No one answered. "Mrs. Daniels?"

She stepped inside, earring in hand, and headed for the stairs. As she entered the living room a cat exploded out of a chair in a hissing frenzy, then scrambled into the master bedroom. Fey's mom lay on the couch, mouth open and drooling, a can of Coors Light spilled in her lap. *Not even eight o'clock. Nice.*

She shambled up the stairs to Fey's room and knocked twice. She tried again, banging on the door with her fist to be heard over the noise. The door shook, but there was no response. She turned the knob and walked in.

"Fey, I found your—"

Fey lay on her bed in flannel PJs, propped up with a pillow, covered in bloody vomit. A surgical tubing tourniquet lay slack around her bicep, and a needle protruded from the vein in her elbow. Ani rushed forward and dropped to her knees next to the bed. *Oh, you stupid girl.*

She put her cheek in front of Fey's mouth, felt hot breath even as her stomach growled at the smell. *That's so gross.* She put her hands to Fey's neck and felt a weak pulse. *Very weak.* She patted Fey's cheek.

"Hey, Fey. Wake up." She patted harder. Nothing. "Fey?"

She snatched the phone off the nightstand and called home. Her mom picked up on the first ring. "What's taking so long?"

"Fey's in trouble, Mom. I think she OD'ed on something."

"I'll be right there. Call 911."

"Okay." She hung up and dialed.

"911?" A pleasant male voice answered. "What's the nature of the emergency?"

"I think my friend had a drug overdose." She was surprised how calm her voice was. She gave the address as she watched Fey's chest rise and fall.

"We're sending an ambulance. Stay with her until they arrive."

"Okay," she said. Fey's chest rose, then fell, then stopped. *No no no.* Ani waited for it to rise again. It didn't.

She pulled Fey off the bed and started CPR. She scooped vomit out of Fey's mouth with her fingers, tilted her head back, took a deep breath, and blew into her mouth until her chest rose. No response. *Except for a growing desire to bite Fey's tongue.* She did it again. No response. *Come on!*

She straddled Fey and compressed her chest thirty times, then breathed in her mouth again. A shadow fell across her vision—her mother stood in the doorway.

"What the hell are you doing?" she asked.

"CPR!" Ani said, then re-straddled her to continue chest compressions. She was twelve counts through when Fey coughed, spluttered, and gasped. She didn't regain consciousness, but she was breathing.

"That was incredibly stupid," her mom said, dropping to her knees.

"What?" Ani asked.

Her mom didn't meet her gaze. "You're on an old serum, Ani. We haven't tested your saliva since...." *Since I burned up the old guy in the basement.*

Ani looked down at Fey. *No.* She wouldn't let it be true. She burst into tearless sobs. "No, Mom, it can't—"

She started to shake.

Her mom knelt in front of her, pried her mouth open, and swabbed her tongue. "Done is done. You deal with the EMTs when they get here. I'll let you know." She turned and walked out.

Fey's mom was still passed out, so Ani rode with Fey to the hospital. She seemed stable in the ambulance, but was whisked away through the ER doors, leaving Ani in the waiting room alone with her thoughts.

Six hours later she was paged to the nurse's station. Her mom was on the phone. Ani's mouth went dry, the world slowed to a stop. Standing next to an expectant nurse, she schooled her voice to neutrality.

"What's up, Mom?"

"You need to come home soon so you can be ready for school tomorrow." *School?*

"I thought I'd stay here with Fey," Ani said.

"Straight A's, remember? I'm not going to back off on that. I don't care what happens. I called you a cab, so don't leave the waiting room." *Oh, great, she's punishing me.*

"What about Fey?"

"She doesn't need you right now. Doctor Banerjee is looking after her. He has some experience with these kinds of things." She'd never met him, but this was the second time her mom had mentioned him. Ani made a mental note to Google the guy.

"What about..." She looked askance at the nurse. "...that thing?

You know, that problem?" If she was paying attention, she didn't show it.

Her mom snorted. "These tests take time. We won't know conclusively until tomorrow, but the fact that she's not dead yet is a good sign. Trust me, if everything's okay you'll be the first to know. And if it's not... Well, we'll deal with that if it happens." The line went dead.

Ani handed the nurse the phone, then went back to the waiting room and waited.

CHAPTER
26

It felt weird riding to school without Fey. The reprieve from her iPod was nice, but kids she barely knew kept harassing her for details. It seemed that everyone on the planet knew that Fey—no, it was Fey's mom—no, it was really Fey—was dead, in a coma, OD'ed but was okay—no she's in the ICU, no it's jail, no it's a rehab facility. They were positive that it was crack, meth, alcohol, crunk, cocaine, acid. *God, people are stupid. "Crunk" isn't even a drug.*

The more Ani deflected their questions, the more they pressed, until she shrieked at the top of her lungs. In the stunned silence she murmured, "I said I don't want to talk about it." When they got to school, Mrs. Sidlauskas pulled her aside and gave her a lecture about the dangers of startling the bus driver.

She was mobbed anew when she got off the bus and again at the beginning of each class. Even teachers asked her for details, which she didn't share. As she limped her way to the bathroom—just as an excuse to escape Trig for a few minutes—she heard hushed voices from around the corner.

"I heard that she and Ani were shooting up when she passed out...." *Leah.*

"Bobby told me that Ani sold him bad drugs last fall...."

"I heard that she called her mom before the ambulance to help her hide the evidence...."

"Yeah, that's why her mom's not in school today...."

Ani stepped around the corner. Two senior boys she recognized but didn't know were talking to Leah. The boys saw her and looked away, red-faced. Leah met her eyes and stepped forward in challenge.

"Yeah, we're talking about you and your meth-head girlfriend, freak. Are you sad you didn't kill her, so you'd have an excuse to cut your wrists for real?" *I might have.*

Ani averted her gaze and walked around them. Leah grabbed her arm and the boys stepped back. Ani looked at the hand on her arm, then down to the floor.

"Let go of me," she said through gritted teeth. Adrenaline—or something like it—surged through her, but it was somehow flat, muted.

"What if I don't?" Leah asked.

"Just let go." Her hands balled into fists.

"Or what?" Leah said, twisting. "You'll kill me, too?"

Ani allowed her face to go slack and looked Leah in the eyes. *A pretty girl for such a cruel look.* Ani grabbed her wrist and pried it off her arm. Behind Leah's gelatinous eyes, Ani could smell her brain, pink-gray and glistening and so, so inviting. *I wonder how she'd taste?* She licked her lips. "Yeah. Maybe I will," Ani said.

Leah tried to pull away. It was like wrestling with a doll. Leah clawed at her hand, gouging her skin, but Ani barely felt it. She stepped forward, forcing Leah back into the wall. Leah punched her in the gut, a vague sensation in the back of her mind. Ani grabbed her other wrist and stepped forward again, pinning her against the wall. As Leah struggled her eyes widened, and she started to sweat.

"Jesus, freak, just let me go." Her eyes begged.

Ani bent Leah's wrists backward. Against the wall, she was forced to her knees.

"Please let me go. Please."

Ani looked down at her—she was crying now—and smiled. "Don't ever touch me again, Leah. Ever."

The bell rang, shocking Ani out of her funk. She let go and stumbled away, shoving past the gaping boys. She looked back when she reached the end of the hall. Leah sobbed on the floor. The boys were comforting her, but their eyes were on Ani.

What the hell is wrong with me?

* * *

After school she went with Jake to visit Fey in the ICU. After several pints of other peoples' blood and a couple of liters of plasma, Fey looked pretty good. Peaked, too skinny, and weird without her makeup, but good. She was conscious and talking, and her vitals looked good. *She'd be at death's door if...* Ani couldn't even bring herself to think it.

"Hey, Fey," Ani said. She set the potted chrysanthemums she was carrying next to the bed. "You look pretty good." Jake smiled at her.

"Better than last night, huh?" She sounded weak.

"How do you feel?" Jake asked. Ani grabbed Fey's hand in both of hers, gave it a good squeeze.

"Achy. Sick. Like I have the flu." *Oh, shit. Shit, shit, shit!*

"No surprise, huh?" Jake asked.

"I guess not... I'm just so...." She closed her eyes and sank deeper into her pillow. Her lips murmured, but no sound came out. Ani held her hand for a while. When her breathing slowed and she fell asleep, Jake stroked back her hair and kissed her on the forehead. Ani gave her hand a final squeeze, and they left.

When she got home, her mom was drinking coffee at the kitchen table, a color print-out in front of her.

"What's that?" Ani asked. "Fey?"

Her mom took a sip of coffee, then pushed the paper over to Ani. There were two smeary graphs on the page. Her mom pointed to specific blotches. "These are the markers for ZV DNA." Ani's heart jumped into her throat. Her mom pointed to the other graph. "This is the sample I took from Tiffany."

Ani compared the two, her eyes flashing back and forth. Most of the splotches on the left graph were absent on the right, and vice-versa. "So, Fey's okay?"

"Tiffany's okay," her mom said.

Ani's legs gave out and she fell into the chair. "Oh, thank God."

"You were lucky." Her mom took a sip of her coffee. "Very lucky."

"I know, Mom. It won't happen again."

"No, it won't. Now let's test you."

* * *

That Friday morning Fey got on the bus, ignoring the stares and whispers. She sat down next to Ani and shoved her over with her hip.

"So where'd you hide my stash?" Fey whispered.

Ani stared at her in dumb shock. "What?"

Fey lowered her voice even further. "I got home last night, thought I'd take a hit—" Ani opened her mouth to protest but Fey cut her off. "Just a little one, to take the edge off." She rubbed her arms. "I'm all itchy. So anyway, I go to grab it and it's gone. Poof. So what'd you do with it?"

Ani didn't know what to say. "Um... why would I take your stash?"

Fey rolled her eyes. "Why wouldn't you?"

"I'm not a thief."

Fey raised an eyebrow.

You know what? Screw you.

"Look, I didn't touch your stuff. There were a ton of people in there after I saved your life—remember that, me saving your life?—so maybe one of them took it."

"Jake's uncle's on the EMTs, and he said they didn't find nothing except for what I had on me. No cops have been there, my mom said so. That leaves you."

"Or her," Ani said. *Or you forgot where you left it.*

"Mom doesn't know where I keep it."

Neither do I. "I don't know where you keep it. I don't know who took it, but it wasn't me."

Fey's eyes danced back and forth between hers. She frowned. "Fine. That's the way you want to be, after all I've done for you? Fine."

"Oh, that's rich. I save your life and you accuse me of taking your stuff? I should have, because you shouldn't be doing—"

"Who the hell are you to tell me how to live my life?"

"Who do you think you are, calling me a thief?"

Fey stood, snatching her purse from the seat. "Not for nothing, but Keegan's right. You are a bitch." She stomped toward the front of the bus.

What the heck was that? Ani hoped she'd calm down once she went through withdrawal.

* * *

That night Mr. Brown came over for dinner. They had salmon. She had a Mediterranean bean salad, then excused herself to study — and flush it out. When she got up the next morning, he was eating Cheerios at the table, in Buffalo Bills pajamas. *Fan-freaking-tastic.* Mr. Brown and her mom went out that evening. At ten o'clock her mom called to tell Ani she wouldn't be home until Sunday afternoon, that Ani was under no circumstances to leave the house, and that Ani should be careful — Dylan was still out there.

This is getting out of hand... but who am I to keep her from enjoying her life?

* * *

Fey stopped speaking to her, on the phone and in person, and with her went Jake and the rest of the emos. Fey thought she was a thief, Mike thought she was a liar, and everyone else thought she was a drug dealer. *If you only knew the real truth, you'd all run screaming.* Ani was surprised at her own bitterness.

She'd picked a good week to become a complete outcast. The AP US History Exam was that Thursday, the SATs were on Saturday, and Ani hadn't been studying as well as she should have been. *Or much at all.* On Sunday afternoon she opened her AP review book for the first time and took the practice test at the kitchen table.

Her mom walked in when she was mostly done, and insisted on grading it. She took the answer key from the review book and poured over Ani's test, marking with a blue pen. Ani did her best to ignore her until she finished, but each disappointed *tsk* and sour grimace shredded her confidence. At last her mom set down the pen.

Ani looked at her with wide eyes.

"You got a two." *Out of five. Ouch.*

"Alright, give me the review book. I'll get to work."

Her mom held out the book, but didn't let go when she grabbed it. "No piano, no drawing, no painting. No reading except for AP and SAT prep. You need to develop discipline, and now is as good a time as any."

Ani tore the book out of her hands. "Whatever, Mom." Her mom raised an eyebrow. Ani looked down. "Sorry, Mom." Her mom took her coffee cup and went to the basement.

* * *

Ani drifted through school with minimal human contact. No one spoke to her, even to be mean, and she spoke only if called upon in class. She didn't know what Fey had told him, but Jake eyed her suspiciously when he couldn't just avoid her. Leah, Rose, and Devon whispered their whispers and pointed their fingers, but she didn't let it touch her. More and more her thoughts turned to Mike, her former friend, her rescuer, her wrathful angel. *A big jerk who ignores me for a vicious bimbo with big boobs.*

She rode home with her mom, hit the books until ten, and got into the bath. She got up the next morning and did it all again, and again. She skipped the bath and crammed for fifteen hours straight Wednesday night.

Thursday morning was a blur. She sat through her classes and reviewed history in her mind—she didn't know nearly enough. The appointed time came and they were herded into the gym, which had been set up for test taking.

They were given assigned seats, and Ani found herself sitting between Keegan and Mike, filling out the pre-test paperwork. Keegan stared at her, and to avoid him she kept looking the other way—right at Mike, who kept his gaze straight ahead. Mike shuffled his feet and cleared his throat, every tiny motion catching her eye and entwining her thoughts.

It hurt to look at him. It hurt not to. Part of her knew she was better than this, better than letting a boy, even *this* boy, bother her so much. His rejection two years prior had hurt, but after that they had formed a kind of uncomfortable, distant friendship.... But it was still a friendship, still something. But now there was nothing, not even anger. *As if your daddy issues are my fault.*

When the test started, she couldn't concentrate. Mike was a stew of boiling, nervous energy. His proximity unnerved her. She could smell him, rugged and manly but not unpleasant, and it drove her crazy. Every twitch, every shift drew her attention away from the test.

The multiple choice questions were brutal, five right answers where you had to pick the 'most right' one. She finished the essay part with two minutes to spare, and realized that she had no idea what she'd just written. She prayed it was good enough and knew it wasn't.

The timer dinged, so they set down their pens and waited for the tests to be collected. Ani felt like her brain had been curb-stomped by William Howard Taft. A passing grade would be a miracle. *At least this doesn't go on my GPA.*

She left the room in a sea of commiserating babble, none of which was directed at her.

* * *

The SATs were easier than the AP exam. *Way easier.* Ani was good at math, comfortable with analogies, and in a different room than Mike. She finished early, was released at the minimum allowed time, and found her mom waiting in the parking lot.

Puzzled, she got into the car. "Hey, Mom. I wasn't expecting a ride home."

"A boy matching Dylan's description was found sleeping in a barn outside Dansville. The owner confronted him after calling the police."

"Did they catch him?" Ani asked. *You wouldn't be here if they had.*

Her mom peeled out of the parking lot. "No. He punched the farmer hard enough to crack his skull and stole a motorcycle."

"Is the farmer okay?"

She shook her head. "He's in surgery."

"When did this happen?" Trees blew past them as the Audi ate up pavement.

"This morning," her mom said as she blew through a red light. "Before dawn." It was eleven-thirty.

"Why are we in such a hurry?"

"I don't trust what he might do to our home. I lost several months' research when you—" She downshifted to third and hit the brakes. They took the ninety-degree turn at forty miles an hour. "—incinerated it. We can't afford to lose any more, and if he's with it enough to realize he needs more serum, you can be sure that's where he's going."

"What are we going to do if he comes?"

"When. You're going to stay out of the way. I'm going to shoot him in the head." They turned the corner onto their street and slowed to a sane speed. Nothing seemed out of the ordinary.

"What about the cops? When they find out he was ZV positive they'll quarantine the town."

She slowed down and pulled in the driveway. "They're not going to find out."

"You're going to cover up the fact that he's ZV positive?"

"I've already alerted my former associates. They agreed that this would be deleterious to our efforts. This isn't the first time they've had to do that." *Who the hell are you, Mom?*

Before they got out of the car, her mom pulled her pistol from under the front seat and tucked it into her jacket. Ani opened the front door, and they stepped inside. Nothing seemed out of place, so they locked the door, armed the security system, and searched the house. He wasn't there.

Ani spent the night without music, the shotgun next to the bath. Every creak and groan of the house had her frozen, alert, tensed and ready to spring. She didn't need to sleep, but the lack of mental rest left her exhausted.

CHAPTER 27

The next morning Ani put on her best face and her best behavior. It was Mother's Day, after all, and while the woman asleep downstairs might not have given birth to her, she was still her mom. Ani would be long dead if it weren't for her, and even if she couldn't agree with everything her mother had done, she owed her everything. *Don't think about Dylan. Don't think about Dylan. Don't think about Dylan.*

It had to start with breakfast in bed, as was tradition. Ani banged around the kitchen, making eggs with runny yolks and toast with honey from the local farm market, hot chocolate, and orange juice. She opened the bedroom door with her elbow and carried in the tray. She moved the pistol from the nightstand as her mom sat up, and set the tray in its place. Her mom's brown hair was stringy and sparse, and her eyes were tired.

They didn't chat while she ate. They had no secrets they were willing to admit, and each knew everything else about the other. When she'd finished, Ani took the tray to the kitchen and put the dishes in the sink. She heard the shower start, so she hurried up the stairs and pulled the presents from under the bed: a pendant of gold wire in the shape of a heart that Ani had made in art class, a gift certificate to Patti's Pedicure and Spa, and a new pair of high heels that went with her favorite black dress.

She had them arranged on the kitchen table when her mom emerged from the bathroom in a robe, hair wrapped in a towel. She smiled without comment, gave Ani a hug, and opened the envelope. The card had a heart on the front, and was blank inside except for what she'd written. *To my mom. Love, Ani.* She thanked her for the gift certificate, hugged her, then looked at the other two presents.

"Which one first?" she asked.

Ani grinned and handed her the shoes. She tore off the paper and popped open the lid. "Oh, those are beautiful." She slipped them on, took a few steps, then took them off. "Not great eight a.m. shoes, though."

"They go great with the robe." The joke earned her the barest hint of a smile. Ani handed over the smaller box. "I made this one myself."

Her mom again shredded the paper, then raised her eyebrow at the jewelry box. She cracked it open and let loose a tiny 'Oh'. She lifted the pendant out and looked at it in the light. "Sweetie, it's beautiful." A tear rolled down her cheek. "I love it." She put it back in the box.

They hugged. "Happy Mother's Day, Mom."

Her mom squeezed her tighter. "It's metastasized," she said.

Ani pulled back. Her mom's eyes were bloodshot, her face crestfallen. "What?"

"My cancer. It's spread to my lymphatic system."

"Wait." Ani shook her head. "What? I thought that leukemia was a bone marrow thing? You were in remission."

They hugged again. "It is. I was. But now I'm not, and it's spread."

Ani sat against the table as her chest tightened. "What... What's the prognosis?"

"Six months, take or give."

Fury burned through her. *Six months. It can't be.* "What about the treatments? Chemo? Radiation?"

Her mom shook her head. "It's gone too far."

"So, nothing, then." *Nothing.* The world spun, faded, burned. Ani shrieked. Her eyes snapped open as the table shattered against the wall, gouging deep rents in the plaster. Her mom had stepped back, eyes wide.

Ani wrapped her arms around herself. "I'm sorry, Mom. About the table. And... I'm so sorry." It had never hurt so much to be unable to cry.

"Me too, sweetie. Me too."

* * *

They spent the morning talking about the SATs and selecting colleges, ignoring the real issues. *Where do I live next year? What if I'm not cured in time? Can Mom's former coworkers be trusted?* She thought about her birth mother and answered the third question for herself.

After a light lunch her mom went to her bedroom to change, and she came out wearing her black dress, new shoes, and the heart pendant. *And makeup.* "How do I look?"

"You look great, Mom. They really work."

"Good. Mike will be here any minute. You're on your own for the afternoon."

"Whoa, Mom, you're going out?" *On our last Mother's Day?*

She smiled. "Mike's taking me to GeVa Theater for a matinee, then out to dinner."

"What about Dylan?"

"You'll be okay. Just don't get too far from the gun. I'll be back by midnight, and you can get in the bath." A car horn beeped, and Ani was alone.

Ani spent the day trying to read, then trying to paint, her back to the wall and her ears alert for any sign of Dylan. The sun went down and evening stretched to night. Her mom got in at ten after two, full of red wine and apologies.

* * *

The next day her mom called in sick to "protect the house until the backup plans were done." The reason she gave Mr. Bastian on the phone was "under the weather." Looking at her bloodshot eyes, Ani believed every word.

"Do they know, Mom?" Ani asked her. "About the cancer?" The word stuck in her throat, but she forced it out. Ani didn't think it would ever get easy to say.

"A few of them. Mr. Bastian does. Not about the... new development, though."

"Oh."

"It's seven-thirty. Get your shoes on."

Ani got on the bus and spent another day at school, where she might as well have not existed. With her mom's permission, she stayed after for Mr. Frazer to organize exhibitions for the spring art show the following night. He trusted her artistic vision and gave her free reign on the floor displays while he covered the walls with student work. She tried to group them by period and style, but was thwarted by the lack of a theme. Joe Stuber's seven-foot "Guitar Man" sculpture got the center of the room, with art grouped by student in radial beams around it. She put her own work as far from the piano as possible so that she didn't have to watch peoples' reactions.

She spent the evening making photocopies with her mom—she didn't trust her files to digital format, but was creating a backup system somewhere she wouldn't disclose. It took hours to copy everything and collate it into binders. Once that was done, they started loading the binders into cardboard boxes for transport. At ten fifteen, the lights in the basement flashed.

The security alarm!

Her mom grabbed the pistol and crept upstairs. Ani followed, empty-handed. They got to the top of the stairs, and Ani slammed open the door, scattering books across the living room. Her mom circled around her, pistol extended two-handed like you see on cop shows.

The kitchen door was latched. Ani peeked around the bookshelf, then ducked back. "Front door's locked." She kept her voice just loud enough to be heard.

Her mom whispered back, "We need to check the windows. Don't split up." They stepped away from the basement door, closed it and triggered the keypad lock. Ani slid the bookcase back into place and they circled through the downstairs. Finding nothing, they moved upstairs. All of the windows were closed and locked.

They searched every nook and cranny before settling down in the kitchen, where her mom checked the alarm system. It said 'Code 1551', which they looked up online. *Front door trigger.* Ani covered her mom while she checked the locks, inside and out—nothing seemed amiss.

"Maybe it was the wind," Ani said, picking up the books and

putting them back on the shelf. She didn't believe it either.

To be safe, her mom slept in Ani's bed next to the bath, snuggled up under the pink comforter with the pistol. They kept the door locked, and the music off.

*   *   *

The next day her mom called in sick again. Mr. Bastian approached Ani at the end of second period and asked if everything was all right. He was so blasé he might as well have screamed, "Hey, everybody! Something juicy is going on with Ani!" to the class. Jake even asked her what it was about until he remembered that she was supposed to be a pariah. His curious, apologetic shunning was almost funny.

She stayed after school to set up the art show. Once everything was ready, she'd walked home, pepper spray clutched in white-knuckled fingers, and changed. She was responsible for the evening's music, and wanted to look professional while she played. With some thought she settled on the black dress she wore to the Hearts on Fire dance. *Might as well reclaim it.*

She chose some of Chopin's mellower compositions for the evening to compliment the desired mood and kept it pianissimo to keep from distracting the crowd from the art. She played with her eyes closed, as usual, but visions of Dylan appearing behind her distracted her, and she started making mistakes. It didn't matter that her back was to the wall.

She opened her eyes and kept playing, her eyes wandering the room. A few minutes later saw Mike and Devon staring at one of her paintings, his mouth agape, while she gritted her teeth. *What the heck?* She hit a B-flat instead of a C. *Dammit.* They started to argue, Devon haranguing him as his face flushed. Clearly embarrassed, he hurried out of the gym.

Devon pulled one of her canvases off the display. Ani's playing faltered as Devon threw the painting on the floor and stomped on it, shredding the canvas. "Hey!" Ani said, vaulting off the bench to protect her art.

As Ani lurched toward her, Devon hocked, then spit. Ani

flinched as mucus spattered her face. "Get your own boyfriend, you goddamned freak!" Ani wiped off her face, smearing black mascara onto her fingers, as Devon stormed out.

Ani looked down at the painting Devon had ruined. Mike's green eyes stared up at her, blazing with internal light beneath wings of feather and flame. He held a small woman, her arms wrapped around his neck. The woman's face—Ani's face—was ruined, destroyed by Devon's foot.

Mr. Frazer put his hand on her shoulder, his face twisted in grief. "I'm so sorry, Ani. That was a beautiful painting." *That painting was rolled up in my locker.* Ani had brought it in to put in her portfolio, but had yet to show it to Mr. Frazer.

"How...? I never submitted that painting for display."

Mr. Frazer cocked his head. "Miss Daniels brought it to me this afternoon, after you left to change, said you'd forgotten to." *Fey. I'm going to kill her.* "It's the best work I've seen from you, so I swapped out the frame from your impressionist poppies."

Ani knelt down and tore the ruined canvas from the frame. Crumpling it into a ball, she noticed the crowd. Everyone looked at her. Everyone. *Yeah, go ahead and stare.*

She looked at Mr. Frazer, but spoke for the room. "He saved my life." *And I love him.* "That's what inspired me." *He's my angel.* "That's all." *And I want him.*

"Well," Mr. Frazer said, frowning at the crumpled canvas as he scooped the frame from the floor. "It was impressive. I hope you can recreate it." They both knew that art rarely worked that way.

Ani went to her locker, pulled up on the handle and kicked the bottom to pop it open, and gasped. Strips of canvas and paper tumbled to the hallway floor. Her portfolio. Six years of her best work in tatters. She knelt, picked up the shreds and held them to her chest. Fey had spared nothing.

Ani was halfway to Fey's house when headlights blinded her. A car screeched to a halt ten feet in front of her, and her mom got out. "Ani, get in the car." Her breath fogged. *It must be chilly.*

She stopped. "No. I'm going to go talk to Fey."

"No, you're not. Mr. Frazer called, told me what happened. You need to get a hold of yourself."

"I'm fine," Ani said. She started to walk around the car and her mom got in her way.

"No, you're really not. Look at your hand."

Ani held her hand up and looked at it. The palm looked fine. She turned it around and hissed in surprise. White bone flecked with green paint protruded from the ruined skin on her fingers. "What—" Her middle finger bone was cracked, a jagged line from knuckle to knuckle.

"You ruined your locker. Put your fist right through the metal." Ani stared in wonder at the damage she'd done to herself. "You need to get in the car and calm down. I'll make sure Tiffany is disciplined, but you can't confront her yourself. You might kill her."

"And that would be a bad thing how?"

Her mom grabbed her shoulders and shook. "You're not thinking right; you're too angry. Now get in the car. We're going home."

Ani got in the car. When they got home, her mom cleaned her hand, smeared it with regenerative paste, and wrapped it in gauze. She spent twenty minutes reassuring Ani that she had a year to rebuild her portfolio, and that she had plenty of pieces at home and in Mr. Frazer's room that could serve almost as well as what was ruined. Ani spent the next ten hours in the bath, fantasizing about cracking open Fey's skull and feasting on her brains. This time she let the thoughts come.

* * *

The next morning she asked her mom to give her a ride to school. The thought of even being on the same bus as Fey made Ani's face burn, but she was calmer than she had been, more resigned than homicidal. *She'd just better stay away from me.*

Her mom was going to work anyway. She'd finished transferring their copies to the mysterious off-site location, and besides, it was School Nurse Day. They arrived, and she was escorted straight to the office.

Fey had been suspended—at least five days out of school, with possible expulsion for vandalism. Devon got two days of out-of-school suspension, plus three of in-school. Ani was given two days detention for the locker damage.

When she got to her locker, it had a brand-new door. Jake lurked next to it with a sullen, apologetic look on his face. She lifted the handle and kicked. Nothing happened. *Oh, crap...* She bit her bottom lip and thought, ignoring Jake. Her combination came to her, and she opened the door with her bandaged hand.

"Ani—" Jake began.

"Don't presume you can talk to me," she snapped, slamming her bag into the locker.

"That's not fair."

"Oh, isn't it?" she asked, jerking out her first period supplies. "You mean like 'not talking to me for weeks because Fey told you not to' unfair, or some other kind?"

"I didn't realize—"

"I don't care. I thought you were my friend. You proved otherwise. End of story."

"Ani, please. You know how Fey can get."

Ani sighed and turned to face him. "You know what? I do. I do know how Fey can get. She's a schizophrenic bitch who uses friendship as a weapon." She saw the agreement in his eyes and went for the kill. "And if she ever told me I couldn't be your friend, I'd tell her to get over herself. You just went along. Coward."

He flinched. "I'm really sorry." He sounded it.

"I still don't care." She realized it was true.

She walked away, ignoring the sympathetic look from Mrs. Weller, standing in her doorway. Jake didn't follow.

She walked around the corner and bounced off Mike. She stumbled back and looked up at him, eyes wide. "Oh, Mike, no one was supposed to see that."

He scowled down at her, face flushed. "Yeah. Whatever." He sidestepped and kept walking. She watched him go.

Ani was pulled out of band so that her mom could be appreciated by the administration in front of a tiny and coerced audience. It was just as well—she couldn't play with her hand bandaged anyway. She was the first person in the nurse's office and put on a fake smile.

"Yay, Mom," she deadpanned.

Her mom put a hand to her head. "Oh, great. This again."

"Yeah. Happy School Nurse Day."

She closed her notebook. "I assume the horde is impending?"

"Probably. I was just called down." It amazed Ani that the same people responsible for making every student a slave to bells could never manage to be on time.

"How's your hand?" her mom asked.

Ani flexed it. "Not bad. My middle finger hurts a little."

"It should hurt more." She frowned. "The staff is abuzz about how strong you are. You need to be more careful."

Ani was saved from a reply by the arrival of Mr. Bastian and Superintendent MacIlwaine. They said their hellos, then stood around in awkward silence for a few minutes before three adults Ani recognized but didn't know came in. *School board members?* They presented her mom with a cupcake with a red cross on it and a certificate of appreciation.

Mr. Bastian said, "We want you to know how much we appreciate you, Sarah."

"Oh, go to hell," her mom said. The board members gasped.

"Mom!"

"Miss Romero," growled the superintendent.

Her mom rolled her eyes at Mr. MacIlwaine. "*Doctor* Romero. I don't get paid enough to take false platitudes from that ass." She looked at Mr. Bastian. "You can get out of my office."

Ani tried to melt into the background.

"Sarah," the superintendent tried again. "Apologize to Geoff."

"Not even if you fire me," she said. The room faded into tense silence. Her mom smiled. "You know what? I quit. Life is too short to put up with his crap for one more minute."

"Mom..." Ani said. *I need you here.*

"Good," Mr. Bastian said. "It's about time."

"Are you sure you don't want to think about this?" the superintendent asked. "Take the afternoon—"

"No, I'm done." She yanked the lanyard off her neck and dropped her nametag on the floor.

"Your health insurance—"

She barked a harsh laugh. "I can pay COBRA for as long as I have to. Forget two weeks. I'm going home." She picked up her purse and walked out. They stared after her, stunned.

"Can I go back to class now?" Ani asked.

* * *

By the time she got home, her mom had cleaned the whole house, and was busy folding laundry.

"Hey, Mom," she said.

"Hi, honey."

No maniacal laughter. That's a good sign. "So, how are you feeling?"

She dropped the last pair of jeans onto the pile and smiled. "I feel great. Better than I have in two years." Sweaty, and flushed, she looked downright frail.

"Are you sure about this?"

She laughed. "It's too late for second thoughts. Geoff wouldn't take me back for a million dollars, and Jim dodged a bullet on health insurance costs. It doesn't matter. I hate that place."

One more thing you've done for me. "I know, Mom, but you took that job to protect me."

She stacked the laundry in the basket and picked it up. "You'll be fine, sweetie." She smiled. "I need to get in the shower—I have a date tonight."

Of course you do.

She carried the laundry basket into the bedroom and kicked the door closed.

Ani checked the medicine cabinet after her mom had left with Mr. Brown. There was nothing inside that would explain her behavior.

CHAPTER
28

The next two weeks were a blur. Her mom stayed home all day doing research and spent every evening out with Mike's dad. Ani tried to recreate her portfolio from the scraps, but her muse had abandoned her. Everything she painted became a nightmare of aggressive smudges, every drawing a study of chaos in black and white. Her bouncy compositions turned angry, spiteful. *Festering Rage in D Minor.*

Devon came back to school unapologetic and vindictive, flanked by Rose and Leah. Every comment seemed to be a passive-aggressive attack on Ani, every look a glare, but they never approached, never did anything overt. Mrs. Weller noticed and tried to talk to her about it, but Ani just gave noncommittal replies until she left her alone.

Fey called six times in two weeks. Ani screened her calls, and didn't return her rambling messages, begging forgiveness and pleading intoxication. No apology could atone for what she did. Ani was alone and she needed to accept it. *Water, water, everywhere; nor any drop to drink.*

She did her homework, practiced for the spring concert as her fingers healed, succumbed to her mom's increasingly intense research experiments, and read. She started and put down four chick-lit novels before giving up on the genre—it didn't speak to her anymore. Nothing did.

* * *

Ani changed her clothes for the spring concert and sat on the couch waiting for her mom to get out of the shower so they could go. She flexed her middle finger to limber it up—the bone might never heal, but the flesh around it was firm and it didn't hurt much. "It should hurt more," her mom had said.

The doorbell rang. She peeked out the window. Mike stood there in his chorus uniform, black pants and a white collared shirt that showed off his muscled figure. In his left hand he held a single red rose, and he shifted his feet as he waited.

Ani blinked, expecting the apparition to disappear. He was still there. *You have to remember he's still a jerk.* The flower was still there. Her ears flooded with static. *You have to breathe.* She forced herself to inhale and exhale and yanked open the door.

"Mike!" she said. She couldn't contain a smile. He held out the rose, which she took and held to her nose. "It's beautiful." She took a deep breath, savoring what little of the delicate aroma she could. There was an unpleasant finish, like the garbage truck had just gone by. She smelled it again, and the unpleasant scent was gone.

He swallowed. "Hey, Ani. I just talked to my dad. For, like, the first time in weeks. It made me realize how much I missed you. I was so angry I couldn't think straight, and I took it out on you. I thought you knew and hid it from me, and I should have talked to you." *I can forgive those eyes anything.*

"I—" A figure tackled Mike from the side, barreling him off the stoop and into the yard. Ani shrieked as they rolled across the grass, the fetid, rotten stench almost overpowering. The shadowy figure moaned, and it sounded like "mine." Mike's scream cut off in a sickening gargle.

Dylan bared his teeth on top of Mike, his drooping face half-covered with moss. He held the larger boy down, strangling with both hands. Mike beat and raked at Dylan's face, and a gob of bloody flesh sloughed off into the grass, exposing white skull beneath.

Ani lurched forward as Dylan opened his mouth wide and leaned in toward Mike's face. She grabbed his hair, matted and stringy, forcing his head back. Her grip started to slip, so she tangled the other hand in the greasy mess and pulled. Dylan was strong—so strong—but she was strong, too, and had better leverage.

Dylan's back arched. He moaned in despair as she pried him away from his meal, his drool spattering Mike's chest. "Mine." Ani pulled harder, bending his whole body backward. His scalp tore free from his skull. Ani pinwheeled and fell flat on her back.

A shotgun fired. Ears ringing, Ani looked up. Dylan's headless corpse collapsed onto Mike, who gasped for air on the ground. Ani's mom stepped over him, shotgun in her right hand, meat cleaver in the left. "Did he bite you?"

"Um..." he said. He worked his mouth and nothing came out.

She dropped the shotgun and backhanded him. "*Did he bite you?*" she yelled.

Mike held up his right hand. His index finger bore teeth marks, ragged and bloody. Her mom stepped on his wrist and brought the cleaver down, she had a deadly aim. There was a wet sound, and Mike screamed. "Is that the only place?"

She pulled the cleaver up, spattering blood across the lawn. "*Is it?*"

"Yes," he screamed. "Yes, that's it."

Ani scrambled on all fours to his side. Mike was spotted with blood and drool, each drop a death sentence if ingested, or if it seeped into a cut. Hot blood spurted from where his index finger used to be.

"Ani," her mom said. She looked up. "Bleach. Now. And get my medical bag." She turned to Mike. "Close your eyes and your mouth and turn your head to the side."

Ani ran into the house as Mr. Washington came out onto the porch. "I called 911!" he yelled. Ani bolted through the door, grabbed the bleach from under the kitchen sink and her mom's bag from next to her desk. Sharp pain stabbed through her hip as she ran, but she ignored it. In the distance she heard the fire-house siren wail to life.

She tossed the bag to her mom and tore the cap off the bleach. Mike's eyes and mouth were closed as tight as he could make them. Her mom jerked her head toward him. "Cover him with bleach. Make sure to get his eyes, nose, and mouth, then his finger."

Mike whimpered as Ani poured the bleach onto his face. He breathed out violently as it went in his nose. "Sorry," she said. Her mom knelt next to her and injected him in the neck. "What's that?" Ani asked, pouring bleach on his hand. He writhed beneath her and she put her hand on his chest. "Shhh. Lie still. As still as you can."

"It's a sedative and a paralytic." She pulled out the needle and dabbed at the stump of his finger, then wrapped it in a bandage. She rolled Mike onto his side as his face went slack. "For horses."

"What's going to happen to him?" Ani asked as her mom inspected him for other wounds.

They locked eyes. "They're going to quarantine the block and triage everyone. Anyone who has so much as the smallest cut or infection will be further quarantined and tested for ZV. Anyone positive will be shot in the head and incinerated."

Ani looked down at her hand. The skin was raw and shiny, but it had scarred very little. "I think I'm okay," she said. She looked at Mike. *Please be okay. Please.*

"Go inside and shower," her mom said. "I'll inspect you in a minute." She pulled her cell phone out of her pocket.

A shadow loomed over Ani, and she turned around. Mr. Washington stood behind her, his hand over his mouth against the stench. "Is that...? Is he...?" Behind him a crowd gathered, their friends and neighbors interrupting their dinners to see what the commotion was. Fey stood in the back, mouth open in shock.

"We don't know," her mom said. "But it looks like it." She looked at Ani. "Go." She stepped to the side and hit speed dial.

Ani went inside, into the bathroom, and took off her clothes. She couldn't see anything in the mirror aside from old, healed wounds. The scar from the pacemaker, the little pucker from the branch that had run her through... Nothing new. She showered, scrubbing every trace of blood from her skin. Toweling off, she heard sirens.

By the time her mom finished inspecting her, there were police everywhere. They'd strapped Mike to a stretcher, loaded him into an ambulance, and carted him off to the hospital under heavy escort. Someone had covered Dylan's body with a sheet, the red soaking into the white fabric in pools of infection and death.

Her mom hugged her tight and whispered in her ear. "We're in trouble, but it's going to be okay. Whatever you do, don't panic, don't say anything, and don't act surprised."

* * *

Police in riot gear blocked off the street, and bullhorns warned everyone back to their homes. The black helicopters arrived less than a half-hour later, their backwash shaking the trees. Everyone was rounded up by armed military personnel and herded into hastily-erected individual cells, like chain-link Have-a-Heart traps for people.

Stern-looking men and women in white hazmat suits started at the end of the block, inspecting people for dings, cuts, bites, or other signs of trauma. Most were left in their cells, but some were carted off in black vans emblazoned with neon green biohazard symbols.

In the cell next to Ani's, Mr. Washington took out his cell phone and dialed. He put it to his ear, listened for a moment, and frowned. He pulled it away from his face and held it out, squinting down his nose at the screen. He looked at Ani's mom. "No bars."

Her mom checked her own phone and shook her head. She winked at Ani when no one was looking. Her mom looked confident, but it was hard to stay calm.

Ani sat and worried as the sun went down, glad to not be hungry, thirsty, or cold like everyone else stuck in their cages. Soldiers in rubber suits gave out water, passing the bottles through the cage. An incineration team immolated their front yard, charring Dylan's corpse, both trees, and all of the grass into white ash in a matter of minutes. They didn't leave, but sat waiting, still dressed in full gear, eyeing the cages as nervously as those inside eyed the flame throwers.

The triage team got to Mrs. Washington, and Ani got a better look at what they were doing. They took the old woman out of her cell and allowed her to undress behind a portable privacy screen. Ani could see her feet, and her wrinkled face from the nose up, but nothing else. The shielded face of the quarantine officers hovered over the nylon curtain. A white-gloved hand came up and touched something to her forehead.

Ani gasped. *Is that a gun?*

Mr. Washington cried out.

The device beeped three times. The triage man's voice was muffled, but Ani heard "fever." *No no no no no.* They dressed her in a hospital gown, then escorted her to a van and loaded her into the back.

They can't take my temperature. Mr. Washington started to cry.

Ani looked at her mom, trying not to panic. *I can get out. These cages aren't that strong. If I can destroy a locker, I can get out of these things. Right?*

"It's okay," her mom said. *Trust me,* she mouthed.

Ani forced herself to breathe to the pacemaker's beat, in for four, out for four. In for four, out for four. Her eyes kept flashing to the incineration team, lurking by the ashy remains of her front yard.

Mr. Washington was next. He was inspected and then put back in his cage. The same with her mom. Finally, it was Ani's turn.

They were gentle, as gentle as they could be under the circumstances. She was ordered out of the cage, stripped naked behind the makeshift curtain, and examined. She shook uncontrollably. *Please think I'm cold. Please.* They prodded the terrible scar on her ribs, examined the cuts on her wrists and thighs, inspected her damaged knuckles. Whatever they thought they kept to themselves. They removed her wig and ran gloved hands over her scalp.

A dark-skinned man gave her the wig back, then held the IR thermometer up to her forehead. As he did so his thumb flipped a switch and the red LED on the front died. He looked her in the eyes, pulled the trigger, then thumbed the switch again. The light came back on. He turned to his partner and nodded. "No fever," he said.

She got dressed and was escorted back into the cage. Her mom breathed a sigh of relief, and Ani collapsed to the ground, mentally exhausted. *I'm alive. Alive! Well... Sort of.*

* * *

ZV was easy to diagnose because it killed and reanimated so fast. Six hours later no one was symptomatic, so they were released. The military personnel loaded up and left. Aside from the ashy remains of their landscaping, at three in the morning it was hard to tell that much of anything had happened.

They canceled school, of course. Ohneka Falls was under general quarantine for the next eighteen hours just to be safe.

CHAPTER 29

Ani rushed into the hospital room, her left foot dragging worse than ever—her mom hadn't had the opportunity to assess the damage from the night before. Mike lay on the bed, wrapped like a mummy over his hospital gown. Off-white canvas straps cinched his biceps, thighs, wrists, ankles, chest, and head to the mattress. Gauze covered his right hand, and a wire bite guard encased the lower half of his face.

She let out a low whistle. "You're way past the danger window. Not taking any chances, are they?"

Mike's eyes—one of the few body parts he could move—turned toward her, and a smile lit up his face. "Ani, hey, it's good to see you."

She stepped forward to hug him and heard a throat clear. She looked up to find a camouflaged guard standing in the corner, an assault rifle slung on his back. "Sorry, miss, no physical contact until the all clear."

Ani smirked and took a step back. "Really not taking chances." *I can't blame them.*

Mike's hand twitched. "Neither was your mom."

Ani clenched her teeth. "Yeah, that sucks." *But I can't blame her for saving your life.*

"It could have been a lot worse," he said. "That was quick thinking." *And years of experience.*

"Yeah, Mom's pretty sharp." *And ruthless. Maybe psychotic.*

"She bring you here? I want to thank her."

Ani nodded. "Yeah, she'll be up in a few minutes." *Delayed at my request, if only for a few minutes.*

Mike chuckled. "I never thought I'd want to thank someone for lopping off a body part."

"I never thought I'd be glad my mom mutilated you." *Holy crap you need to change the subject.* "Hey, I never got a chance to thank you for the rose."

Mike smiled, then schooled his face to a careful blank.

"What rose?" Devon said from behind her. *Speaking of psychotics....*

Ani widened her eyes at Mike, then stepped to the side so that she could face them both. She opened her mouth, but before she could think of a reply, Mike spoke.

"I went to Ani's house yesterday to apologize."

Devon's mouth twisted in distaste. "Is that why?"

"Yes," Mike said. "That's why."

"What would you possibly have to apologize for?" Devon flicked her fingers at Ani. "Be someplace else, Cutter. You're not wanted here."

Mike scowled. "I want her here."

Devon turned crimson. "Do you want her here, or me here, lover?" She stepped toward him, hand stretched out to touch his face, and the guard cleared his throat again. She dropped her hand but didn't step back. She lowered her voice. "And if you want this later, you'll choose your next words very carefully."

Mike closed his eyes. "Okay, Devon. Okay."

Ani wanted to tear the triumphant smile off Devon's face. And eat it. Anger and hurt boiled in her gut, and she lost her breath.

"Ani," Mike said.

No, Mike, don't do this.

"Would you please..."

No.

"...please... "

NO!

"...punch me in the face if I ever talk to that stupid bitch ever, ever again?"

A laugh escaped before she could stop it. Devon's face darkened to purple, and she started to shake. Incoherent syllables escaped from her lips. Ani laughed harder, catching herself against the wall. Devon growled in rage and stormed out of the room, grinding her teeth.

Mike's smile vanished. "Ani, you've always been there for me, for as long as I can remember. Even when I didn't deserve it. Especially when I didn't deserve it." Ani's heart soared even as her laughter died. "When I thought that maybe I'd die, I lay here, thinking about what I'd miss most, and I thought of you."

Ani's mouth opened. Nothing came out.

"I love you, Ani. I always have. When you changed, I was all mixed up in my head. My priorities sucked. I don't care what other people think. I don't care how you dress, who your friends are. I care what you think. I want—"

"Ani," her mother said from the doorway. "It's time to go."

"Hi, Mrs. Romero," Mike said.

"Michael." She didn't smile but grabbed Ani's arm.

"I wanted to thank you for—"

"You're welcome," she said, dragging Ani to the door. "I'd hope you'd do the same for me." Ani walked backward until her mom spun her by the shoulders and pushed her out the door.

"Bye, Mike!" she called out behind her. Her feet barely touched the ground. She couldn't stop smiling.

"I know that look," her mom said, propelling her down the hallway. "Every girl on the planet gets that look when she's gone boy-stupid. You know the rules. You will follow them, for your safety and his."

"Yeah, Mom, I will." *He loves me. He said it, he meant it.* "Of course I will." *He loves me.*

* * *

The spring concert had been delayed a day for the zombie quarantine. They packed the gym; the town turned out in droves in a celebration of life and rebirth. *And love. And severed fingers.*

* * *

The next day Ani floated through school. Alone in the crowd, she wasn't lonely for the first time since she'd died. Devon lunged at her in the hallway, but Rose restrained her until Mrs. Slocombe intervened and escorted her to the office. Ani laughed. She'd probably just realized that she didn't have a date for the prom on Saturday.

The school buzzed with rumor, but this time the story mirrored the truth. Most people left Ani well enough alone, but she threw a bone to Jake by giving him a few details. She ignored Fey, who returned the favor with a sullen pout. Keegan approached her after Trig, acknowledging her with a tiny lift of his chin. "Mike's out," he said.

"Oh, good," Ani said. "Is he home already?"

"On his way. They left the hospital about twenty minutes ago. He wants you to stop by after school."

Ani beamed. "Thanks!"

He looked at her a moment, his lips twitching in the barest hint of a smile. "Sure." He walked away.

She took the bus home, but when she got off, she turned around and crossed the street. She glanced at the empty windows in her house. *Stay in the basement, Mom, just for a while.*

She rang the doorbell. As the door opened her stomach lurched. *Devon, fastening her bra.* She shook away the image and smiled at Mike's mom. "Hi, Mrs. Brown. Is Mike available?"

"Hey, Ani!" he called from the kitchen. He came around the corner and his dazzling smile weakened her knees. "Thanks for coming over." He scratched the side of his face with the back of his hand, the bandage abrading the skin raw and red, then sat on the couch. "It's going to take some getting used to." He patted the seat next to him as his mom made herself scarce.

Ani sat down on the far side of the cushion, not daring to get too close. *Not yet.* "Just as well you play soccer and not football, huh?" *So lame.* But he smiled.

"Sure." They sat, smiling at one another. A minute stretched to two. "I'm glad you're here."

"Me, too." Her desire was like hunger, only beautiful instead of horrific. Her eyes traced his jaw line, speckled with stubble, and flitted to his mouth. She forced herself to look out the window. *Phew!* "So will you be back in school tomorrow?"

He shook his head but inched closer to her. Now less than a foot separated them. "I'm seeing a psychologist tomorrow." She raised an eyebrow. "You know, nightmares."

She'd been euphoric for two days, and it hadn't occurred to her how the attack might have damaged Mike. "I've had trouble sleeping, too," she said. *Nightmares.* The word felt strange to her. She hadn't slept in two years, and had forgotten what it was like to dream.

"I'm sure," he said. "I can't imagine watching my mom do... what your mom did." He shifted his weight. Six inches between them, maybe less.

"I'm just glad she did." Ani swallowed. Her mouth was dry, and it was hard to concentrate.

"Ani?"

"Yes?"

"Will you go to prom with me on Saturday?" The universe exploded in bliss. She couldn't bite her lip and smile at the same time, so her mouth hung slack. He leaned in and she stopped breathing, her lips inches from his. An inch. Less.

She put a hand on his chest and turned away. "I can't. There's no way my mom would allow it."

"Why not?" He looked hurt.

She shrugged. "It's the rules."

Mike smirked. "She doesn't have to know."

Ani bit her lip. "How could she not know?"

Mike smiled. "I gave my dad tickets to the Journey concert in

Buffalo this Saturday."

A laugh escaped her mouth. *That's happening a lot lately.*

He leaned in again, and she put her finger to his lips. "Not too fast." He frowned. She smiled. "We've waited a long time. We can wait a little more." He returned her smile.

She dragged herself away from him, shambled to the door, and blew him a kiss. "See you Saturday," she said.

"I'll pick you up at seven," he replied.

* * *

As Ani came down the basement stairs, her mom looked at the clock. Blond wig on the floor, her bald head hidden under a Bills cap, she had an ink smudge on her nose and bags under her eyes. She looked back at the chemical equipment in the lab. "You're home late."

"It's nice out. I walked now that it's safe." Ani strangled a pang of guilt.

Her mom turned the stopcock on a burette, and fluid trickled into an Erlenmeyer flask set on a magnetic stirrer. "You're supposed to avoid sun exposure."

"I wore a hat," Ani said. "A big hat."

Her mom sucked some of the solution into a transfer pipette and dripped it onto a microscope slide. "Come here, sweetie." As Ani approached she picked up a scalpel. "Arm." Ani put out her arm and her mom grabbed her wrist with her left hand.

She drew the knife across her arm, expertly removing a nickel-sized flap of skin almost down to the muscle. Ani winced, but she endured much worse on a regular basis. Her mom sliced a vertical section out of what she took, placed the skin on the slide, put on a coverslip, and slid it into the incubator. A digital stereoscope displayed the images on the computer screen. "Don't go anywhere." Ani waited five minutes, then ten, then twenty, then an hour while her mother stared at the monitor. Without looking up, her mom crooked a finger at her.

As Ani approached, her mom stepped out of the way, eyes

ablaze. "What do you see?"

Ani looked. She recognized the cell membrane and the nucleus. Some of the nuclei looked funny, barbell-shaped, with smeary nuclei. "Mom, are those cells dividing?" She looked up, mouth open. "They're alive. Those are my cells, and they're alive."

They hugged, and Ani's heart felt fit to burst. Her mom pulled back, and she wasn't smiling. "Don't get too excited. It's a huge step, but the division is way too fast, faster than anything we've ever seen, and we don't know what it will do uncontrolled. I'm going to let it grow overnight and then test it for ZV."

"What then?" Ani asked.

She ignored the question. "It might take a while to iron out the kinks. Either way, I have some big news for you." *What does 'a while' mean? And what could be bigger than this?*

"Rishi—that's Doctor Banerjee, the man from the other day—has been sharing our data since I had to tell him about you. He's been very careful and hasn't shared our identities. One of his colleagues, Doctor Bhim Raychaudhuri, developed this serum. He's invited us to his lab to continue this research."

"For what, like, the summer?" *She'd miss Mike, but it'd be worth it.* "That's awesome!"

Her mom shook her head. "Indefinitely." Ani's stomach lurched. "Someone needs to look after you when I'm gone."

"Uh..." Ani couldn't put her thoughts together. "Um... Where is his lab?"

"Tempe. It's just outside Phoenix."

Ani sat. "Arizona." Her heart died, but the machine in her chest kept it pumping.

"You'll like it there. They've agreed to all my demands. Your secret will be safe. You'll go to school, be a normal girl."

"But my friends..." *Mike. You can't take Mike. Not now.*

"You don't have friends, you have cover. You can make friends out there, and they can be real friends, Ani. You won't have to pretend anymore. These people are going to cure you."

She realized then how much she missed Fey. *Petty,*

vindictive, angst-filled bitch that she is. "I do have friends, Mom. Fey and Mike are my friends."

"Regardless," her mom said. "Done is done. This is necessary and we're doing it."

Ani tried to speak through her broken heart. "When?"

"The movers will be here Monday."

"Monday." *So soon.* Ani couldn't wrap her brain around it. Ohneka Falls was the only place she'd ever known. "So tomorrow's my last day of school?"

She shook her head. "No, tomorrow you're staying home with me to pack up the basement ahead of the movers. One day either way makes no difference to your education, but we need this place looking normal."

CHAPTER 30

Friday morning the printer hummed, and her mom snatched the paper from it. Ani raised her eyebrows and she handed it over. Ani had seen something like it before, when they'd tested her saliva. The markers for ZV were absent. The sample was clean.

They hugged, danced, and packed, giant smiles plastered on their faces the entire time. The Zombie Virus could be cured. Dead flesh could be reanimated. Sure, they weren't quite there yet, but they were close enough to taste it. It felt weird to hope.

* * *

That afternoon Ani managed to escape the endless packing while her mom took a quick nap. She went to Fey's house to say goodbye. She rang the doorbell and Mrs. Daniels answered the door. "Ani, what a surprise!"

Fey sat on the couch watching TV, a bowl of chips perched on her stomach. "Tell her to go away," Fey mumbled. Ani stifled the hate she still felt when she looked at her. *Let it go, Ani. Let it go.*

"Tiffany Michelle, you get over here and greet our guest like a civilized human being!" *This is starting off on exactly the right foot.* Fey rolled her eyes, set the chips on the coffee table, and grumped her way to the door, arms crossed.

"What do you want, Ani?"

Fey's mom rolled her eyes and stole Fey's spot on the couch.

"I'm moving," Ani said. "I wanted to say good-bye."

"Good-bye," Fey said. Ani stopped the closing door with her foot.

"I'm sorry things went so sour with us. I only ever wanted to be your friend, even if you are an insufferable bitch."

Fey smiled. "Not for nothing, but you can be quite the bitch yourself." *I'm the walking dead. What's your excuse?* They looked at each other a moment. Fey broke first. "So where are you moving to?"

"Arizona. We leave on Monday."

"Mom get a new job?" *Something like that.*

"Yeah, some research position at a big hospital."

They stood in companionable silence for a minute, then Fey said, "Well, get a freaking cell phone and we can keep in touch. I've missed you."

"I will," Ani said.

* * *

Ani snuck across the street to Mike's house and peeked in his bedroom window. He sat in his jeans on the bed, topless and barefoot, playing Xbox. He was all tan skin and lean muscle, the angel of her paintings in the flesh. It hurt to look at him, to want him, crave him so much.

She tapped on the window. He looked up and smiled, paused the game, and tiptoed to the door. With a furtive glance down the hall he closed it, then opened the window. His face darkened when he saw her expression.

"Hey," he said through the screen. "Who died?"

"I did," she said. "Or I may as well have."

"What happened?"

"We're moving. Mom got a new job."

He leaned against the windowsill. "Moving? Where?"

"Arizona."

Tears sprang to his eyes. *I wish I could cry for you, too.* "At the end of the school year?"

"Monday."

He squeezed his eyes shut. "Ah. God. This can't be happening."

His house phone rang. He looked at the screen, then showed it to her. 'ROMERO'.

"I need to go. I'll see you tomorrow night."

"Okay," he said. "Bye, Ani." *Not goodbye. Not yet.*

When she walked in the door her mom was still on the phone.

"Ah, okay then. Thank you very much. Good-bye." She hung up and slammed the phone into the charger, her voice turning accusatory. "According to Jennifer, Mike and Devon are no longer a couple."

"So I heard," Ani said. "It's about time they broke up."

"And yet Mike is still going to the prom." *Shit.*

Ani tried to look blasé and crestfallen at the same time. "Oh? Did she say who with?"

"She did. And you're a terrible liar." *I can fool everyone but you, Mom.*

"Mike asked me. I didn't say 'yes.'"

"You apparently didn't say 'no' either, so you're either lying to me or leading him on, and neither is acceptable." *Nothing but complete honesty ever was, but it's always been a one-way street.*

"Aren't we packing tomorrow night anyway?"

"You can finish up your stuff. Mike's father is taking me out." She grabbed Ani under the chin and turned her head to face her. "I'm putting a great deal of trust in you. Don't screw it up."

Ani widened her eyes. "I won't, Mom."

"Promise." Her mom squeezed her cheeks.

"I promise."

"Good, 'cause I'll know if you try anything stupid." She kissed her forehead. "You want to be a headstrong teenager, but you don't have that luxury. If you think I've been restrictive before, try lying to me again. You'll never leave the lab until you're cured."

Her mom never bluffed. Ani would be chained to a chair. She thought of Arizona, of leaving Ohneka Falls, of leaving Mike. *Does it even matter if I am?*

* * *

They spent the rest of the evening and most of Saturday

packing the basement and turning it into something more nearly normal. A bare concrete floor swept clean, whitewashed walls, and a hot water heater were all that remained. Even the 'just in case' room had been turned back to its original purpose, the washer and dryer ensconced where a shackled recliner once sat.

They talked of research advances from her mom's new colleagues, improvement ideas for her serum they could try, advanced regenerates that could repair bone, and promising antiviral therapies. When her mom tried to talk up Arizona's virtues, Ani moped until she gave up. They stopped at three so her mom could get ready.

* * *

Her mom left at four-thirty. Ani waited a half-hour to call Mike. The phone rang once.

"Hello?" Her throat closed at the sound of his voice, tight and breathless. She closed her eyes against the hollow gnawing in her chest. *Is this how I'll always hear it, on the phone?*

The words rushed out. "It's me. There's no way I can go to the prom. Mom has spies who will rat me out in a second. It will literally ruin my life like you have no idea."

Silence brooded on the other end of the line. "Do you want to go?"

"Yes, Mike, more than anything I want to go."

"Well, I have an idea. I'll pick you up at eight-thirty."

"Why eight-thirty?"

"It's dark out by then. No one will catch us. I'll see you soon."

"They'll catch—"

"Trust me."

"Okay. I trust you. I'll see you soon." She licked her lips. "I love you."

"I love you, too, Ani. I wish it hadn't taken me so long to see it."

"Me, too. See you soon." *I'm babbling.*

"Okay."

"Bye."

"Bye."

She hung up the phone and opened her eyes. The world blazed

with color and life.

*   *   *

Ani took a hot bath and cranked the heat in the bathroom as high as it would go to raise her body temperature. Her mom called at six-thirty. She called again at seven. And again at eight. Ani checked online, and the concert started at eight-fifteen. *Good call, Mike.* She listened to Katy Perry's *One of the Boys* on repeat while she got ready.

Ani's only dresses were black, and that couldn't be helped, but she used her mom's makeup. Glossy pink lipstick and pink rouge over a very light foundation made her look more human. It made her look like a girl.

She quashed the butterflies in her stomach, or tried to. *If I know this is the right thing to do, why do I have to keep telling myself it's the right thing to do?* She shoved the thought away, touched up her lipstick, and waited on tenterhooks. At eight-thirty sharp she went downstairs.

A soft tap on the kitchen door startled her. She leapt up when she saw Mike, dapper and handsome in a black tuxedo with a pale green bowtie that matched his eyes. She disarmed the alarm system and pulled open the door, confused.

She pointed at the front door. "Why are you...?"

He stepped forward and kissed her, his lips warm and rough and gentle. He tasted like mint and honey. It lasted a moment. It lasted forever. She stepped back, breathless, and shared his boyish grin.

"You look beautiful. I don't know if your mom's spies include the neighbors, so I thought I'd do things this way." He grabbed her hand, his bandage soft against her palm, and led her out the door. He closed it behind her and she reset the alarm. They walked through the back yard and onto the adjacent block, where Mike's dad's rusty pickup waited. "It's not a limo, but it'll do."

"It's perfect," Ani said. For what, she still wasn't sure.

He opened the door for her and helped her up. *At least the inside is clean.* He started the engine and drove toward school, but hung a right instead of a left. Ani wanted to ask, but the tiny smirk on his face told her everything she needed to know—it wasn't polite to ask about surprises.

Mike pulled onto the access road that stretched behind the school, then into the unmowed field. He killed the lights and drove the truck through the tall weeds, right to the edge of the soccer field. He turned off the engine, got out, circled the truck and helped her down. He kissed her again, and she resisted as he pulled away.

He took her by the hand and his touch electrified her. He led her through the darkness toward the school, where they could hear music. They neared the back of the gym, and he pulled her into an embrace. He held her, then began to sway.

They danced, first to one song, then another, staring into one another's eyes under the starlit late May sky. He kissed her, a bare brush of the lips. She kissed him, pulling him down to her, devouring his taste and his touch. He pulled away, gasping, then circled behind her.

Another song started, and he put his arms around her waist, his chest pressed against her back. He leaned over her shoulder and kissed her ear, and then her neck. She closed her eyes and felt the passion grow inside, an all-consuming rush of energy. She'd never wanted anything so much.

"We need to slow down—" She almost didn't get the words out.

"No," he said. "I've wanted this, wanted you, too long. If we only get one night together, I want it to be this night." *I do, too.*

He ran his finger down her neck, slipped her dress off of her shoulder and kissed her naked skin.

"This isn't right," she gasped. *I don't mean it. Tell me otherwise.*

"It is. There's never been anything more right." His hands moved on her body as his mouth danced on her neck. She started to pant, to gasp, to moan. He talked to her, low and loving, and she fell into his voice. "Yeah, Ani. I love you so much. I need you. I've always needed you. You don't have to pretend anymore. Let go." His words carried her to euphoria, guided by his hands, and she surrendered to it.

* * *

Ani wiped her hands on her dress. They were sticky with something, red and pungent with the tang of iron. She licked her fingers, sucked the delicious fluid from them.

She knelt down to the thing on the ground. It was all legs and arms and meat, nothing good. She saw a gobbet of something gray nestled in a tangle of its hair and she cooed in excitement. *Brains!* She pulled it out and put it in her mouth, then pushed it out with her tongue. *Why so good before, but now so bitter?* She moaned in anguish. *MORE! Where?*

She heard music, laughter, talking, as the meat thing on the ground struggled to its feet, bowtie askew and splattered with blood. She looked at it, warm flesh and hot blood, and wanted it. *Bitter. No good.* She looked up at the moon and groaned in denied hunger, then turned toward the laughter. *More.* She lurched toward the gym door, licking her lips, the tuxedoed corpse at her side.

The End

THE
DEVIL
OF
ECHO
LAKE

DOUGLAS
WYNNE

Tied for 1st Place in the 2012 JS Horror Writing Contest.

Billy Moon would have given his life for rock 'n' roll stardom, but the Devil doesn't come that cheap.

Goth rock idol Billy Moon has it all: money, fame, and a different girl in every city. But he also has a secret, one that goes all the way back to the night he almost took his own life. The night Trevor Rail, a shadowy record producer with a flair for the dark and esoteric, agreed to make him a star... for a price.

Now Billy has come to Echo Lake Studios to create the record that will make him a legend. A dark masterpiece like only Trevor Rail can fashion. But the woods of Echo Lake have a dark past, a past that might explain the mysterious happenings in the haunted church that serves as Rail's main studio. As the pressure mounts on Billy to fulfill Rail's vision, it becomes clear that not everyone will survive the project.

It's time the Devil of Echo Lake had his due, and someone will have to pay.

In the deepest reaches of space, on a ship that no longer exists, six travelers stare into the abyss...

Man has finally mastered the art of space travel and in a few hours passengers can travel light years across the galaxy. But, there's a catch—the traveler must be asleep for the journey, and with sleep come *the dreams*. Only the sleeper can know what his dream entails, for each is tailored to his own mind, built from his fears, his secrets, his past... and sometimes his future.

That the dreams occasionally drive men mad is but the price of technological advance. But when a transport on a routine mission comes upon an abandoned ship, missing for more than a decade, six travelers—each with something to hide— discover that perhaps the dreams are more than just figments of their imagination. Indeed, they may be a window to a reality beyond their own where shadow has substance and the darkness is a thing unto itself, truly worthy of fear.

"The work is as tidy as the town and as pat as a familiar horror film." -

Publishers Weekly

Diagnosed with a brain tumor, Geoffrey returns to his hometown for a reunion of the Jokers Club (his childhood gang) with the hopes of unearthing the imagination he held in his youth.

Unfortunately Geoffrey's tumor quickly worsens, bringing on blackouts and hallucinations where he encounters the spectral figure of a court jester who had been his muse as a child. The jester inspires Geoffrey's work on his manuscript, fueling his writing at a ferocious pace. The dead and the living co-exist in the pages of Geoffrey's story, in a town where time seems to be frozen in a past that still haunts the present.

Will the pounding growth in Geoffrey's head be held at bay long enough for him to discover who is targeting his friends, or will the pages in his unfinished novel rewrite history?

"This is a novel full of visceral, intense moments. It will keep you holding on until the brilliant end." - Richard Godwin, author of *Mr. Glamour* and *Apostle Rising*.

An evil force is at work at the Hospital where Nathan is recovering from injuries he received at the hands of his Mom's abusive ex-boyfriend. Demonic looking men with pale faces and glowing eyes lurk in the shadows. Someone is harvesting skin and organs from living donors against their will.

In his dreams, Nathan can see these demons in their true form -- evil creatures who feed on the fear and hatred they create in their victims. Nathan's only ally is the Doctor who cares for him. Bound together by their common legacy, they alone seem to share the ability to see the demons for what they truly are.

Together they must find a way to stop these creatures before they, and their loved ones, become the next victims.

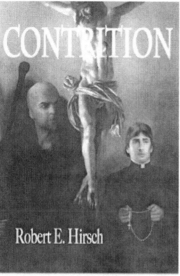

In a tiny community on the Mississippi Gulf Coast, Brother Placidus finds little Amanda LeFleur sacrificed below a crucifix, in the attic of The Brothers of the Holy Cross. It is not the first body he's found there.

Assigned to the investigation is detective Peter Toche whose last case was that of a murdered child, a child that has been haunting his dreams, forcing him to face his worst fears and the evil that has targeted his town.

As additional victims are discovered, Tristan St. Germain, a mysterious man who was rescued by a parish priest from the waters near his home, may hold the key to the safety of all mankind.

Little Amanda was only the beginning...

"Faherty's latest novel provides readers with as much fun in a graveyard as the law will allow." -Hank Schwaeble, Bram Stoker Award-winning author of DAMNABLE and DIABOLICAL.

Rocky Point is a small town with a violent history - mass graves, illegal medical experiments and brutal murders dating back centuries. Of course, when Cory, Marisol, John and Todd form the Cemetery Club, they know none of this. They've found the coolest place to party after school - an old crypt. But then things start to go bad. People get killed and the Cemetery Club knows the cause: malevolent creatures that turn people into zombies. When no one believes them, they descend into the infested tunnels below the town and somehow manage to stop the cannibalistic deaths.

It's a race against time to find the true source of evil infesting Rocky Point, as the Cemetery Club ventures into the cryptic maze, to face their demons in a final showdown.

CPSIA information can be obtained at www.ICGtesting.com
Printed in the USA
LVOW06s1615070813

346784LV00007B/883/P